1

JERUS

OTHER TITLES BY CONRAD JONES

FIRST PUBLISHED 2010

BY GERRICON BOOKS

Copyright 2008 Conrad Jones

CONRAD JONES HAS ASSERTED HIS MORAL RIGHTS TO BE
IDENTIFIED AS THE AUTHOR

http://ebookpublishingexpert.com/index.html

OTHER TITLES BY CONRAD JONES

Soft Target II 'Tank'

Soft Target III 'Jerusalem'

The 18th Brigade

Blister

The Child Taker

Criminal Revenge

Criminally Insane

Nine Angels

A Child for the Devil

Hunting Angels

Frozen Betrayal

Chapter One

Tank

John Tankersley switched on the wipers to clear the drizzle from the windscreen of his black four by four. It had been raining heavily for the last three days. The sky was a dark shade of gunmetal grey, which indicated that it wasn't going to stop raining any time soon. Suddenly, forked lightening illuminated the ominous clouds, and Tank wondered at the sight of a million volts of electricity snaking its way across the sky to find the earth. Tank counted in his mind, one-second, two seconds, three seconds, four seconds, then the clap of thunder roared above him and the drizzle became torrential rain. He had counted the seconds after a lightning strike since he was a small boy. His father had been a Chief Petty Officer in Her Majesty's Royal Navy during the Second World War, and he spent hours explaining to Tank the maritime myths about the weather. Red sky at night, shepherd's delight, red sky in the morning, sailor's warning, and so on. Every second you counted following a lightning strike represented one nautical mile that the thunder had travelled from its epicentre. By counting the seconds you could tell if the storm was coming toward you or not. The shrill polyphonic ring tone of his car phone interrupted his thoughts.

"Hello John, I am terribly sorry to disturb you, today of all days, are you on your own?" said Major Stanley Timms. The Major was Tank's commanding officer, and head of the Terrorist Task Force. John Tankersley was the Task Force lead agent. He stood over six feet tall and weighed around seventeen stone. Most of his considerable size was packed around his upper body; his physique was unusually muscular and his colleagues nicknamed him Tank. His shaved head and Desperate Dan jaw line made him a fearsome looking man. Only Major Timms called him by his Christian name, and when he did it usually meant there was trouble coming.

"Hello Major, what`s the problem?" answered Tank, he slipped his fingers inside his shirt collar to try and loosen its grip on his eighteen inch neck. He hated wearing collars and ties but he was heading to a funeral, so there was no choice in the matter.

"We've had a communication from our man in Israel. He's received information that an assassination attempt is imminent," the Major was purposely vague because they were talking on civilian telephone networks. Any number of undesirables could monitor their calls. He would never discuss official business under normal circumstances, but this was urgent.

"Is something planned here in the UK?" Tank asked.

"We're not sure about that yet. The information has come direct from Jerusalem. All we have so far is that key tier one personnel from a leading Palestinian terrorist organisation have slipped off the radar. These particular individuals have a penchant for assassination," the Major couldn't be any more specific. The finer details would have to be ironed out later on, where enemy agencies couldn't listen in on the conversation.

Tank wanted to know why the Israelis suspected that the terrorists in question had headed for the British Isles. He knew that the Major would have all the details, but the line wasn't encrypted. The funeral would have to wait five minutes while he stopped the vehicle to change channels.

"Give me two seconds Major," Tank said. He indicated that he was turning left off the dual carriageway. The spray from passing vehicles was making visibility poor, but he could see an exit and he needed to park up. He had lost his bearings in the pouring rain, and talking to the Major wasn't helping, so he looked down the carriageway for a landmark. There was a brown sign above the exit with a white elephant embossed in the centre of it. Tank smiled to himself as he realised he was driving into Knowsley safari park. His parents had brought him here many times as a child, and if his memory served him correctly, the weather had been similar to this on every occasion. He remembered that the animals always looked cold and wet and completely fed up, longing to be back on the sunny plains of Africa, or wherever they were originally from.

Another bolt of lightning streaked across the dark sky. Tank counted in his mind again, one second, two seconds, three seconds, the thunder rumbled above. The storm is moving closer, he thought. Tank pulled the car to a halt in a lay by, just before the park entrance. He removed his cell phone from its cradle and then opened the glove box. Inside was cable, which he plugged into the bottom of his phone. He then switched his stereo onto a preset frequency. The car was equipped with encryption equipment, but it could only be used if the vehicle was stationary.

"We are secure Major. What do you know?" asked Tank. The rain intensified and the car's wiper blades were struggling to keep up with the deluge. There was a steady stream of cars passing him on their way to see the miserable animals in the rain.

"Mossad have been interviewing a known operative of the Axe group," the Major began. Mossad was the Israelis version of our Britain's MI5 or America's NSA, and they didn't interview anybody in the traditional sense of the word. An interview is something you experience when applying for a job or a telephone loan, basic polite questions and answers. The Israeli security agencies do polite. They do however use extreme interrogation techniques and torture to extract information, as do most Western agencies if the truth were known.

"It seems that since we captured Yasser Ahmed, the Axe group has splintered into several factions. At the moment, they seem to be concentrating their efforts in Gaza and the West Bank. Some known associates have been spotted meeting with senior officials from Hezbollah in Lebanon. Several of Ahmed's senior lieutenants have cropped up in Afghanistan, and there are at least three still in Chechnya, but the Israelis have lost track of six of the others, two marksmen and four explosive experts," the Major left the information to hang in the air for a second so that Tank could digest it.

"What makes them think that they're headed here?" asked Tank, he was thinking at a thousand miles an hour. The possible connotations of the chaos that could be caused by such a highly skilled group of terrorists were infinite. Yasser Ahmed had demonstrated that terrible carnage could be created by just a few determined suicide bombers during the first 'Soft Target' campaign. Osama bin Laden had achieved equally devastating results by attacking the Twin Towers.

"Mossad extracted the outline of a plan from the Axe insurgent, he'd indicated that there was a plot to assassinate key personnel in Britain, but we're not sure who or when," the Major explained.

"Can't they get more specific information from him?" Tank asked. He was well aware of the interrogation, or interview techniques that Mossad employed. If the Axe man had specific information then the Israelis would extract it, there was no doubt about that.

"It would appear that the insurgent died during the interview. Apparently he suffered a massive heart attack and couldn't be revived. That's all we know," the Major said.

"Bloody typical, you would think that they would learn to temper their interview techniques. The Israelis' over enthusiasm leaves us with a conundrum Major. Do you need me to come in now?" Tank asked. The funeral was due to start in twenty minutes.

"No John, you need to be there today. I know how much she meant to you. I will call the team together later on this afternoon, turn up when you're up to it," the Major knew Tank had to attend the funeral. There was no way he could miss it.

"Thanks Major, I'll see you later on," Tank terminated the call and placed the cell phone back in its cradle. Another bolt of lightning exploded across the darkening sky. One second, two seconds, then the thunder roared and the rain came down harder.

Tank selected drive and indicated. He turned the car one hundred and eighty degrees and drove away from the safari park. It was three miles further on to the church. Tank stopped at the traffic lights at the junction of Burrows Lane. On the left was an imposing war memorial dedicated to those who had fallen in the Great War. A ten feet tall bronze infantryman stood on top of a stone podium, bayonet fixed and his gun at the ready. The bronze figurine of his sweetheart reached longingly with her arms outstretched toward him. It was a poignant effigy dedicated to those who lost their lives and loved ones. The statue was cast from bronze, and oxidation had turned the metal the colour of jade. The First World War or the Great War as it is often called was supposed to be the war to end all wars, 'How naive', Tank thought. The traffic light turned green and he drove on through the rain, the roads awash with surface water, his tyres produced a loud splashing noise as he accelerated.

Tank turned round a long sweeping left hand bend. The church stood in a small copse and had an arched wooden gate leading up several smooth stone steps to a huge studded wooden door. The building was made from red sandstone blocks with tall stained glass windows placed symmetrically down each side. There was a pub called The Griffin situated a few hundred yards from the church entrance, at the edge of the graveyard.

Tank parked next to the curb at the end of a long line of vehicles. He could see that the hearse was arriving closely followed by the black limousines that carried close family members. The coffin was decked with red roses. Tank felt his stomach twist, a feeling only the bereaved can truly identify with. There was a tremendous feeling of loss and emptiness, hopelessness and anger. He felt warm tears filling his eyes and he blinked to try to clear them. He reached for a tissue from his pocket, and his hand bumped his Glock 17 in its holster. Tank removed the 9 mm pistol and placed it into a lock box, which was situated between the front seats. He slipped out the bullet magazine and placed that away from the gun in the glove box, which he also locked.

Tank turned the engine off and opened the door, taking a deep breath to compose himself. The rain hammered down and bounced off the pavement soaking the bottom of his trousers in seconds. Rivulets of water ran from his bald scalp down the back of his neck saturating his collar and the back of his shirt as he approached the funeral party. The faces of some of the bereaved family were familiar, but much older than he remembered. Wrinkles, grey thinning hair, double chins and expanding waistlines were attacking his relatives on mass. He had not seen some of his cousins for thirty years or more, not since they were young children playing in his grandmother's garden.

Tank nodded hello to two familiar faces in the throng. Clive and Martin Henderson, his cousins were much older than the last time they had met, but their features still looked the same. Clive was with his wife Fiona, but Martin was alone. Tank couldn't remember what Martin's wife had been called, and he wondered if they were still together. He nodded hello to them across the throng of mourners. The coffin was carried into the church on the shoulders of pallbearers, supplied by the funeral directors. None of the family carried her because it was too upsetting. Tank couldn't have done it even if he had been asked. As the mourners entered the church, lightning flashed again and the thunderclap was instantaneous this time. The storm was directly overhead.

Tank was the last person to enter the small church. There was a musty old smell as he entered, age and woodworm combining to leave their distinctive odours. He was soaking wet and distressed. Tank wasn't scared of any man alive, and he wouldn't think twice about killing a wanted terrorist, but he was still only human. He'd been born under the star sign of Cancer the Crab, which his sisters reliably informed him meant that he had an extremely tough exterior, but was soft once you got inside the shell. The news that Major Timms had imparted to him earlier was already at the back of his mind as there was an aura of grief around the mourners that had already infected him. He needed to deal with the funeral first then the terrorists would have his full attention, which was something that they would not enjoy.

The church was warm as the funeral party entered it, relieved to be out of the thunderstorm. Visible puddles were forming on the ancient wooden floorboards as umbrellas were closed, and raincoats dripped on the floor. They were greeted at the door by a portly man dressed in a simple long black religious robe. There was a plaited rope tied around his ample belly and a wooden cross, hung from his neck, on the centre of his chest. He welcomed the guests with a solemn greeting, which suited the occasion.

The last guest entered the church and the usher noticed that he was an unusually large man with a shaved head. He looked like his suit would split down the back if he moved too quickly. The holy man noticed rainwater forming tiny rivers that were running down the bald man's scalp, and for a second he thought he had seen a red dot of light on the back of his head. As the church usher closed the door, he noticed a dark panelled van driving slowly past the church, the driver was of Middle Eastern appearance. That in isolation wasn't so unusual, but the fact that he was wearing dark sunglasses in a thunderstorm was odd.

If Tank had noticed it then he would have realised that something was afoot. He hadn't noticed the van, nor did he notice that there was a man aiming a sniper rifle at the back of his head. The sniper had been about to take the shot when the lightning flashed, blinding him for a second through the telescopic sights, and distracted him. When his vision returned, he looked back through the scope but Tank was inside and the door was being closed behind him. They would have to wait for the funeral party to emerge before they could complete their mission.

Chapter 2

Chen

Chen stood on the huge stone breakwater, which separated Holyhead harbour from the Irish Sea. The breakwater had been built jutting out one and a half miles into the sea to protect shipping from the devastating storms that rolled in from the Atlantic. It was built from huge blocks of granite and stands thirty feet above sea level. An access road runs the full length of the structure and it's wide enough to carry articulated wagons along it. Despite the breakwater's size and robust stature, it needs to be protected from the crushing waves that batter it relentlessly. Trucks arrive daily, which carry huge blocks of slate and granite. The rock is lifted by crane over the sea wall and dropped into the ocean to act as a buffer. They were piled up to protect the breakwater from the destructive power of the crashing surf. At the end of the huge marine edifice was a lighthouse, which warned shipping away from the treacherous rocks. Chen had parked his vehicle at the beginning of the access road and had walked five hundred yards along it. It wasn't the first time the Task Force had been called to investigate shipping incidents. The Welsh port of Holyhead was one of Europe's deepest harbours and it serviced super-tankers, which brought minerals for the manufacture of aluminium from the Middle East. There was absolutely no way of monitoring who was aboard the foreign vessels that arrived in port.

Chen was from Chinese origin and had been part of the Terrorist Task Force since its formation. He had been sent to Holyhead to investigate reports that several men had been seen jumping from a Syrian tanker while it unloaded its precious cargo. From where he stood on the breakwater, Chen could see the tanker jetty across the harbour where the ship was anchored. The harbour was a busy ferry port through which over two million passengers a year travelled to Ireland. Both foot passengers and heavy goods vehicles utilised the route. Busy ports like Holyhead were almost impossible to police, because of the sheer volume of international shipping that called there.

Two uniformed officers were stood a hundred yards further along the breakwater; they noticed his arrival and approached Chen. They looked wet, bored and disinterested; one of them was kicking stones off the edge of the huge seawall into the stormy ocean.

"The dingy was found just there, and the clothing was found here," one of the officers said pointing to a section of the sea wall. There was a rusted metal ladder attached to the wall, which descended into the murky ocean. The water was a deep green colour topped with white tips as the waves rose and fell against the breakwater. There were the remains of a four-man inflatable on the road, next to a pile of wet clothing.

"Have they been touched?" asked Chen pointing to the discarded clothing. There was a slim possibility that DNA samples could be recovered from the material. Cross contamination at the crime scene could cause confusion at the crime laboratory. It could also cost thousands of pounds of wasted man-hours to investigate useless evidence.

"Yes, we were looking for identification. We thought they belonged to swimmers or sailors that hadn't returned," the officer said defensively. The harbour was home to a busy marina, which was used as the berth to hundreds of expensive yachts. Unfortunately, not all the boat owners were as responsible as they should be, and the local police were often sent on a wild goose chase looking for people that weren't even missing. Alcohol and high spirits had often ended in tragedy at the marina.

"The Syrian sailors seen deserting were only reported two hours after we found this lot," said the second officer shrugging his shoulders and slurring a Welsh accent.

"What's your name officer?" asked Chen smiling.

"PC Frank Burton sir," the uniformed officer replied. He was ruddy faced and looked like he had spent many years in the boxing ring, the disfigured shape of his nose indicated that he needed to work on his defence.

"Ok Frank, have you interviewed anyone on the Syrian ship yet?" Chen asked.

"No sir, we haven't, because they have refused us permission to board, and no one on the ship seems to speak English," officer Burton replied, flushing red with embarrassment.

"When is she due to leave dock?" asked Chen. He was reaching for his cell phone. He flipped it open and waited for officer Burton to answer.

"Today sir, that's why I said it was so urgent when we spoke on the telephone. They're stalling us hoping that we'll just leave them alone, but marine law states that we can't board a foreign ship when it's harboured, without the captain's permission," the policeman replied, proudly quoting verbatim from the maritime legal code.

"Good point Frank, but don't worry. That ship is going nowhere until we know who jumped off it. We suspect the people who left that ship could be wanted terrorists, which means your men can board it with my authority," Chen explained as he dialled the Task Force headquarters. "I want your officers to impound that vessel until we can get Task Force agents here. Don't take any nonsense, use an Armed Response Unit and arrest everyone onboard. I want answers." Chen was connected to headquarters and the uniformed officers headed back toward where the vehicles had been parked. It was a long walk in the pouring rain and they jogged most of it.

"Hello, it's Chen, is Tank there?"

"I'm afraid not sir, he is at a funeral today. The Major is in the office and he's asked me to contact you. Shall I connect you?" asked the operator.

"Yes put me through."

"Hello Chen, have you made any progress there?" the Major came on the line.

"There is evidence of a number of people leaving a Syrian vessel Major, they had an inflatable and fresh clothing waiting for them. It's not your average asylum seekers jumping ship, this was a well planned, well executed operation," Chen said, "I have ordered the local uniformed guys to board her and impound the crew. I need two squads to meet me at the boat as soon as possible sir."

"I will despatch red and blue teams to you immediately, we need to be thorough Chen. We've received information from our man in Israel that six members of Axe have dropped off the radar, and could be heading here. We can't substantiate the information, but they could be trying to carry out a high profile assassination attempt." There was a link forming and it was beginning to look like the two situations were connected. The fact that the terrorist cell had possibly already arrived was very worrying indeed.

"Do you think that they could be here already? How old is the information?" Chen asked as he started walking back toward his Jeep. He pulled up his collar to keep out the driving rain.

"We have no way of knowing, I'm afraid the informant was under Israelis interrogation and is no longer with us. We must assume that they're already here, worst case scenario," answered the Major sternly.

"We'll be onboard within the hour Major, I'll establish coms as soon as we have something to report," Chen closed his phone and put it in his trouser pocket before it could be soaked. He waved to PC Frank Burton and his colleague as they left in their police car, their wheels span in the gravel as they drove off. The uniformed officer was using the radio microphone as the car pulled away from the breakwater, already organising an armed unit to board the Syrian vessel. A huge wave hit the breakwater and Chen was splashed with salty sea spray. The wind was picking up and it started to rain even harder. The weather was closing in as he reached his Jeep. Chen opened the door and climbed into the driver's seat, pleased to be out of the rain. He'd got to the Jeep just in time as he inserted the ignition keys the heavens opened and torrential rain battered his vehicle, and the wind shook it.

He was about to turn the keys and start the engine when he noticed a strange fragrance. Chen's father still owned a Chinese restaurant in Liverpool's China town. Chen was familiar with the many herbs and spices that were used in Chinese cooking, as he had spent countless hours in his father's kitchen watching the chefs creating their culinary masterpieces. This smell reminded him of the kitchen but it was alien to his Jeep. It was the wrong smell in the wrong place. His expert intuition clicked into overdrive, something was wrong. Something was very wrong indeed. The spice that he could smell was Turmeric, a bright yellow powder with a very distinct fragrance. Chen looked around the vehicle, searching for anything that appeared to be out of place. Chen recalled that the spice was widely used in curried food, especially the type of food cooked in Asia and the Middle East. Its fragrance was so strong that the people that consumed it on a regular basis often smelled of the spice because it is excreted from the pores in the skin.

Someone had been in the Jeep while he was on the breakwater. He started to sweat. The wind blew and the rain poured. The Jeep trembled slightly as the Atlantic winds blew around it. Chen lowered his head slowly beneath the dashboard, trying to see if the steering column had been tampered with. The plastic casing was offset; it had been removed recently and not replaced properly. On the floor of the foot well, beneath the brake pedal, was a tiny piece of plastic coated wire filament. The coating was bright yellow with a black spiral running around it. The Jeep had been valet cleaned two days earlier. Chen hadn't been exposed to any electronic materials since it had been cleaned. Someone else had dropped that wire in his Jeep, and the only reason anyone would need wire filament was to plant a sophisticated explosive device.

The wind howled beneath the Jeep, rocking it. Chen sat up in the driver's seat and reached for his cell phone very slowly, the slightest vibration could trigger a motion sensor. He was absolutely convinced that there was a booby-trap bomb attached to his vehicle.

Chapter 3

Nasik

Nasik parked the battered old Citroen van in a multi-storey car park on Mount Pleasant, Liverpool city centre. He had stolen it the day before from outside a house in a suburb of Warrington called Orford. It looked like a million other work vans that took to the roads every day, spotted with rust and dented. The van had belonged to a self-employed tradesman who ran a small carpet cleaning business. The unfortunate owner was still sunning himself on a beach in Florida, completely unaware that his livelihood had been stolen. The terrorist cell, that he belonged to, would be able to use the van for days before it would be reported stolen. Nasik had covered the advertising decals with aerosol paint, and swapped the registration plates to complete the disguise. Even if it were reported stolen, it would be like looking for a needle in a haystack.

He turned off the engine and stepped out of the vehicle. Nasik was wearing a white canvas boiler suit, the type that painters favour, and a new pair of Adidas training shoes. He opened the rear doors of the van and removed a tough resin toolbox. Home improvement warehouses advertised them as tough boxes. The box was the size of a large suitcase, fitted with wheels and a pop up handle so that it could be moved easily. It was also designed to be used as a makeshift seat or a stepladder, and could comfortably withstand the weight of an adult male. Nasik put a baseball cap on his head and was a little shocked when a tuft of hair came away from his scalp in his fingers. He looked at the strands for a long moment, and then folded cotton dustsheets over his arm and carried on as if nothing was wrong. He extended the handle on the massive toolbox and set off toward the busy town centre.

When Nasik stepped out of the car park the persistent rain intensified, large raindrops bounced off the pavement soaking the bottom of his overalls immediately. He looked around to find his bearings and referred to a tourist map that he had been given the night before. To his right, up the hill was the Catholic cathedral, known to the locals as Paddy's wigwam, because of its distinctive conical shape. It dominated the skyline and looked like a giant chess piece topped with a stained glass crown weighing hundreds of tons. Nasik was fascinated by the building, but he had to blink to clear the pelting rain from his eyes.

To his left, down the hill, the busy metropolis was already buzzing with life, despite the early hour. A twenty feet tall naked statue of a man stood above the door of a large retail building. It was situated at the junction of a major traffic intersection. Nasik found the volume of traffic intimidating, as it was completely alien to him. The concrete landscape that surrounded him was a strange, noisy frightening world. He walked through the rain past a colossal hotel called the Adelphi, it was built from white marble blocks and tall roman columns adorned the front of the building, atop wide sweeping stone steps.

He pulled up the collars on his overalls to try to stop the rain from seeping in, but to no avail. The temperature in his homeland never dipped below thirty degrees Celsius, and he was struggling to acclimatise. He'd seen rain only twice in his life. The wind blew off the river and seemed to penetrate his clothes; he hadn't been warm since he had arrived in this god-forsaken country. Nasik jumped with fright as lightning forked across the dark sky, thunder rumbled seconds later. He steeled himself against the wind and rain, and walked faster toward his destination.

Nasik was born in the part of Israel known as the West Bank. Muslims, Christians and Jews had fought over this disputed territory for centuries, but in 1948, religious conflict resulted in millions of Palestinians being forced from their own country and being exiled in the West Bank. It became a breeding ground for suicide bombers in recent years, and they have taken a terrible toll from the Israeli people. Israel adopted a policy of zero tolerance against the Muslim populations in the West Bank and Gaza strip. When a suicide bomber was identified, the Israelis launched brutal search and destroy missions into Gaza and the West Bank, which targeted their families. The homes of the bomber's families were demolished by tanks and bulldozers, in retaliation for any attack on Israeli soil.

Nasik was born to one such family, who were distantly related to a Muslim extremist, who chose to blow himself up on a bus packed with

Jewish workers. Nasik and his family were dragged from their home and could only watch, helpless as the Israelis demolished it. The search and destroy missions were supposed to send a message of warning to the wider Muslim community, that insurgency would not be tolerated. Homeless, Nasik left the West Bank and headed for a religious camp situated in the deserts of northern Somalia. It was there that he became a dedicated follower of the legendary Yasser Ahmed. He trained for four years in the camp under the direct supervision of Yasser.

Nasik had a forte with a sniper rifle, and he became an excellent marksman, eventually teaching the newer recruits how to shoot. For many years, he had been focused on the Muslim struggle that affected him the most, Israel. The wider struggle only became an issue when Yasser Ahmed was captured. Now he had been given the opportunity to use his skills on a mission that would have a global impact, and take revenge for his leader.

Nasik dragged his toolbox half a mile across the busy city centre, all the time keeping his destination in clear view. As he approached it, the sheer size of it shocked him. He stood beneath it and stared upward, his jaw hung open slightly. The St. John's tower was attached to a large two-storey shopping mall. The tower was seventy-five feet in diameter and over two hundred feet tall. It was a perfect cylindrical shape, until near the top of the structure, where there was a large disc shaped section. It looked like a flying saucer had landed on top of the tower. The disk shaped section had originally been a restaurant, which revolved imperceptibly offering breathtaking views of the city. In more recent times, it had become the home of a local radio station, called Radio City. The building was currently undergoing major refurbishment, which ousted its tenants to a temporary site, and that's what Nasik's plan depended on.

At the base of the tower at street level, there was a stainless steel door. The door concertinaed to reveal a goods lift. To the right of the door was a keyhole, which activated the service elevator. It was used to transport deliveries and heavy equipment to the old restaurant area situated at the top of the tower. Nasik fumbled in his pocket for the bunch of keys that he had been given the previous evening. They'd been labelled and marked with coloured plastic tape to save him time on the mission. He flicked through them until he found one that had been labelled, 'lift 1'. His hand was visibly shaking as he inserted the key into the lock and twisted it. It didn't budge. Nasik cursed under his breath and twisted the key in the opposite direction. The key turned and he heard the lift spring into life behind the steel doors. The elevator car clunked into its place in the lift shaft, and a bell rang as the door slid open. He stepped inside, dragging the toolbox out of the torrential rain. Nasik opened the dustsheets that he had carried with him and used the dry pieces to wipe the rain from his hands and face. He was cold and wet through; his hands were numb and still shaking. He took a deep breath to compose himself. Nasik took a packet of cigarettes from the toolbox. He flipped open the lid and tried to remove one with his fingers but they refused to work. He put the packet to his lips and used his front teeth to take out a cigarette. Nasik lit the cigarette with a match and inhaled deeply. The warm smoke soothed his jangled nerves momentarily and he held it in his lungs as long as he could, enjoying the sensation and its calming effect.

Suddenly the lift jerked and started to ascend as if it had a mind of its own. Nasik pressed the buttons on the panel to stop it, but it carried on upward. Someone in the old restaurant at the top of the tower had pressed the call button; it was supposed to be empty today. Nasik dropped his cigarette on the floor and stood on it. He reached into the toolbox and removed Colt .357. Then he opened a small compartment in the box, and took out a two-inch suppressor, which he screwed onto the barrel. He slipped the silenced gun inside his overalls, and closed the toolbox. It felt like an age passed as the elevator climbed two hundred feet toward the old restaurant. Nasik was stood facing the doors when the bell rang and they slid open.

Chapter 4

Grace Farrington

Grace Farrington was the Terrorist Task Force's number one agent below Tank. She was in a critical condition in a high dependency unit, at Liverpool's Royal hospital. The hospital specialised in long-term coma care. Grace had been shot twice during an incursion into Soviet held Chechnya, on a top-secret mission. The high velocity bullets, which ripped into her body, had been fired by the nefarious terrorist leader, Yasser Ahmed. The surgeons had removed her spleen, which had left her susceptible to infection. The physical wounds had healed well, but her body had gone into traumatic shock and switched off her brain as a defensive reaction. She was breathing for herself but nothing more.

Despite strict Task Force regulations about interdepartmental relationships, Tank was her lover and soul mate. He had spent every spare minute at her bedside reading newspapers aloud, or just telling her what was happening at work.

Tank didn't really believe that Grace would wake up, and neither did the doctors that were honest enough to be straight with him. What they didn't know was that she was becoming more aware of what was going on around her. She knew when visitors were next to her bed, especially Tank. She could recognise his voice. Grace had heard her father and mother fussing around her bed, as if she were a little girl, not a senior member of the Terrorist Task Force. There were other voices but she couldn't distinguish them all. Grace knew in her subconscious that something bad had happened to her, but she couldn't remember what it was. There were vivid memories of terrible pain and a noisy helicopter journey, then nothing. Her body still hurt sometimes but not as bad as it had. Grace sensed that she was healing and would become more aware as time went by. She also knew that she needed to wake up soon, but not just yet.

On the morning of the funeral, Grace was aware that her father was sitting next to the bed, and that her mother was fussing around putting water into a vase. Auntie somebody had sent fresh flowers. She was also aware that Tank hadn't been there today, which her subconscious told her was unusual. Grace was stressed, and her heightened awareness knew that something wasn't right. Her brain was starting to function again, as if someone was walking through an empty building turning on all the lights.

Her right hand twitched, she wasn't sure how she'd made it move, but it felt good. The movement shocked her father so much that he wasn't sure if she had actually moved at all, or if he had imagined it. Grace had an overwhelming sense of dread and she felt that she had to escape the dark helpless world that she dwelled in. She needed to return to the real world because something bad was going to happen. Her index finger twitched again.

"Doctor, nurse, someone get in here quickly!" her father pressed the emergency button next to Grace's bed. A nurse entered wearing a starched white uniform, which didn't flatter her curvy hips, and black nylons. She had black hair pulled back harshly from her face, and tied up on top of her head in a bun. Her forehead was covered in acne, large red angry spots clustered across her skin, reaching into her hairline. Her shoes clicked on the vinyl floor as she walked. She looked tired and disinterested, there was little to no hope that this coma victim was going to recover. She couldn't understand why the visitors were making such a fuss. She silenced the alarm.

"What's the problem Mr Farrington?" the nurse asked. She picked up Grace's hand and checked for a pulse in the wrist. It seemed much stronger than it had earlier that morning, which was unusual for a patient in this condition.

"She moved nurse, she moved her hand twice, I thought it was a mistake the first time but she did it again," Grace's father was rambling. Her mother was stood frozen rigid by fear, holding an empty vase and staring at her daughter, watching for a sign of life. She was cautiously excited, but also fearing the worst. Her husband could have been mistaken.

"I don't think that is possible Mr Farrington, you're well aware that Grace has been comatose for a very long time," the nurse didn't finish the sentence. Grace moved her fingers again. The nurse reached over the bed and pressed the alarm button. This time nursing staff came running into the room, along with a senior consultant who had been starting his rounds on the ward.

"What's going on nurse?" the doctor asked as he placed two fingers against Grace's neck, feeling for the jugular vein.

"There was definite movement in her right hand," the nurse answered.

"She did it twice before that doctor, I thought it was a mistake but she did it twice before," Mr Farrington was becoming very agitated.

"Sister, could you take the relatives to the family room while we have a good look at Grace please," the doctor wanted the parents out of the way, it could just have been a muscle spasm, which was unusual but not impossible. Mrs Farrington started to cry as her husband led her away from the ward, helped by a nursing sister. Several doctors and consultants had been paged to attend to Grace, and they passed by the Farrington family on their way to give their expert advice. It was all a bit of a shock for Mr Farrington as they had repeatedly been told to expect the worst.

They had come to see their daughter everyday that she had been in hospital, even though they'd been given little hope. They timed it so that when they were leaving, John Tankersley was arriving. Mr Farrington blamed Tank for what had happened to his beautiful daughter. She should never have been placed into a combat situation as far as he was concerned. On the odd occasion that they ever crossed paths in the hospital, Tank always said hello to them, and they always ignored him, gathered their things and left. Grace's father opened the door to the relatives' room and he ushered his distraught wife into a comfortable chair. He gave her a paper tissue from a box on the table.

"Would you like some tea Mrs Farrington?" asked the nurse. It doesn't matter what type of disaster was about to unfold, tea was Britain's answer to all evil.

"I'll go and get some, thank you nurse," said Mr Farrington. He needed a little space to clear his thoughts. He thought that he should phone John Tankersley to tell him about Grace, but the hatred ran too deep. Grace's father was still in turmoil when he reached the vending machine in the corridor. He was so confused that he dropped his change on the floor. He didn't notice the cleaner that passed by him. The cleaner looked to be from the Middle East somewhere, and he wasn't wearing any blue plastic overshoes. The wearing of plastic overshoes had been made compulsory for all external employees because of the spread of the MRSA virus. Of course, any genuine cleaning contractor would be well aware of that, and there was nothing genuine about this particular cleaning contractor.

Chapter Five

Yasser Ahmed

Yasser turned over in his sleep and knocked the septic stump of his amputated arm on the edge of his metal cot bed. He awoke with a scream of pain as the nerve endings in his wound went into a terrible frenzy. The pain brought tears to his eyes every time he accidently caught the stump. He had been shot in the arm and shoulder by John Tankersley, leading to his capture and brutal imprisonment. The arm had never been allowed to heal properly as his interrogators focused all their attention on the tender appendage. Eventually gangrene took hold and the arm had to be amputated. His tormentors still used the wound to cause him as much pain as they could during his daily interrogations. They plied him with antibiotics to stop any life threatening infections taking root, but his shoulder never healed and became a festering sore.

Yasser Ahmed was the spiritual leader of the terrorist organisation known as, Axe. His formative years had been spent in his native Iraq, where after surviving two allied invasions and witnessing the chaos they had inflicted upon his people, he had joined in the Islamic struggle. Once a protégé of bin Laden Yasser formed a splinter group of his own. He focused all his considerable resources into attacking the Western coalition on their own soil. In time, he had become the most wanted terrorist on the planet. His untimely capture in Chechnya didn't put an end to his organisation's activities, it only fuelled their resolve.

The American intelligence agencies had demanded first crack at him when he was captured, despite the fact that British forces had actually caught him. Yasser had been handed over to them in the Turkish city of Istanbul; from there he had been taken to a Chechen prison that specialised in extraordinary rendition. Most of the information that they extracted was useless or made up. Yasser knew that they would never release him, and a slow lingering death was all he had to look forward to. He would never betray his followers, no matter what agonies he suffered, and he had endured more pain than you could imagine in your worst nightmares. He would never surrender. Yasser had given them names. He had also given them detailed information about imminent plots that were yet to unfold, but they were always the names of rival militias, people that he wanted dead.

Yasser sat up in his stinking cell and gritted his teeth against the pain in his shoulder. It radiated through his entire body. He could tell by the amount of daylight that entered through a tiny barred window, high up the wall of his cell that the sun had been up for a while already. His torturers would come soon. Their routine was like clockwork. An hour after sunrise every day they came down the corridor of the medieval dungeon opened the metal door and dragged him into the interrogation suite, or torture chamber. They were late today. There was a noise and he heard the metallic scraping of a door being opened in the corridor, and then the sound of boots running down the dank passage toward his cell. There were at least three sets of boots, maybe four or more. Normally there were never more than two guards and they didn't run anywhere. Perhaps this was the end. Yasser closed his eyes and said a silent prayer.

The door was unlocked and four uniformed guards entered the cell. The first guard punched Yasser in his bad shoulder and yelled at him in Chechen to stand up. The pain was unbearable and Yasser felt consciousness slipping away. The men dragged him to his feet and a hessian sack was thrown over his head. They strapped his one good arm to his torso with an elastic bungee, and dragged him out of the cell into the dark passageway. Yasser was too weak from the pain to carry his own weight. The guards lifted him and his feet dragged along the dank stone floor.

He was taken through three sets of thick metal gates; they screeched open and then slammed shut as they passed, which was the normal routine. As they approached the torture chambers Yasser could hear the demented screaming of his fellow detainees, whose daily interrogation had already begun. The guards dragged him passed the interrogation rooms and through another set of gates, which was not part of the usual routine. The sound of screaming was fading into the distance as he was dragged further on through the maze of corridors. He was convinced that they were taking him to be shot. He was no longer any use to them.

A metal door clanged open and Yasser felt the wind on his skin for the first time in years. The cold air-cooled the raging pain in his stump, and he breathed in the fresh air. Yasser felt a leg restraint being fixed around his ankles; then he was picked up and thrown onto a raised metal floor. He heard more voices around him but the hood obscured his vision. There was a muffled scream and another man landed on top of Yasser crushing his infected shoulder. Yasser screamed through gritted teeth and waited for the surging pain to subside a little before he wriggled away from the other body to a more comfortable position.

Angry voices continued to bark instructions to unseen prison guards then a door was slammed shut and the voices faded. There was a deep reverberation as the unmistakable sound of a helicopter engine filled the air. Yasser felt the vibration generated by the rotor blades turning. He didn't know why, but he was being moved. A twinge of hope entered his world of despair.

Chapter Six

Eccleston Church/ Tank

Tank shifted uncomfortably on the narrow wooden church pew, his suit was damp and his collar was rubbing his thick neck. The congregation had just finished singing the hymn, 'Abide with me'. The vicar had positioned himself in a carved wooden pulpit, and he began to deliver his sermon when Tank felt his pager buzzing against his thigh. Only Major Timms and the consultant at Grace's hospital had his pager number. He was seated alone at the rear of the church, so it wasn't difficult to check the message without attracting attention, or offending anyone. Tank read the message and panicked; he stood up and walked to the back of the church. He felt his blood pressure rising and his face reddened. He approached the church usher at the rear of the church, and showed him his badge.

"I need to make an urgent call, is there somewhere quiet I can use?" Tank whispered without disturbing the requiem.

The usher opened a narrow wooden door and indicated that he should go up the stone steps. Tank started up the staircase and heard the usher closing the door behind him, the sound of the vicar's sermon became a muffled drone. The stairwell was plunged into darkness when the door closed, and Tank had stop to allow his eyes to adjust. The steps had been worn smooth by centuries of use. There was a sharp turn to the right at the top of the stairs before Tank reached another wooden door. He groped for the handle and felts its cold metal surface against his skin; he opened the door and stepped into a large loft room conversion. The ceiling followed the contours of the steep slate roof above it, and the floor was made from polished piranha pine planks. There was a window set in the far wall, which overlooked the graveyard at the side of the church. Tank headed toward it and removed his cell phone from his jacket pocket.

He punched in the telephone number of the high dependency ward, fearing the worst.

"Get me Dr Morris please, its John Tankersley speaking," he said to the switchboard operator. The pager message had told him to call the senior consultant urgently regarding Grace's condition. Tank felt his stomach knotting with dread. He had anticipated receiving this dreadful news, and rehearsed what he would say when it came a hundred times. Tank stared out of the window at the rain, and his mood matched the appalling weather beyond the window. He could see a freshly dug grave in the near distance that would soon be the final resting place for his grandmother. The undertakers were moving flowers from the hearse to the rain soaked graveside.

"Hello John, I'm sorry to use your pager number, but your mobile was going straight to answer phone," the consultant said.

"It's not a problem Dr Morris, what's happened?" Tank felt stupid asking the question. Grace was dead, what else could possibly have happened? Tank felt his eyes welling up again. He was very vulnerable today. He stared at the churchyard trying to occupy his troubled mind, when he noticed a black Mercedes panel van parked at an odd angle on the graveyard's access road. There was something not quite right about it. The rear passenger window was open about six inches, and cigarette smoke was drifting from it. One of the worst thunderstorms Tank had witnessed was in full flow, yet someone needed the window open. Who took the time out to relax and smoke in a graveyard?

"I don't want you to get unduly optimistic but Grace is moving her hands, it may be nothing it's too early to tell, but it is very unusual for a patient in Grace's condition to demonstrate any motor function at all," the doctor explained. Tank hardly heard a word, because he was focused on the Mercedes. He reached into his inside jacket pocket and took out a telescopic sight glass that was no bigger than a ballpoint pen.

"I know it must come as a shock to you John, but it's a very positive sign, are you alright?" the doctor was trying to breach the silence at the other end of the phone. Tank focused the telescope on the window of the van and saw the business end of a Bushmaster sniper rifle, which had a silencer built in to it. The barrel was unmistakable.

"John, are you alright John?" the consultant was becoming concerned. "We have moved her to an assessment ward for neurological tests to see if there is any brain activity. Her parents are here John, I know you don't see eye to eye but I thought you would want to know immediately."

"That really is great news. I need to call you back Dr Morris, I'm afraid something has come up," Tank ended the call and touched the empty holster beneath his armpit. His Glock 9 mm was locked in the car two hundred yards away. He couldn't get to it without passing the sniper.

Chapter Seven

Holyhead Breakwater/ Chen

Chen had activated the personal alarm function, which was built into his Task Force cell phone. He couldn't risk making a conventional call or even sending a text message in case the explosive device was sensitive to SMS signals. Chen figured that it would take fifteen minutes for a reaction team to respond to the alarm, locate it and then launch a rescue. Holyhead was situated twenty-one miles from the Welsh mainland, off the northwest coast of Anglesey. It is one hundred and twenty miles by road from the Task Force headquarters in Liverpool. A helicopter flight would half that distance and cut the two-hour drive time to forty minutes. He had to try to survive for at least one hour, without triggering the bomb.

Chen had found a fragment of wire filament in the foot well of his vehicle, which indicated that there was a bomb attached to it, fitted with an electrical detonator. If he was correct then the device could be detonated either remotely or by a trigger switch. Remote detonation requires the bomber to remain close to the target; they can use infrared or another source of electrical impulse such as a mobile phone to ignite the explosive. Trigger switches generally contain mercury, which possesses the qualities of both a liquid and a metal. Its metal qualities give it the ability to conduct an electrical charge, whilst its liquid qualities make it behave like a fluid. Even the slightest vibration makes the substance move. The motion of a moving vehicle, or even opening the door could make the mercury move enough to complete an electrical circuit, triggering the bomb. This could be the longest hour of Chen's life, if he lived that long.

A bolt of lightning streaked across the dark sky and struck the earth somewhere on Holyhead mountain, in front of him. The mountain rose fifteen hundred feet from the sea, grassy lower slopes gave way to bare grey rock at the summit. Thunder rumbled overhead and the wind rocked the vehicle. Chen froze as he waited for the wind to subside, but it seemed to strengthen and rocked the Jeep even more. He tried desperately to think of a way out of this predicament. Chen focused on the sea for a moment. The water had turned an angry deep green colour, and the swell was rising to form huge peaks and troughs. A wave crashed against the breakwater, spraying the vehicle with tons of saltwater. The Jeep lurched violently and Chen squeezed his eyes closed, waiting for the imminent explosion. He gripped the steering wheel so tightly that his knuckles turned white, but nothing happened.

Chen heard sirens in the distance. Across the marina, he saw a convoy travelling along the Newry beach road, heading toward the breakwater. The beach had a ten feet wide strip of gritty sand, and then a rock shore led up to manicured grass slopes, which reached the beach road. The road was lined with wooden wind shelters that resembled little cottages; he could see tourists sheltering from the rain sat inside them. The police vehicles reached the end of the beach and disappeared into a single-track lane hidden from view by tall trees. The remains of an old air force stronghold peeped above the tree line, looking like a huge grey stone cube with windows. The convoy stopped on the breakwater approach road, and set up a roadblock to stop any unsuspecting tourists stumbling into a bomb scare. The Task Force must have alerted the local law enforcement agencies; therefore, they must be on their way. He thought that he had heard the unmistakable oscillation of helicopter engines approaching, but he couldn't be sure. The wind gusted again and the engine noises faded. He was starting to panic, hearing rescuers that didn't exist. A wave exploded against the breakwater and spray covered the Jeep, obscuring his view again. The wind dropped momentarily and he heard the engines again; this time he was certain that it was the noise of a twin engine Chinook. He rotated slowly in his seat and lowered his head, trying to get a glimpse through the rear window. The black clouds were too low for him to distinguish anything, but the sound was coming closer. Chen strained to look, and then slowly returned to face the windscreen.

Two Chinooks emerged from the thunderstorm. One of them flew toward the mountain and then turned one hundred and eighty degrees to position itself in front of the Jeep. The summit of the mountain was now covered by low storm clouds. The helicopter struggled to manoeuvre with any degree of accuracy against the winds. The immense downdraft created a cloud of dust and gravel. The side cargo door slid open and four ropes were thrown clear, landing on the breakwater fifty yards away. Task Force agents used the ropes to abseil from the helicopter onto the sea wall. They were on the ground in just a matter of seconds. The second Chinook peeled away from the breakwater and headed across the harbour toward the Syrian vessel that was still anchored to the jetty. Chen watched agents descending onto the cargo deck of the ship in his rear view mirror.

Four Task Force men approached the Jeep cautiously. The team leader pointed to the ground and then to his eyes, and the Task Force men dropped to their knees. They lay prone on the sea wall looking for explosives beneath the vehicle. The agents stood up and the team leader summoned them to look beneath the engine block.

An explosive device was identified. It had been fitted to the electrical coil, on the engine block. The coil amplified the Jeep's electric current, which powered everything fitted to the vehicle. The explosives would be detonated if Chen used the electric windows, central locking, ignition, stereo, heated seats or any of the other bells and whistles. Moving the vehicle or opening the doors was out of the question. The reaction team stood huddled together in the torrential rain, machineguns slung over their shoulders, concocting a plan. Chen wished he could hear what they were saying but they couldn't risk opening a window to communicate with him.

The agents looked to be concerned and rushed, which was unusual for a unit selected for their professional expertise. They broke and approached the front of the vehicle. One of the agents indicated to Chen that he must put his head down beneath the dashboard. Chen wasn't sure what they had in mind, but they had seen the bomb, he hadn't. Two of the agents took rolls of silver duct tape from their haversack and began sticking long strips of it across the windscreen. Even the torrential rain couldn't stop the duct tape from bonding tightly to the glass. Layer upon layer was placed horizontally onto the glass, then vertical layers were placed over them, and the process was repeated until the duct tape was used up.

Chen was lying across the two front seats. He jumped when an agent tapped gently on the window. He signalled one, two then three, with the first three fingers of his right hand. Whatever they were planning he would have to move quickly. Chen stared at the agent as he began the countdown for real. He counted mentally as the agent's fingers flicked up, one then two. As the third finger appeared six, nine millimetre bullets ripped through the windscreen. The glass was fractured into a thousand pieces but remained in place held still by the duct tape. The agents dragged the shattered glass away from the vehicle and reached into the Jeep to grab Chen out. The wind and rain howled into the smashed window. Chen kicked against the dashboard trying to gain purchase, but he lost his footing and slipped. Strong hands pulled him through the windscreen and across the bonnet.

He cleared the Jeep and landed with an unceremonious bump onto the concrete and gravel, his hips and legs submerged in a puddle. The agents didn't stop there. Chen tried to regain his feet but they were pulling him too quickly, his legs dragged behind him through the puddles of rainwater and sea spray. He was pleased to be away from the booby trap, but surely, they were a safe distance away now. Chen was about to protest when the timer on the bomb reached zero minutes, and detonated the explosive charge. The shockwave lifted Chen and his rescuers off their feet, and blew them off the breakwater into the Irish Sea.

Chapter Eight

Nasik/ St. John's Tower

The lift door opened to reveal two slightly surprised businessmen. One of them was an estate agent the other was the refurbishment project manager. They had agreed to bring forward a scheduled meeting, so that they could inspect the building progress without interruption from the contractors who worked there. Several contractors had hired cheap foreign labour to work on the site, resulting in friction from local trade union members who refused to work alongside them. The tower was completely empty of workmen, except for the dark skinned painter stood in the elevator. Nasik could tell from their surprised expressions that the businessmen were not expecting to encounter any contractors. He could try to bluff his way through the situation, but his English wasn't good enough. He didn't have the required paperwork to give him authorised access to the tower either.

"Step away from the door please, and you won't get hurt," Nasik spoke quietly, his pronunciation wasn't perfect but it was said with conviction. The expressions of surprise turned to fear as the businessmen realised that the painter was holding a firearm, and it was pointed at them.

"What the bloody hell is going on? What do you want?" spluttered the estate agent. He stepped backward instinctively trying to get away from the weapon and stumbled into a workbench. The sawhorse toppled over and a claw hammer fell at his feet. The estate agent stared at the hammer trying desperately to make a decision. Then he looked at Nasik, his eyes locked stares with the Palestinian for long seconds, sweat ran down his forehead. He was debating if he could reach the hammer and disable the gunman before being shot, or not. The odds were stacked heavily against him. The Palestinian read his thoughts. Nasik pulled the trigger twice and the silenced gun spat death. Two jacketed slugs slammed into the businessman's abdomen, and he crumpled to the floor, all thoughts of picking up the hammer were gone forever.

Nasik turned his attention to the second man. He gestured with the weapon and the project manager raised his hands and stepped away from his dying colleague.

"Turn around and kneel down, I won't hurt you as long as you follow my instructions," Nasik said. The man knelt and placed his hands behind his head, his body shuddered as he started sobbing with fear. Thick black fluid was leaking from his colleague's abdomen onto the workmen's dustsheets. Nasik removed a thick roll of tape from his toolbox and fastened the man's hands behind his back; then he stuck a strip across his eyes.

"Stand up," Nasik ordered. He grabbed the man's arm roughly and guided him to a roof support, which was situated in the centre of the circular restaurant. He taped the businessman to the scaffold pole, and then forced him into a sitting position. Nasik noted with disgust that the man had urinated in his trousers. The man continued to sob as Nasik walked back to the lift. Nasik pulled the toolbox from the elevator into the empty restaurant. The estate agent groaned as he passed. Nasik pointed the pistol at the prone man and shot him again, he stopped groaning. The Palestinian's plan had been compromised, so he needed to adapt the situation accordingly. He picked up the dead man by the ankles and dragged his body into the lift. Then he removed the pin from a fragmentation grenade and fixed it beneath the armpit of the corpse. If anyone moved the body, the grenade would explode two hundred feet below at street level, giving Nasik an early warning of approaching danger.

Nasik reached inside and pressed the ground floor button inside the elevator. The doors closed and the lift descended with the booby-trapped corpse in it. There were lights above the lift doors and they illuminated, indicating that the elevator had reached street level. Nasik picked up the claw hammer and used it to force open the lift doors. He righted the workbench and wedged it between the doors exposing the long dark shaft, rendering the lift useless. He was back in control of the situation but time was running out, he had to be quick if he was to successfully complete his mission.

Nasik wheeled the toolbox across the deserted restaurant to a booth next to the windows. The radio station that now occupied the old restaurant had built a soundproof broadcasting booth. It was made from glass. Inside were a mixing desk and a comically big foam covered microphone. The old restaurant was a circular shape, with walls made completely from glass. Situated hundreds of feet above the city centre it was a perfect viewing gallery. It was also the perfect sniper's nest. He took four sections of a Cheytac-200 sniper rifle from the box and assembled them with expert speed. It was an exercise that he had rehearsed hundreds of times, blindfolded. The rifle was completely assembled and loaded with 7.68 mm bullets in under two minutes. He attached a long-range telescopic sight and pointed it toward the river. Nasik used the huge bronze Liverbird statues, which were perched on top of the Liver buildings, to focus the sights. The Liverbird statues were half a mile away, next to the river. As the image became crisp, he panned the rifle left toward the Albert docks, and focused them again. The docks were old converted grain storage buildings, built at the height of Liverpool's maritime domination. The port was once the busiest in the world, and was the centre of the slave trade at its height. Nasik was happy with the distance, now he needed to find his target. He panned the rifle right, until the police headquarters at Canning Place came into sight.

The structure was built from prefabricated concrete slabs. Every corner of the building had narrow slit shaped windows fitted into the stairwells. The windows were adopted from medieval castle architecture, and were designed to be used as sharpshooter positions if the building ever became under siege. He raised the barrel until it was pointing at the top floor. The image was slightly blurred so he adjusted the sights again. There was a man stood in the window, holding a telephone to his ear. The image cleared, and Nasik lined up the crosshairs of the sights, directly on the forehead of Major Stanley Timms.

Chapter Nine

Tank/ Eccleston Churchyard

Tank dialled the Task Force hotline but it was constantly jammed. The congregation would soon be heading outside into the graveyard and into the path of a sniper; he was going to have to deal with this on his own. He activated his emergency beacon twenty minutes after the reaction team had left to rescue Chen. An armed response unit would be dispatched by the local uniformed division, but they would not arrive before the requiem was finished. Tank scanned the Mercedes van with his telescope again. He could make out the silhouettes of two men, a driver and a shooter. The rifle was not standard issue for any Western agency; it was a model more commonly used by African and Middle Eastern militias.

Tank opened the door to a small store cupboard, which was situated in the corner of the converted loft. He studied the contents of the cupboard quickly, and formulated a plan of action. There was a five-litre container of methylated spirit, which he removed along with some cleaning rags. Tank twisted the top off the container and stuffed the rags into the purple liquid. The smell of the spirit reminded him of chemistry lessons at school. The church used the spirit to fuel its lanterns. He carried the container toward the door and paused at the desk. On the centre of the leather topped desk there was a heavy glass paperweight, holding down a pile of documents. Tank slipped it into his jacket pocket and sprinted down the narrow stone stairs.

The church usher seemed concerned as Tank entered the main body of the church. Tank summoned him over.

"Do you have the keys to the main doors?" Tank asked in a hushed voice, so as not to disturb the mass.

"Yes, I have them here. What's the problem?" the usher was confused by the strange question.

"Is there any other way into this building?" Tank asked guiding the usher toward the main doors by the arm.

"There's a leper door behind the altar," the usher replied. The church had been built in medieval times when lepers were not allowed to mingle with the public, even during worship. Small-secluded entrances were built into churches as standard features, to accommodate the infected members of the community.

"Lock the doors, and do not open them under any circumstances until you hear my voice," Tank squeezed the ushers arm to emphasise the urgency in his request.

"I'm afraid that's against health and safety regulations. I can't lock the church with people inside. What are you doing with that methylated spirit, you know that it's highly flammable don't you?" the usher blustered, offended by the big policeman. He was not the type of public servant that was easily intimidated by anyone, police officer or not.

"Lock the doors, or I'll place you under arrest, and then lock them myself. Do I make myself perfectly clear?" Tank raised his voice slightly and members of the congregation noticed the fracas at the rear of the church. People turned to look at the altercation and the vicar stopped his sermon. Tank could feel the withering looks he was getting from members of his own family. There wasn't time to explain, he needed to move now.

"Lock the door," Tank stared at the little man, and he did as he had been instructed. Tank walked down the aisle. The congregation was sat in stunned silence.

"You will need to continue the sermon until I return, vicar, there's police business outside I'm afraid," Tank flashed his badge and the vicar nodded open mouthed in response. He knew that Tank was in law enforcement and he sensed that the situation was urgent. The vicar cleared his throat and continued, although no one was listening anymore. They were far more interested in their relative's behaviour. There's nothing like a relative misbehaving at a funeral to get tongues wagging. Some of the congregation turned to each other and whispered conversations could be heard throughout the church. Tank entered the vestry and headed toward the leper door at the far end. He noticed spare robes hanging from hooks on the wall. They were long black gowns used for Eucharist services, beneath them were ceremonial mortarboards, which were worn on the head. Tank removed a set and put the biggest robes that he could find on over his suit, and he placed the mortarboard on his head. He unlocked the leper door, opened it and headed into the thunderstorm, carrying his impromptu Molotov cocktail.

As Tank stepped into the torrential rain, lightening flashed again. Tank counted silently in his mind until the thunder clapped. He left the church from the opposite end that he had entered it. The section of graveyard he was in was hidden from view by trees and undergrowth. A hedgerow ran along the edge of the graveyard for a few hundred yards, and offered him cover from the men in the black van. The urge to run and close the distance quickly was overwhelming, but if the men in the Mercedes turned to look in his direction, they would find it a little odd to see a priest dashing around the graveyard in the rain. Tank strolled briskly over the graves, hiding the container of methylated spirit behind his cassock. He kept his head bowed and his face obscured. Three minutes later, he was twenty yards away from the Mercedes. The driver moved position and looked in the direction of the church. Tank turned away, froze and placed his free hand on a headstone, as if he were praying for a departed soul. He read the inscription silently in his mind, trying to appear as authentic as possible.

The driver saw Tank move from the corner of his eye, and turned in his seat to get a better look. There was movement in the back of the van too. Tank turned his face away from the van, knelt down and hunched his shoulders as if in prayer. He removed the glass paperweight and a lighter from his pocket, using his obscured hand. Tank lit the rag, and the spirit ignited with a whooshing sound. He turned quickly and launched the paperweight with all his might. The heavy glass ornament shattered the driver's window and struck the terrorist on the side of the head, knocking him over the gearstick. The second man panicked and tried to turn his rifle toward Tank, but his movement was hampered by the headrests. It gave Tank precious seconds. The sniper was still wrestling with the gun when the burning container of spirit was launched through the broken window of the van, splashing the occupants with its contents. The container ruptured spraying the flammable liquid around the van. There was a delay of two seconds before the methylated spirit burst into flame.

The interior of the vehicle became a raging inferno. Tank sprinted to the side door of the Mercedes and pulled open the door. The flames licked at him as he reached in, and pulled the burning terrorist from the rear of the van. The driver managed to open his door by himself, and he staggered from the vehicle and fell burning onto the road. Tank grabbed the sniper and punched him hard on the jaw. His body went limp. The driver was still alight, and he tried to regain his feet. Tank threw a powerful low roundhouse kick, which swept the drivers legs from beneath, and he crashed to ground. The Task Force agent dragged him onto the road and rolled the terrorists over through the puddles, trying to extinguish the flames, as half a dozen armed response vehicles screamed to a halt, their sirens blaring.

The armed police surrounded the suspect Mercedes and began to search it for weapons and explosives. Tank turned toward the little stone church. The entire Tankersley clan were stood aghast in the pouring rain staring at him dressed in vicar's robes, stood over two smouldering bodies, and surrounded by armed police.

"It looks like our Tank has had a spot of bother," his uncle whispered to the priest.

Chapter Ten

Yasser

Yasser tried to make himself comfortable. The helicopter had been flying for over an hour, and his legs were becoming cramped. He shifted his weight and blood circulated back into his limbs. The pain in his infected shoulder was present, but it was bearable for now. He sensed that there was someone lying next to him, not far away. The stench of stale sweat that pervaded from him told Yasser that it was another prisoner. The smell was male. Yasser could hear that the prisoner's breathing was laboured, either because of injuries sustained during torture, or the onset of a serious respiratory disease. Tuberculosis was rife in prisons that were built in the eighteen hundreds, such as most of the Eastern European jails that are used by the West for rendition. Yasser stretched his legs toward the sound of the breathing, and his foot made contact with a body. Yasser poked the prisoner gently with his foot, but he got no response. He kicked harder and the prisoner groaned audibly, but there was no communication from him.

The helicopter engines drowned out any noise, so Yasser didn't hear the footsteps approaching him. He still had a hessian hood over his head, which dulled his senses even further. Suddenly a size twelve combat boot crashed down on his shoulder and unbearable pain wracked his body. Yasser gritted his teeth together, and screamed in agony. He rolled away from his attacker and curled up in a ball, trying to shield a further attack. There was a tirade of abuse hurled in his direction, but it wasn't in a language that he understood. The engine noise was deafening, but he thought his attacker might be speaking in a Greek dialect. Yasser had heard that several Eastern European countries were sympathetic to the West's rendition programme. The guard could be from Macedonia or Albania, he wasn't sure, and it didn't really matter, but his survival instinct was telling him to gather as much information about his surroundings as he could.

Yasser had trained several victims of American rendition in Pakistan, and he had learned some important facts from them. There was a consistent modus operandi. Victims were never transported by road, always by aircraft. Helicopters were used to carry prisoners to and from the jails. Commercial jets were chartered to transfer them across the international borders of sympathetic countries, where they would meet the helicopters to complete the journey. Victims of rendition were usually given enemas to negate the need for toilet breaks. They were fitted with a nappy and then drugged to make them compliant. If Yasser's information was correct then the helicopter flight would be the first leg of a longer journey. At some point, his captures would strip him and subject him to an enema.

When they did he would make his move, it wouldn't matter if he died, because he was already as good as dead. If he reached his new destination alive then he would be locked up deep in a filthy dungeon, with a new set of interrogators and a new set of torture techniques. Once inside, its impenetrable walls and iron gates, the opportunity to escape would be zero. Yasser knew that he was too weak to endure any more torture, and his amputated arm was so infected that he could barely stand the smell of his own flesh rotting. He would soon succumb to septicaemia without medical attention. He would not allow himself to be imprisoned again. He would die first.

Chapter Eleven

Major Stanley Timms

The Major was sitting at his desk when the telephone rang. It was the control room giving him an update on the developing situation in Holyhead. The agents that had rescued Chen were cold and wet, but otherwise uninjured. Chen was on the line to the control room.

"Patch Chen through to my direct line," the Major said. He was aware that a device had been planted on Chen's vehicle, but the circumstances were confusing.

"Hello Major," Chen came on the line.

"What happened there Chen?" asked the Major. "I have the preliminary reports, but they don't make sense."

"I parked the Jeep on an approach road to the breakwater, about five hundred yards from where the dingy was found," Chen explained. "I was walking through the scene with the local uniformed officers, for about forty minutes."

"That's not enough time for the attack to be random. Did you notice anyone following you there?" the Major asked.

"I didn't notice anything untoward, but then why would there be?" Chen answered. "As far as I was concerned I was there to confirm the evidence was of genuine interest to us."

"Was the vehicle compromised, or had you secured it?" the Major pressed.

"The vehicle was secured Major," Chen replied. "Whoever attached that device was an expert. Obviously, we'll know more when the forensic boys have finished, but our men said the device was fitted to the coil, wired into the electrics. It comprised of a mercury motion sensor and a timer. The device was high tech and the bombers were quick."

"Someone must have manufactured the bomb, and then followed you, waiting for an opportunity to attach it," the Major speculated.

The line buzzed indicating that there was another call coming through.

"Sorry to interrupt Major," said the switchboard operator, "Tank is on the line, he's using the emergency channel."

"Put him through, and leave Chen on the line too please," the Major ordered.

"John, what's happened?" the Major asked. He was aware that Tank had been attacked too, but wasn't party to the facts yet.

"Major, I've just taken out two insurgents armed with a CheyTac sniper rifle," Tank began, "they were positioned in the graveyard, outside the church. Both men were Middle Eastern in origin. I can only assume they were targeting me."

"Are you injured John?" the Major asked, he stood up and walked to his office window, "Chen has been attacked this morning too."

"I'm fine Major, how is Chen?" Tank answered, concerned.

"I'm okay Tank," Chen answered for himself, "it sounds like the two incidents could be connected, and it's too much of a coincidence for them not to be related."

"There's no doubt in my mind that the attack here was well planned and aimed at me," Tank said, "what happened to you Chen?"

"I was investigating the men that jumped ship in Holyhead. When I returned to the Jeep it had been rigged," Chen explained, "plastic explosive attached to a mercury switch and a timer."

"We need to assume that Task Force agents are being deliberately targeted Major," Tank said, "We've got to make sure everyone is accounted for."

"We know where everyone is at the moment, but there's one person that springs to mind as being very vulnerable," the Major said. The line remained silent while they digested the information and then figured out the possible connotations. The Major turned away from the window and walked toward his desk. Out of the corner of his eye, he thought he'd seen a flash in the distance.

"I had to think about that for a minute," Tank said, "you're talking about Grace Farrington aren't you?" Tank's stomach twisted. Grace was lying helpless in a hospital with absolutely no security whatsoever.

The Major was just about to answer, when a CheyTac bullet crashed through his office window, and hit him between the shoulder blades. It was like being hit with a sledgehammer. He was catapulted forward onto his desk. The Major tried to hold onto the edge of the desk, but consciousness was fading fast. He could only think about Grace being on her own, unprotected, when a second bullet smashed through his left shoulder, sending him into a spin, which landed him on the floor behind a metal filing cabinet. The Major crawled as close to the wall as he could, hiding his body from view of the window. As he drifted into unconsciousness, he could hear high velocity bullets slamming into the filing cabinets.

Chapter Twelve

Abu/ Grace

Abu waited for all the commotion to quieten down before he decided what to do. This was supposed to be a straightforward assassination. The target was a cabbage; surely, he couldn't possibly get this wrong. He wasn't sure what was happening, but his target was surrounded by medical staff. Her family had been taken away crying, hopefully, she was dying anyway and he would be saved the job of killing her. He doubted it though, because he wasn't that lucky.

Abu's family were once rich Palestinians and had lived in Jaffa, which is now part of Israel's Tel Aviv. They once owned miles and miles of orange groves and orchards, which they farmed. Their fragile existence was shattered in 1948 when war broke out between the Arabs and the Israelis, and they were forced into exile in the West Bank as refugees. Abu had grown up in poverty, constantly reminded by his parents that they were once rich. His father couldn't accept the loss of his wealth and he died from a broken heart when Abu was very young.

Like many disenfranchised young Palestinian men, Abu's only ambition was to join the Palestine Liberation Army and fight the Jews. When he reached the tender age of fourteen, Abu left home to fight. He had travelled to a training camp in Syria to learn how to use explosives, and that's when he'd met Yasser Ahmed. Abu became a dedicated follower of Ahmed's teachings. Although Abu had been a dedicated soldier of Islam since an early age, he hadn't received the recognition that he felt he deserved. Other Palestinians had climbed through the ranks of his organisation, while Abu was still a foot soldier. He was convinced that his family was cursed, forever unlucky.

There was a sudden flurry of activity in his target's room. To his dismay, his target was wheeled from her ward toward a large elevator, surrounded by a scrum of white coats. She couldn't be dead; unfortunately, something else had happened, which was just Abu's luck. The medical staff pushed her bed into the lift and the doors slid closed. He stood and watched the lights above the lift doors illuminate. The lights stopped at number five. She had been taken to the fifth floor.

Abu headed back toward the stairwell and started to climb up to the fifth floor. As he began his ascent, the lights above the lift doors moved again. He passed visitors and hospital staff en route but no one paid the lowly cleaning staff any attention, as long as he didn't loiter too long in one place his disguise rendered him invisible. He reached the door, which led into the ward, and he stopped to catch his breath. A combination of nerves and physical exertion was taking its toll. The doors to the stairwell burst open and two young doctors sprinted passed him down the stairs on their way to a critical emergency somewhere. Their voices faded as they turned on the stairs, quickly going out of sight. Abu's heart was pounding with fright. Instinct told him to abort the mission, report to the others, and then assess if the woman was still a viable target. Abu and his affiliates were not on suicide missions, they were soldiers of Islam, assassins. Failure to complete a simple mission such as this would only add fuel to Abu's self-loathing. He was always unlucky. This was another prime example. His target was supposed to be in a coma, helpless and easy to access.

The ward doors stopped swinging, and Abu looked through the round porthole window to assess the situation. There was a wide-open area beyond the door, starkly illuminated by a raft of strip lights. Three beds were lined up along the walls to the left, only one of which was occupied. The occupant was white skinned. This couldn't be his target. To the right was a metal machine, it was shaped like huge anvil with a tunnel bored through the middle of it. There was a throng of white coats standing next to it, and he could just see the feet of someone who had been put inside the machine. The feet were black with pink soles, but were dainty enough to be female. Abu guessed that his target was inside the big scanning machine. The group of doctors and nurses seemed to be discussing the situation; Abu watched them nodding their heads as there seemed to be a general consensus of opinion, and two nurses were headed straight toward him.

Abu jumped up three stairs at a time to reach the sixth floor landing before the nurses entered the stairwell. He paused at the top of the flight of stairs and held his breath, waiting to see which direction they took. The doors opened and the nurses headed down the stairs toward the fourth floor. Abu breathed out and wiped the beads of perspiration from his forehead.

"I've never known anyone to show signs of motor neurone activity after so long comatose, have you?" the nurses chattered.

"Never, it's very unusual, but we'll see what's what when she's done in the scanner, she'll be in there an hour at least."

Abu checked his watch. He had heard what the nurses had said and deduced that his target was going to be in the scanner for an hour at least. Apart from the doctors who were initially around her, the ward only had one other occupant. Two of the doctors had already gone elsewhere, as had two of the nurses. He tiptoed back to the fifth floor doors and looked in. There was only one woman near the scanner, and she was sat behind a protective screen looking at a computer terminal. The other doctors were huddled at the far end of the ward, heading toward an alternative exit, which seemed to lead into an anti-ward beyond the doors. His target was inside the machine and the other patient was unconscious in her bed. He reached inside his cleaner's overalls and touched the cold handle of his revolver.

He decided to wait fifteen minutes. If the scan took an hour the doctors would probably leave, and then return when it was completed. He headed back up to the sixth floor landing and looked for the cleaner's cupboard. Abu needed a mop and bucket to get him into the ward without arousing suspicion. He found it just to the side of the elevator doors on the sixth floor, but unluckily it was locked, typical. Abu used a pocketknife to twist the lock open. Inside the cupboard, he found three empty mop buckets, red, yellow and green, and the corresponding mops. He wasn't sure why they were different colours but it didn't matter. He grabbed the nearest one and waited inside the cupboard, relieving himself in the cleaner's sink while he had the opportunity. He hadn't realised how badly he needed to urinate until he saw the sink. His nerves were taut and the next fifteen minutes would feel like an age.

Abu opened the cupboard door fifteen minutes later, and headed down the stairs to the fifth floor, carrying his red mop bucket and yellow mop. He reached the ward doors and looked inside. He couldn't believe his luck. The ward was empty apart from the two patients that he had seen earlier, one white asleep in bed, the other black in the scanner. The doctor that had been studying the computer readout had gone. Abu pushed the doors open with his mop bucket and stepped into the ward. He double-checked that the ward was empty and then headed toward the scanner.

The machine was emanating a humming noise as he approached it. He took his revolver from his waistband, clicked off the safety and checked that the noise suppressor was screwed on tightly. He pointed the gun into the scanner aiming for his target's abdomen and fired. The gun clicked and nothing happened. Abu stared at the pistol in disgust. How much bad luck can one person possibly have? The bullet was a dud. He pointed the gun into the scanner a second time and pulled the trigger. This time the gun worked perfectly. Abu kept pulling the trigger until the remaining five bullets had been discharged into his target. The protruding black feet twitched every time a bullet slammed into the body.

Chapter Thirteen

Tank

John Tankersley didn't need a picture drawing to tell him that the Terrorist Task Force was under attack from a resourceful and determined enemy. Chen had survived being bombed, Tank had foiled two snipers, and the Major was en route to hospital in a critical condition. If it hadn't been for the thunderstorm at his grandmother's funeral, then Tank wouldn't have spotted the snipers in the Mercedes van. The Task Force had dispatched two combat units to impound the Syrian vessel in Holyhead harbour; another was heading to the high dependency unit at Liverpool's Royal hospital, to protect Grace Farrington. Chen and Tank had agreed to meet at the hospital, after all, the Major and Grace would already be there. His cell phone rang.

"Tank, where are you? We think the shooter was positioned in the St. Johns tower," said Ryan Griffin. Ryan was on secondment to the Task Force from the Royal Signals regiment. Using reverse trajectory, they could pinpoint where the sniper had fired his shot.

"Good job Ryan," Tank said. "Set up a cordon around the city centre. I want the bastard found."

"Roger that Tank. We're there now, my men are surrounding the place, and uniform divisions are evacuating the area as we speak."

"Be sharp Ryan, these people are very good, very good indeed. Keep me posted I'll be at the hospital until I know the Major and Grace Farrington are safe," Tank said, ending the call. The rain was still hammering down, making driving conditions dangerous. He needed to concentrate on the road ahead. He needed to reach Grace. He dropped the Shogun into fourth gear and stepped on the gas, accelerating the vehicle past the safari park toward Prescott Road. The road led directly into Liverpool city centre, and the Royal hospital, where his two colleagues were clinging to life by a thread. The route through Huyton was painless but the traffic thickened as he approached the McDonalds drive thru in Page Moss.

Tank opened his window and stuck a magnetic blue flashing light on the roof of his Mitsibushi. He switched it on and floored the accelerator, reaching eighty miles an hour in seconds. Tank turned up the heater, trying to dry off his damp suit. He felt chilled to the bone, but he didn't think it was anything to do with the constant thunderstorm. Ten minutes later, he was pulling into the hospital car park. He headed for the main entrance and screeched to a halt in front of the revolving glass doors.

A security guard stepped out and was about to object when Tank flashed his badge. He gave the guard his keys and told him to park the vehicle, and leave the keys behind reception. The guard nodded and climbed into the driver's seat. Two agents in full combat gear approached him, carrying Mossberg pump action shotguns. They were Task Force men. Across the reception area, Tank saw uniformed policemen carrying weapons. They nodded but looked confused and concerned to see Terrorist Task Force agents on the scene. Tank hadn't asked an armed response unit to attend, so someone else must have called them. Uniformed armed response only attended confirmed shooting incidents, and as far as Tank was aware, no one in the hospital had been shot.

"How's the Major?" Tank asked the first agent.

"He's in pretty bad shape Tank, he took two in the back. He's lost a lot of blood; they're operating on him now."

Tank frowned as he listened to the prognosis and nodded sternly. There was a uniformed officer talking to hospital security guards near the reception desk. Hospital security must have had a shooting incident in the building, prior to Tank arriving. His stomach wrenched.

"What about Grace Farrington?" Tank asked.

The agent was about to answer when one of his men burst into the reception area from a stairwell, his weapon was raised in a combat posture.

"We've got an incident on the fifth floor, possible agent down, suspect must still be in the building," the Task Force man shouted to Tank and his colleague as he scanned the reception area with his weapon. The reception area was half the size of a football pitch, surrounded by shops selling hospital stuff, flowers, magazines, fruit and the like. Dozens of people were milling around oblivious to the danger. Tank removed his Glock nine-millimetre and chambered a round.

"Cover the exits. Who's been hurt?" Tank shouted to the agent as he headed toward the stairwell.

"We think that it's Grace," the man replied without emotion. He was concentrating on locating a suspect and neutralising them. Tank felt like he had been kicked in the guts. He barged through the swing doors and pointed his gun up the stairwell. There was an agent on every landing above him, up to the seventh floor.

"Situation report," Tank shouted to the nearest agent.

"Casualty on the fifth floor Tank, five bullets in the chest," the man on the first floor landing replied. Tank nearly vomited. No one survived five bullets in the chest, especially in Grace's already weakened condition. Tank bounded up the steps, taking them three at a time without pausing, until he reached the fifth floor. The agents stationed on the landings remained silent as the big man sprinted passed them. They all knew what losing a fellow Task Force agent felt like, but losing a fellow officer who was so defenceless was mind numbing.

He reached the doors and looked through the glass porthole. A doctor was washing blood from his hands at small porcelain sink, lots of blood. Tank pushed the ward doors open and held his breath as he entered, with his gun still in his hand. Two doctors were walking away from a gurney. A starched white cotton sheet had been draped over the victim; bloodstains were spreading across the material where it touched the wounds beneath it. Tank put his hand against the wall and vomited into a red mop bucket. He could feel his knees trembling as shock started to set in and sap his strength. The doctors reached him and guided him to a seat.

"Sit down and take a deep breath. It really is a shock," the doctor said.

"I got here as quick as I could, when did she die?" Tank asked, feeling like he was going to vomit again.

"She died immediately, there was massive trauma, and she was so weak anyway," the doctor answered passing Tank a paper cup of water from the bloodstained basin. Tank shuddered at the sight of the blood-streaked porcelain.

"Why would anyone want to shoot an old lady like that, she was riddled with cancer, it's disgusting. I hope you catch the bastard."

"What do you mean, old lady?" Tank said regaining his composure somewhat.

"Well, sixty two is not that old, I suppose. I bet she wouldn't have thought so anyway," the doctor rambled.

Tank shook the doctor's hand off his arm and walked over to the gurney. He pulled back the sheet and stared at the grey haired lady. Her black skin had already lost its pallor making her look a grey colour. Tank looked at the doctors in disbelief, then at the red mop bucket, and the yellow mop, then back at the doctors.

"Where is Grace Farrington?" Tank said.

"Who?" asked the doctor, confused.

"Grace Farrington, the gunshot victim," Tank explained.

"Oh, you mean the coma victim, don't you?"

"Yes, Grace Farrington the coma victim," Tank was becoming agitated. Two of his agents entered the ward and Tank held up his hand to stop them from interrupting.

"She's been taken up to the seventh floor to be prepped for a brain scan. I believe she demonstrated some muscle activity earlier, which is quite remarkable really. It's been a bizarre day really," the doctor was starting to waffle. Tank found himself staring at the mop bucket. There was a red bucket, with a yellow mop, any self respecting cleaning contractor wouldn't make that mistake, especially not in a hospital.

"It's a cleaner," Tank turned to his agents. "The shooter is disguised as a cleaner, and he's fucked up, that's not Grace Farrington, she's on the seventh floor, so get your men up there."

The two agents turned and shouted their orders down the stairwell. The sound of combat boots thudding up the stairs faded as the Task Force men ascended.

"Is there any other way off this ward?" Tank asked the doctors.

"Through the anti-ward, there's a stairwell and a service elevator."

Tank rushed through the small anterior ward, which was virtually empty, and he entered a narrow stairwell beyond. He carried the Glock next to his right cheek, barrel pointed toward the ceiling as he tiptoed to the handrail. He looked up the stairwell, then down, checking for any escaping assassins. It was empty and silent. The service elevator was to his left, and he saw that the lift was in motion. It stopped in the basement. Tank jumped the steps down to the next landing then took two steps and repeated the process again descending the staircase rapidly.

"I need backup in the basement," Tank said into an open coms channel. "We are looking for a dark skinned cleaner." It would be like looking for a needle in a haystack. Cleaning companies the world over exploited the use of ethnic minorities for their underpaid workforce.

"Roger that, Tank. We've located Grace's position and she's secure."

Tank felt his nerves relax a little. Someone had tried to kill the Task Force's senior officers, and that someone was going to pay. He slowed his pace as he reached the first floor landing. A seventeen stone man descending the stairs at speed was not stealthy, to say the least. As he reached the basement doors two agents entered the stairwell, shotguns at the ready. The three men positioned themselves. Tank pointed to the agents and indicated that they were to branch right; he was going to go left.

They entered the basement area and moved swiftly, crouched low and they were sticking close to the walls. The basement was hot and steamy. It was separated into several service areas, an incinerator, a delivery bay and a laundry. Tank and his agents had entered the laundry section. There were four employees visible. They were all dark skinned, two afro Caribbean and two even darker, probably African. The employees looked frightened and concerned by the presence of men in combat gear, armed with shotguns. Tank pressed his index finger against his lips with one hand and pointed toward the exit with the other. He indicated that they had to remain silent and leave.

The cleaners walked slowly toward the doors until they were a few yards away, and then they ran and clattered through the swinging doors tripping over each other as they rushed to escape. As the laundry workers reached the steps, two more Task Force agents entered the laundry. Tank gestured them to progress through the middle of the basement, parallel to the others. The rest of the laundry was deserted.

At the far end of the laundry was the incinerator room. It was a huge area filled with immense piles of refuse waiting to be incinerated. There was an army of cleaning staff sorting the refuse into organised piles, sheets and linen, contaminated sharps such as syringes, food waste and gruesome body parts. At the far end of the cavernous room was the oven, its chimneystack towered above it and disappeared through the ceiling, before emerging again in the hospital car park above. There were contract staff members wandering about everywhere, brushing the floor and moving refuse. Tank and his agents stopped in their tracks when they realised how many of the cleaning staff were working in the basement. It would take an incredible stroke of good luck to identify a fugitive here. The employees were all foreign immigrants, dark skinned. They were all wearing black polo shirts, emblazoned with a gold embroidered logo on the chest. Big C cleaning company, everyone had dark canvas trousers on, and bright blue plastic overshoes, all except one man. It was a minor detail but an obvious one to a trained eye. It was always the attention to detail that gave terrorists away in the end. The suspect cleaner was about one hundred yards away. He didn't have the plastic overshoes on, and out of over twenty other staff, he was the only one.

The odd one out was walking away from Tank toward the delivery bay entrance. If he made it to the delivery bay, he could escape into the busy hospital car park, which was full of innocent members of the public. It was the best place for an armed confrontation. The majority of staff that were milling around had realised that there were armed police in the basement. Most of them stopped working and watched the police fascinated. Some of them moved swiftly toward the nearest exit, fearing that this was an immigration purge. Tank knew that there would be many illegal immigrants working in the basement, and they would be frightened that the police had launched a raid to find them.

He focused entirely on the man that wasn't wearing plastic overshoes, and he started to close the distance between them as quickly as he could without making it too obvious. The sight of Tank running with a gun raised sent a shockwave through the basement. Suddenly, like a flock of frightened birds, the army of cleaners bolted for the exits, mass hysteria fuelled by the lack of immigration papers and social security fraud kicked in. Self-preservation took control and scuffles broke out at the exits as the cleaners battled to escape.

As the cleaners panicked, Abu looked behind him trying to figure out what had spooked them. He spotted Tank fifty yards away, directly behind him carrying a gun, and at least two other armed policemen to his left. Abu couldn't believe that armed police had arrived on the scene so quickly, just another example of his cursed bad luck. He ran as fast as he could toward the delivery bay, and took his revolver from his waistband. That was a huge mistake. Tank dropped to one knee and took aim at the running man. He'd did not intend to shoot him, because he had no proof that he was definitely the assassin, until he saw the revolver. He gripped the gun with two hands and rested his elbow on his knee to steady the shot, and then he fired three times, aiming to stop him in his tracks, but not kill him. The nine millimetre slugs slammed into Abu's legs. His left femur was smashed to pieces by the first bullet. The second shattered his right kneecap as it passed through the joint, blasting cartilage and bone fragments across the concrete floor. The third bullet hit him in the pelvis, and then unluckily, it ricocheted off the bone up through his abdomen into his heart, killing him instantly.

Chapter Fourteen

Nasik

Nasik had lined up the crosshairs of his rifle, targeting the Terrorist Task Force's commanding officer. The shot was aimed at his head when Nasik squeezed the trigger. Major Stanley Timms was half a mile away when the bullet was fired, which meant that there is nearly a two-second delay from the bullet leaving the rifle, and it hitting its target. As the bullet left the rifle, Timms had turned away from the window. When Nasik realised that the first shot had missed the kill zone, hitting the Major in the back, he fired a second shot. The target had been thrown across his desk behind some metal filing cabinets by the force of the impact. Nasik had emptied the entire magazine into the cabinets but the bullets had failed to penetrate the metal and compressed paper inside them. He was disappointed not to kill his mark with a headshot, but sure that the Kufur would not survive the injuries that he had received. Now he had no more than ten minutes to affect an escape, before the police setup a cordon around the city centre. It would not take them long to realise where the shots could have been fired from, and then narrow the possible sites down to the exact spot.

Nasik dismantled his rifle and put it back into the toolbox. He stuffed his pistol into his overalls and wheeled his box toward the fire exit, which led into one of the world's longest stairwells. Nasik analysed the scene. The old restaurant looked like any other building site, apart from the businessman sat on the floor tied to a roof support in the middle of the room. That definitely looked out of place. Nasik stared at the man, thought things over for a moment, and then made a plan.

Nine minutes later, he stood at the same spot near the fire exit and surveyed the scene again. It was almost identical to the first time, apart from the man tied to a roof support, who was now dressed in painter's overalls. Nasik had stripped him and swapped clothes. The project manager was now secured, standing with his back to the upright scaffold pole. He was sporting Nasik's baseball cap and sunglasses. Nasik forced a three-foot length of wood up the right hand sleeve of the overalls, through the material at the shoulder, and then taped it to the pole. The effect was to leave the businessman with his arm fixed in a pointing position. Then he used the same gaffer tape to attach a six-inch piece of copper pipe to the extended right hand of the project manager. From a distance away, it would look like he was pointing a gun. Nasik smiled at his creativity, turned off the lights, switched on the gas, which fuelled the old ovens, and headed toward the exit. The lift doors were still wedged open. Nasik dragged a five-foot propane gas cylinder, which was attached to a blowlamp that the plumbers used. He turned the gas tap to open, and then tossed it down the seemingly bottomless lift shaft. It was still falling when he reached the fire exit.

The shirt and tie he'd put on were a little too big but they would pass for now. The suit trousers were warm and wet. The smell of stale urine pervaded from them, but it was unavoidable that he would have to live with. He opened the fire exit door and headed down the almost endless spiral staircase. The staircase was over a thousand steps high, and was built inside the cylindrical exterior walls, so it descended in a wide circular sweep, with no landings. The lift shaft ran up the centre of the tower, encased by the stairwell. There were no intermediate floors for the lift to stop on, just street level and the tower. There were no windows fitted into the stairwell, which meant that Nasik soon lost all concept of how far down the huge tower he had travelled, or what police activity was happening outside. He felt, rather than heard, the oscillation of a helicopter engine approaching. There was no doubt that it would be carrying at least two police sharp shooters on board. The option of reaching the bottom of the staircase and then leaving through the street entrance was completely ruled out. He kept on down the wide curving stairwell until he almost became dizzy. If only the mission had gone to plan, there would have been no one else in the tower and he could have taken the lift back down to the street and disappeared into the crowds.

Just when he was beginning to think the stairs would never end, he reached a green exit sign fixed to the curved wall of the tower. It signposted a fire exit which led from above the base of the tower, into the second floor of the shopping mall. It was a lifeline. He pushed the metal door release bars and the door opened immediately, but only a few inches. A thick steel security chain was threaded between the locking bars, stopping access to the shopping centre. A fire alarm began to sound inside the tower, it was deafening in the confined space of the stairwell, as the acoustics of stone steps inside a massive concrete tube amplified the sound. Nasik looked through a rectangular piece of fire glass. Beyond it was a smoked glass panel, which led directly onto a wide marble concourse, which was lined, by shops on either side.

There were two stainless steel escalators carrying the hundreds of shoppers from one floor to the next. He felt inside the suit jacket, removed a pair of reading spectacles, and put them on. Then he kicked the fire doors unnoticed by the shoppers, but they refused to yield, held in place by the thick metal chain. He was trapped in the stairwell.

Chapter Fifteen

Armed Response Unit

Ryan Griffin was organising his squad of fifteen Task Force agents at the base of the St. John's tower. In the absence of a senior officer, he was in charge of the unit. The Terrorist Task Force was a small elite unit, whose remit was international, but focused completely on counter terrorism. They relied on the back up and support of conventional law enforcement agencies and military Special Forces, to provide the numbers required to affect large areas, such as a city centre. Local uniformed divisions were erecting steel barriers around the pedestrianized sectors of the shopping centre, and evacuating the precincts and office blocks. They had also mobilised an Armed Response Unit, which was comprised of uniformed police officers that had received specialised weapons and tactics training. As Ryan was prepping his Task Force team, the Chief of the uniformed police approached.

"Where's your commanding officer?" the uniformed officer demanded, without any introductions. Ryan noticed a battle bus had arrived on the scene and the policemen moved the metal cordon to allow it to pass, and then replaced it to contain the growing number of onlookers that were gathering along the barrier. Liverpool has two hugely popular radio stations, Radio City and Radio Merseyside based within a minutes walking distance of the massive tower, and they had both already dispatched roving news reporters to the scene. The media throng buzzed as they reported that the bus had all the insignia of the Merseyside Armed Response Unit emblazoned on it. It indicated without shadow of a doubt, that there had been a firearms incident in the city centre.

"I'm in charge sir," Ryan Griffin answered.

"Not any more you're not Sonny Jim," the Chief blustered. "This is not a terrorist incident, unless you know something that we don't, then this is a firearms incident, and my armed response men will answer the call."

"Sir, with respect we think that the suspect shot Major Stanley Timms, and....."

"Exactly, my boy, you think that the suspect shot your senior officer, therefore it is not a terrorist attack, it's a firearms incident and it's our jurisdiction, now stand down immediately," the officer was abrupt, arrogant and correct.

"With respect sir, my lead officer John Tankersley warned me that this attack is linked to several others, and that the perpetrators are highly trained, highly skilled terrorists, sir."

"Respect, respect, John Tankersley doesn't understand the meaning of the word respect, now for the last time stand down. Watch and pay attention sunshine, you might just learn something," the Chief was not backing down. He had been involved in several altercations with Tank before, and had never come off the winner.

This time he was one hundred percent correct, it was not a Task Force incident, at this point anyway. He could barely contain his excitement at finally ousting the mighty Terrorist Task Force and being placed directly in the spotlight of the local media too. The city boasted television studios for the country's two biggest channels, Granada and BBC news, and their camera crews had set up camp next to the journalists from the radio stations.

The Chief summoned the battle bus to set up their command position near the base of the huge tower. The response team had disembarked and made the final adjustments to their kit. They were kitted out in similar combat gear to the Task Force, except their equipment was not designed to withstand military firepower. They were essentially policemen, not soldiers. Their skills and reflexes had never been honed on the battlefields of Iraq, Afghanistan, Kosovo, Bosnia or even Northern Ireland.

The Chief was handed a set of plans, which detailed the layout of the tower. There were just two ways up to the old restaurant, and two ways down, the lift and the stairs. The police helicopter was circling the disc shaped restaurant at the top of the tower. The pilot and navigator were reporting one gunman still on the scene.

"There's one armed suspect on the scene, I'm afraid the restaurant lights are off and the interior is very dark, but our body heat sensors are confirming what we can see, a single gunman," said the spotter from the helicopter.

"Is he causing an imminent threat to the public?" asked the Chief. He needed to know if the sniper was near the windows aiming to take another shot at someone.

"Negative, he's in the centre of the room, but the weapon is raised. We have a clear sight of the target. Do you want us to take the shot?"

"Negative, if he's not near the windows then stand down and retire to a safe observation point." The Chief placed them on standby and the helicopter swerved away from the tower a safe distance away, where they could maintain observation on the target, without being shot at. The Chief gathered his team around him for a briefing.

"We need to disable the lift, and send one team up the stairs, and another smaller unit will be airlifted onto the restaurant roof," the Chief began. "They'll abseil the short distance from the roof and enter the restaurant windows, simultaneously timed with an attack from the stairwell."

It seemed to be a win-win situation. There was one suspect isolated in a deserted tower hundreds of feet up in the air. If they disabled the lift then there was only one way out, which was down the stairs. He could already see the headlines in tomorrow's newspapers. The Chief was pleased that he had chosen his best uniform to wear today; the smooth black drill and shiny silver buttons would look good on the front pages tomorrow. It might even speed up his promotion to Police Commissioner.

"Any questions," the Chief asked sternly, daring one of the lower ranks to question his plan of attack. His men remained silent and waited for the order to go.

"What if it's been rigged?" asked Ryan Griffin who had been ear wigging from the back of the group.

The Chief flushed a crimson colour and didn't even turn his head toward the Task Force man. He found it typical that one of Tank's men would question his orders. Any insubordination in the uniformed ranks was stamped out immediately.

"You have your orders, let's move," he said. The response team sprang into action.

"What if the tower has been rigged Chief?" Ryan shouted as the policemen noisily grabbed their gear and followed their orders.

Ryan Griffin shook his head in disgust. The policemen could be walking into a death trap, but there was nothing he could do but watch and hope that he was wrong. From what Tank had told him about this foe, they were experts. They would not make a situation like this one as simple as it seemed. The sniper had hit his mark, and then decided to hang around waiting for the police to shoot him; it just didn't make sense. His attention was distracted by the sound of a twin-engine troop carrier. The black Wessex helicopter approached the huge disc at the top of the tower and four armed policemen abseiled onto the roof. The tower was so high that they were barely visible from the ground. A squad of around a dozen men entered the stairwell from the street, while four more approached the elevator doors and waited. Ryan`s cell phone vibrated in his webbing.

"Ryan, it's Tank," said his boss, "what's the situation there?"

"It's pretty desperate Tank, we're stood down," Griffin answered.

"Stood down by whom exactly? What's going on?"

"Chief of Police himself, Tank. He's sending his muppets into the tower. They could be walking into god knows what in there."

"He's a fucking idiot. That tower will be rigged, there's absolutely no doubt about it," Tank raised his voice but there was not much that he could do about it right now.

"He's put four men on the roof, a squad climbing the stairs and four men are about to disable the lift," Ryan relayed the scene to Tank, because it was obvious to a soldier that there could be half a dozen booby traps in the towering structure.

Chapter Sixteen

Yasser

Yasser was woken by a change in the engine noise. He was curled up in a protective foetal position against the bulkhead of the helicopter. The constant pain in his shoulder made him feel very vulnerable. He felt the engine noise intensify and then felt the undercarriage touching solid ground. It was the fifth time that the aircraft had landed since he had been thrown into it. The last time it landed the side doors had been opened, and Yasser felt the blast of downdraft through the hessian hood. He couldn't see a thing but he heard the other prisoner being dragged out of the cargo hold before the door was slammed closed again.

Yasser was feeling stronger mentally than he had done in months. The daily routine of relentless pain and torture had all but broken him. He hadn't had anything to eat or drink for twenty-four hours but he wouldn't swap that for his stinking cell and another session with his tormentors. The engine noise dissipated steadily and slowly wound down to a complete stop. They had kept the engine running since he had boarded it, even when it had landed. He listened intently trying to identify anything that would help him, any voice or accent, but all he could hear was muffled tones.

The doors slid open and a blast of heat engulfed Yasser. It was an intensely dry heat that Yasser identified with the desert climates of the Middle East. The aircraft shook and he felt movement as people climbed aboard. The sound of footsteps approaching made Yasser curl up and tense his body, anticipating an assault. Rough hands grabbed at his feet and dragged him toward the fresh air and scorching sunshine. The world became brighter even through the hessian hood. He felt himself being tipped over the edge of the hold, feet first, where more hands supported his weight and then dragged him away from the helicopter. Yasser let them carry him along without wasting any of his meagre energy reserves on walking. It didn't hurt to let them think that he was completely incapacitated either. He heard the clink of a key turning in a metal lock, and then the screeching of metal hinges protesting at being opened. Yasser was dumped unceremoniously onto a sandy floor.

He gritted his teeth and grunted as his infected stump scraped on the floor. He was slightly confused because the heat was still incredibly strong and he could feel the sun on his skin. The hessian hood was roughly removed from his head, and he had to squeeze his eyes closed while they adjusted to the intense sunlight. There were three soldiers stood over him. They could have been first, second and third place in a Saddam Hussein lookalike competition. They had short wavy black hair, gelled back from their faces and thick black moustaches. They were wearing olive green military shirts with epaulets fixed to the shoulders. There was no insignia attached to the uniforms. Their dark green combat pants were tucked into high-laced army issue boots. Yasser decided they were Egyptian, probably from the Sinai Desert region, because their facial features were soft and rounded. Egyptians from Cairo, and the Nile delta area, have sharp hooked noses and high cheekbones, different to these men.

One of them raised his hand and Yasser flinched away in fear. The soldier raised his hand again slowly; in it was a canvas water bottle, which he put to Yasser's lips. Yasser drank greedily from the canteen, he hadn't realised how thirsty he was until water was offered. The soldier pulled the water away when Yasser had quenched his thirst, and he poured some gently over the terrorist`s head to cool him down. Yasser nodded his appreciation.

"Shukraan," Yasser whispered under his breath. He had used Egyptian Arabic to thank the guard.

The soldier nodded imperceptibly to his colleagues, turned away and locked the gate behind him without speaking. Yasser looked at his surroundings for the first time. He was outdoors locked inside what could only be described as a cage. He had seen similar cells on news film of Guantanamo`s camp x-ray, but the climate was not tropical like Cuba, he was definitely in the middle of a desert. There were low dark mountains far away in the distance. The foreground was blurred as a heat haze rose from the parched earth.

The helicopter that he had arrived on was standing on a square of compacted sand, next to a single storey building that had a flat felt roof. On the opposite side of the building was a metal hut made from corrugated sheets, and beyond that was a short runway. There was a hanger situated at the far end of the runway, and three bright yellow passenger aircraft were stood idle next to it. The planes had a dusty unused appearance to them. A warm breeze blew in from the desert and sand and dust was blown from the airplane wings and fuselage. Yasser deduced that they had not flown for a long time. He sat up and put his back against the metal bars staring at the mountains in the distance. Despite the agonising ache in his infected shoulder, he felt more alive than he had done for as long as he could remember.

Chapter Seventeen

Abdul Ahmed

Abdul Ahmed was a rich hotel owner. He had owned his first hotel at the age of twenty-two in the Eygptian holiday resort Sharm el Sheikh. Situated at the southern tip of the Sinai Peninsula on the shores of the Red Sea, the resort had guaranteed sunshine three hundred and sixty five days a year, combined with the most breathtaking reefs in the world. The coastline of the Red Sea grew so much in popularity that construction work could be seen along its entire length, as far north as Israel. As the resort expanded Abdul`s empire grew with it. Although capitalism had made him a rich man, he was a fanatical supporter of Islamic Jihad.

As a small boy, he had witnessed the Israelis invasion of Sinai, which they occupied for many years before eventually handing it back to Egypt in 1982. The Jewish state of Israel, armed with Western military technology destroyed the Egyptian air force in less than a few hours, before they could even launch an airplane in retaliation. Abdul was hell bent on the annihilation of Israel and the liberation of Muslim Palestine and the West Bank. He was focused and extremely clever. He knew that his talents lay in business and finance; he was not a warrior or a military genius. Abdul had immense political influence within the Middle East, which he used to aid the Islamic cause. He was also a multi-billionaire and he used his financial muscle to supply and support many terrorist militias in his own country and abroad.

Abdul had searched the world over for the whereabouts of his hero, Yasser Ahmed, but it seemed that he had disappeared off the face of the earth. Until one day, he received a telephone call from one of his hotel managers.

Two months prior Abdul had been on the fifteenth hole of the Conrad Hotel golf course, near Sharm, when his caddy handed him his cell phone. The call was from his hotel in a resort called Taba, which is situated at the north tip of the Red Sea. The resort is the only place in the world where you can see four countries from your sun bed. Sitting on the Egyptian beach if you look to the north, you can clearly see the Israelis port of Eilat, and the Jordanian sea port of Aqaba, which are separated only by the River Jordan and a few miles of sand. Ten kilometres south of there, on the eastern shores of the Red sea, is Saudi Arabia.

The hotel manger had been alerted by an eagle-eyed receptionist. The receptionist had noticed that a guest's passport had raised a diplomatic red flag when it had been scanned into their system. It seemed that the guest had once worked for Her Majesty's Secret Service, MI5 to be precise. Abdul had the manger investigate further, and it seemed the man had checked in alone. He was booked in for a two-week vacation, all-inclusive, and had been blind drunk since he arrived. The opportunity had been too good to miss. Hundreds and thousands of tourists use the Egyptian resort of Taba as a base to travel into nearby Israel to visit the Dead Sea and the Holy city of Jerusalem. Millions more take the ferry crossing to Jordan, and travel to the lost city of Petra, one of the Seven Wonders of the World. Border crossings are painfully slow and obstructive. It wasn't difficult to engineer a scenario where the ex-MI5 agent seemingly left Egypt on a tourist trip and never returned. No one even noticed that he'd gone.

The agent in question, Mark Garden had been sacked from the service for incompetence a month earlier. In a very short space of time, he had lost his job, his marriage and his home. Despite government warnings, he'd decided to travel abroad for a break, before his employment history could be erased. He had been at the hotel for a week, most of it a complete blur. The hotel employees were friendly and accommodating, especially toward their British guests. In recent years, there had been a massive increase in the number of Russian tourists heading to the Red Sea for their holidays. The Egyptian staff described them as the most ignorant, rude and aggressive people that they had to cater for.

Garden assumed that the reason he was being treated so well was because the Russians were such a bunch of arseholes. The waiters kept coming to his table and he drank whatever they put in front of him. One night after being plied with free brandy all evening, he returned to his room to find all his clothes packed, and his belongings had disappeared.

He remembered a blow to the back of the head and a chloroform smell, then nothing until he woke up.

That was over two months ago. He awoke strapped in a chair with a blinding headache and a raging thirst. At first, he had thought it was just another hangover, until his eyes started to focus. The room he was in looked like the sheriff's office from a spaghetti western, bare walls, a small barred section and a desk. He was sat in front of the cluttered desk facing a wall with posters stuck to it, he'd called for help but no one came. He couldn't see behind him. As his vision cleared, he noticed the posters were prints from a book or manual. The original drawings had been hand drawn in coloured crayons, and then copied to make a book. His blood had run cold when he realised the drawings were illustrations of torture techniques. He recognised them from his time at the agency. They were pages from the al-Qaeda torture manual, even more terrifying because they were hand drawn with such attention to detail. They included most of the power tools your local DIY warehouse stock, being used to inflict terrible injuries to the pencilled characters. Shortly afterward, the torturers arrived, and his nightmares really began.

Abdul didn't know where his men had kept the British agent, he didn't need to know what horrors they had inflicted on him, and he didn't really care. The information that they had extracted from him however had been priceless. Abdul had obtained the names and descriptions of Britain's senior counter-terrorism agents, along with website addresses and encrypted passwords to access their files. Armed with this information Abdul financed the team of assassins to strike at the heart of the Western crusaders, on their own soil. The information they extracted had slowly become less valuable as time went on, until the agent started to divulge the whereabouts of facilities that were used by the West for extraordinary rendition. That was the icing on the cake. From that information, Abdul had a list of possible sites where Yasser Ahmed may have been held and tortured. He paid thousands of dollars in bribes to have the facilities monitored by radar. Every time an aircraft took off or landed, they were tracked by satellite and radar. Eventually Abdul would find the inspirational terrorist leader, Yasser Ahmed.

Chapter Eighteen

Nasik/St. John's Tower

Tank and Chen bypassed the city centre roadblocks and took the dock road back to their headquarters at Canning Place. Armed police encircled the building, and police vehicles were leaving the fleet car park in an uninterrupted convoy. They were stopped briefly at the gate by two uniformed policemen and then waved into the car park. They took the lift to the top floor, which was the home of the Terrorist Task Force. The elevator stopped but the door refused to open without a security access code being punched into the control panel. The top floor was on lock down following the attack on Major Timms. The high wide windows, which normally offered panoramic views of the Albert Docks and its flotilla of beautiful tall wooden sailing ships, were now covered by automated metal shuttering. The Task Force office was virtually deserted. They had units deployed in Holyhead searching the Syrian tanker, at the Royal hospital protecting Grace Farrington and Major Timms, and a small unit on standby at the base of the St. John's tower. Tank felt like he needed to be everywhere at the same time, but without Timms at the helm he had to coordinate operations.

Chen turned on a digital screen and punched grid references into a map function. An aerial view of the city centre appeared. He zoomed onto the tower. Tank walked by the screen and removed his suit jacket. It was still damp. He looked at the images and tried to be objective as he watched the Armed Response Unit preparing to storm the tower. The satellite picture became magnified, and he could clearly see four men on the circular roof of the old restaurant. They were positioned at twelve, three, six and nine o'clock on the circle. Each one was holding onto a nylon fibre rope, which was anchored to the centre column, ready to drop over the edge and crash through the windows. Standard forced entry technique, if the area was clear of explosives. At this moment in time, the policemen didn't know if the area was clear or not. Tank set the coms channel to secure, which prevented all but the Task Force personnel from receiving it.

"Griffin, are the response team set?" Tank asked his unit leader at the scene.

"Roger that, the stairwell team entered five minutes ago, a second team are set to disable the lift."

Chen accessed a file that held detailed plans of the St. John's Tower and the adjoining shopping mall. At first glance, there was nothing remarkable to note on the ground floor layout. Chen clicked on the first floor file. Although the plans showed the structure of the tower there was no shared floor space. He clicked the second floor file and they swapped anxious glances.

"What's that?" Tank asked. Chen was far more clued up on architectural design. He was more clued up on most things, his brain was like a sponge, and he absorbed information at a frightening rate.

"It's a fire escape. The planning department would have stipulated that the tower would have to have an alternative exit, and this point is the first opportunity that the architect has to build an exit from the stairwell. It leads into the second floor of the shopping precinct," Chen looked Tank in the eye. They were both thinking the same thing.

"Griffin, get your team up to the second floor of the mall," Tank said over the coms channel, "there's a fire exit leading from the tower's stairwell into the shopping centre. If anyone wants to escape from that tower, that's the only other way out."

"Roger that, we're on our way, do you think this is a set up Tank?" Ryan Griffin asked. He gathered the unit and in seconds, they were sprinting toward the shopping centre's escalators.

"There's no doubt in my mind, Ryan, someone is going to try and leave that tower through that doorway."

Chen tugged the sleeve of Tank's shirt and pointed to the screen, it looked like the armed response men were opening the lift doors with a wrecking bar. Tank sat down heavily in a chair. He rubbed a big hand over his baldhead slowly, which meant something bad was going to happen.

Chapter Nineteen

David McLean/ Top of the Tower

David McLean couldn't see what was going on around him, because Nasik had put duct tape over his eyes and then put sunglasses on him. There was nothing wrong with his hearing or his sense of smell though. He could hear helicopter engines coming and going. There were two at least, one smaller than the other. He was convinced that one of them had flown directly above the tower briefly; he was sure they were coming to rescue him, but then it moved off and never came back. He could also hear boots far away stomping up the stairs, he wasn't sure at first, it had been a distant rumbling but now he was positive that someone was coming for him.

The problem was that he could smell gas. At first, he thought it was the adhesive on the duct tape that he could smell, but as the odour became stronger, he had to accept that it was gas. He was drifting between controlled concern and complete panic. The men on the stairs would get him and turn the gas off, and then he could go home to his wife and family. When he thought positive thoughts he calmed himself momentarily, but he couldn't help but fear the worst. His colleague had been shot. He heard Nasik firing a gun repeatedly; obviously, he didn't know what he was firing at, not that it mattered. He'd been tied up and was so scared he'd peed himself.

David McLean was sure the dark skinned man had left, but he was confused as to why he had taped a piece of wood beneath his arm, and his hand was taped too. If only he could see what was going on he wouldn't be so afraid, or that's what he thought anyway. The truth was far more frightening.

David McLean heard metal straining. It was being forced and bent. The response team was forcing the lift doors open, hundreds of feet below. The renting grinding sound travelled up the lift shaft to him. Then he heard shouting, frightened voices echoing up the shaft. He was sure he could make out someone shouting the word, grenade. Then time seemed to stand still, and his senses became ultra-aware. He sensed movement on the stairs, and outside the restaurants windows, which couldn't be possible because they were hundreds of feet up. He heard glass splintering, but the noise came from several different locations. Then he felt a wind. It began like a whisper but within seconds, it had become a roaring whirlwind, which grew hotter as it grew louder.

The grenade that Nasik had placed beneath the body in the elevator car had ignited the propane gas in the lift shaft. The enormous shaft acted like a chimney flue and the flames shot skyward in a blazing back draft. David McLean was acutely aware of voices shouting, 'armed police, drop your weapon', but he thought the gunman had gone; he didn't understand that they thought he was the gunman. Then the hot wind turned into a raging inferno, and he felt incredibly calm as his flesh blistered and burned from his bones. He breathed in the flames and he felt a sizzling sensation in his lungs as the delicate tissue frazzled. He was aware of four men screaming, and their screams fading as they were blown back out of the windows that they had entered through. Then everything made complete sense and he was confused no more.

Chapter Twenty

Ryan Griffin/ Nasik

Ryan Griffin led his unit into the St. John's shopping mall and headed for the escalators, which were situated in a central square. The square could have been in any mall, in any big city, anywhere in the Western world. It had polished marble tiles, glass elevators and stainless steel escalators. There were huge terracotta planters strategically positioned around the mall. The square was lined on three sides by fast food outlets from every corner of the planet, Chinese food, Indian food, pizza and pasta, sushi, fish and chips and the obligatory McDonalds. The deserted escalators were running. The only sound in the mall was being made by an ornamental fountain, the splashing water echoed through the empty precinct. Ryan used hand signals to direct the unit to split into two, one team on each escalator.

They headed up the moving staircases to the first floor. They reached a square, which mimicked the floor below, except the food outlets had been replaced by designer shops. The shop doors were open, the lights were on, but the floor was deserted. It had been evacuated in a hurry. There was movement at the far end of the east aisle. A uniformed policeman appeared, looking for any stragglers that needed to be evacuated, and preventing any opportunist looters from raiding the empty department stores. Ryan made an ok sign with his right hand and the policeman waved back and carried on his way.

The Task Force units headed up to the second floor. They reached the top of the escalators and took up defensive kneeling positions; both units protected each other's flank. Ryan Griffin took stock of the situation. He checked his compass. The tower should be situated north east of the escalators, but he couldn't see anything that resembled a fire exit leading to it. He signalled one unit to move fifty yards down the left hand side of the precinct, and the other to take up a firing position on the right. To the left hand side were four wide shop fronts, Primark, Next, Armani and Diesel, but there was nothing that looked like an exit. Long plate glass windows stretched down both sides of the aisle, but there were no breaks in the facades.

"Can you tell from the plans where exactly the tower exit joins the mall?" Ryan asked over the coms unit.

Chen stood up close to the screen in the office and studied the plans. He pointed to the screen as he spoke.

"There should be four retail units situated on the left hand side of the precinct, can you confirm that?" Chen had to ask in case the plans weren't current.

"Roger that."

"The exit should be situated between the third and fourth unit," Chen explained.

Ryan Griffin signalled his men to move down the aisle to the third unit, Armani. Mannequins poised in the window dressed in the latest hideously expensive gear, emblazoned with the famous eagle brand; then there was a four feet wide, floor to ceiling mirror, then the Diesel store. There was no obvious fire exit, it could`ve been built over and blocked off by construction work. He looked at the mirrored section again, and noticed there was a groove running down the centre of it. The surface of the mirror was polished to a gleaming finish with a smoked effect. On the left hand panel there was a smudge. Griffin approached the mirror, and he studied the smudge up close. It was an almost perfect handprint. He put his fingertips along the bevelled edge and pulled. The mirror panel hinged toward him revealing a set of wooden fire doors behind it, they'd been left open and there was a thick chain hanging from the locking bars. At the end of the chain was a heavy padlock with a blackened ragged hole through it. Ryan removed his Kevlar glove and held the padlock in his palm. It was still red hot.

"Tank, you're right," Griffin said. "Someone has shot the lock securing the fire exit. There's no sign of them here but they've left a print." He called one of the Task Force men over and pointed to the print while he was talking to his superiors. The man removed a small haversack from his back and placed it on the floor next to the mirrored door. He unzipped it and took out an A4 sized plastic sheet, which he peeled away from its backing. He smoothed the plastic film over the handprint, and then pressed it firmly. The imprint was then slid onto the screen of a palm top computer and sent to the Task Force headquarters. The computers there would search every international database that existed to identify the owner of the print. The plastic swatch was sealed in a bag to be returned to the forensic lab later for DNA analysis.

"The lock is still hot, they can't have gone far," Griffin said.

"Chen will run the print, see if you can trace them," Tank replied.

"Roger that."

Ryan signalled the unit to head toward the precinct balcony. The balcony ran the full length of the exterior of the mall and was lined with shops. There was a canopy above, which protected shoppers from the rain, and a waist high metal railing to prevent them tumbling over the edge of the second floor. They stepped out of the mall onto the balcony and took up positions covering both directions. Ryan looked to the left; the second floor pavement was empty. He looked right, nothing moved.

Ryan walked to the railing and leaned over it to get a better view of the floors below, still nothing. He looked out over the second floor balcony across Williamson Square. The near distance of the city centre was deserted. There were police cordons in the distance and the odd stragglers running toward them, but the area around the mall was silent. A lone female appeared from the ticket office of the Playhouse theatre two hundred yards away. She looked confused. The normally vibrant city centre where she had worked every day for twenty years was empty, fast food wrappers blew across the deserted square. A uniformed police officer had noticed her from the cordon and he called her to him through a megaphone. His words were lost in the wind.

Ryan signalled for the unit to descend to the first floor. Fifty yards away was a wide, open concrete staircase, which connected the two upper floors. They moved in formation, guns pointed horizontally at the ready, they descended in silence. At the bottom of the wide steps the unit automatically split into two teams, one team stayed on the stairs and covered the first floor from a position of high ground, while the second team scanned the balcony in both directions. The unarmed policeman that they had encountered earlier was twenty yards away down the shopping aisle that led back into the mall. He looked a little perturbed when confronted with a Task Force unit bristling with automatic weapons.

"Any sign of life officer?" Ryan shouted.

"I thought I heard someone coming down the steps where you are, sounded like they were dragging a suitcase with wheels on. You know the ones I mean? Like you take on holidays. They have wheels so you don't have to carry them. You know what I mean, don't you?" the policeman waffled. His voice was very nasal, almost camp.

"I get the picture constable. Where did they go?"

"That's the bizarre thing about it, one minute he was there. At least I'm guessing it was a him. I shouldn't speculate really should I?"

"Look, just tell me where you saw them?" Ryan Griffin looked at his sniggering troopers and rolled his eyes. One of his unit bent his hand at the wrist, limp wristed, indicating that the policeman was a poof.

"Sorry, I'm really sorry, it's all the guns, and they're making me nervous you see."

"Where did you see the fucking bloke, with the fucking wheeled suitcase?" the Task Force man hissed through gritted teeth. The uniformed policeman flushed red and his eyes filled with tears. He looked like he was about to start blubbering when he pointed to a set of double fire doors. Above the doors, it had a sign designating it as a restricted area, authorised personnel only. There was another sign, which had the silhouette of a goods lorry on it; it stipulated that only delivery bay staff had access.

"I didn't actually see him," said the policeman. His voice was trembling now, he was close to crying. He rambled on. "The only place they could've gone was through there, but it's locked so I couldn't follow them. My boss told me not to leave the shops under any circumstances, because they're unlocked, and people will sue the police, so I was worried."

Ryan was about to order the Task Force unit to enter the subterranean delivery area when the gas in the St. John's tower exploded.

Chapter Twenty-One

Tank

Tank put his head in his hands when the armed police team lifted the dead body that Nasik had left in the lift. In the theatre of guerrilla warfare against terrorist extremists, you have to assume that everything left behind by the enemy is a booby trap. Unfortunately, the domestic law enforcement agencies are not trained to encounter enemy soldiers on their own streets. Their behaviour is alien to them. The fragmentation grenade had injured one policeman seriously, which was bad enough, but it had also ignited the propane gas cylinder that Nasik had hurled down the shaft as a parting gift.

The explosion in the lift in turn, ignited the escaping gas from the kitchen area. The Terrorist Task Force men could only watch in fascinated horror as the policemen abseiled through the windows into the old restaurant, only to be blown back out of them in a maelstrom of burning gas and debris. Although the four men were badly burned by the explosion, they twisted and grasped at thin air on their long journey to the concrete streets below. There was no feeling of sour grapes toward the policemen and their ill-advised Chief, just a bitter feeling of sorrow for those men that had just wasted their lives. A gut wrenching feeling of empathy for their families, when they watched the national news later, only to see their loved ones died because of a series of mistakes. They were human pawns in a lethal game of political chess, sacrificed to enhance the ego of an ambitious autocrat.

"Griffin, where are you and your team?" Chen asked over the coms.

"We're currently on the north east side of the precinct; situated on the first floor balcony. We've received information that a possible suspect may have entered the delivery bay, situated beneath the mall."

Tank pulled up the plans for the basement areas. The delivery bay was like a labyrinth of loading platforms and storage areas. The shopping precinct was situated in the centre of a vast pedestrianized zone. Traffic of any description was only given access during the night, outside of trading hours. Two separate subterranean basements serviced the hundreds of shops above. On top of the twenty or so service roads, that Tank had already counted, there were a myriad of stairwells and goods lifts. Stock was inventoried by department store staff in the vast underground warehouses, and then dispatched as needed into the goods lifts.

"Even if that was a suspect, you've got no chance of tracking anyone down there without sensors," Tank didn't want his men walking into another trap. There had been enough surprises for one day. "Bring your men in; we need a debriefing before we launch a response."

"Roger that." Griffin replied. He was disappointed, but they hadn't even had a positive sighting. Better to regroup, and then redeploy a fully equipped response team. It was an odd thing to notice, but he studied a pool of vomit close to the delivery bay, it looked fresh.

Chapter Twenty Two

Nasik/ St. John's Precinct

Nasik slammed the reinforced fire door closed. He leaned against it and caught his breath. A passive motion sensor reacted to his presence and activated the lights in the narrow stairwell that led down to the subterranean delivery area, which was situated beneath the St. John 's shopping mall. The stairway stunk of rotten vegetables and garbage. The stink made Nasik wretch again, but this time his stomach was empty of food. He tasted thick bile at the back of his throat, and his stomach constricted again, making it difficult to breathe. Panic set in for a brief moment as he felt like he was choking. Then his jaw reflexively opened to snapping point and his eyes filled with tears, but still nothing came up. He remained still for a short while gasping for air, and his heartbeat slowed down, allowing him to regain his composure.

There were eight steps down to the next landing then they turned back on themselves plunging out of view. He grabbed the handle of the big plastic tough box and picked it up off its wheels, to carry it down the stairs. He turned the corner at the bottom of the first flight and headed down the next set without pausing on the landing. The second landing was wet, there were empty crisp bags, and chip wrappers piled in the corners. The stench of rotting vegetables grew stronger the further he descended. Nasik paused for a few minutes. He was out of breath again. He wiped cold perspiration from his brow with the sleeve of his stolen suit, and noticed several strands of hair came away from his scalp. The sight of the tufts of hair spurred him on and he grabbed the toolbox and headed down the steps into the dank cellar area.

At the bottom of the steps was a fire door, which had been wedged open with a red fire extinguisher. Nasik stepped through the doors, relieved to be able to wheel the box again, as it was becoming heavier the further he carried it. He opened the top lid of the tough box, removed a piece of paper, closed the lid again, and then sat on it. Nasik studied the paper and then turned it the opposite way round, so that it related to where he was. It was a photocopy of a hand drawn plan of the basement warehouses, and the maze of access roads that serviced them. He reached into the suit pocket and discovered a half eaten chocolate bar that must have been left by its real owner. Nasik peeled the wrapping from it and bit into it greedily.

The sugar gave him an instant energy rush, which he welcomed. It reminded him of the years he had spent in the West Bank and the Lebanon fighting door-to-door gun battles against Israeli soldiers, eating whatever he could whenever he could, because he never knew when the next meal was coming. He was sat on a wide concrete loading bay that stretched a thousand yards in each direction. The edge of the bay was painted with a thick white line to discourage employees falling off the loading dock onto the service road. The service road was wide enough for two trucks to pass each other on opposite sides of the road. Every hundred yards or so, there was a metal roller shutter which secured the warehouse space behind it. The wide loading bays were built to be the same height as the back of a heavy goods lorry, so that forklift trucks could remove the stock pallets and drive them straight into the relevant storage space. The service road was littered with wastepaper and discarded rotten fruit and vegetables, which had fallen during unloading and had never been picked up. Rainwater from the thunderstorm above had made its way down the access ramps and was pooling in the basement.

Nasik stood up and picked up the handle of his toolbox. He wheeled it right toward roller shutter number thirteen, unlucky for some. He approached the metal roller and located the padlock, which held it in place. The key labelled 'roller' opened it at the first time of asking. The roller rattled open noisily. The interior of the storage area was inky black. Nasik couldn't see a thing. He dragged the tough plastic box inside and closed the roller. It clanged into place. Nasik reached blindly for the top of the toolbox and put his hand into a small compartment. He removed a small penlight torch. He noticed a dull blue luminous glow coming from some powdery spots inside the compartment. Nasik touched the powder with his index finger and looked at it. The powder had turned to a blue smudge on the tip of his finger, but it still glowed. He wiped it on his trousers and was a little irked to see that it still glowed.

He switched on the small torch and shone the thin beam across the warehouse to the far wall. It took just seconds to locate a grey isolator box. He crossed the dark room avoiding discarded wooden pallets, and switched the isolator to the on position. A bank of strip lighting buzzed into life, revealing the interior of an unused storage unit. The walls were made from breezeblocks that had been left bare. At the rear of the unit was a metal concertina shaped door, which hid a small goods lift. It had a notice attached to the door declaring it unsafe, and out of commission. Nasik headed toward it, dragging the big plastic toolbox.

The final key in his bunch was labelled, 'lift 2'. The door opened with a quick turn of the key. Nasik dragged the safety gate open and wheeled the toolbox inside the goods lift. He closed the safety gate, and then slammed the lift door, glad to be rid of the cumbersome plastic tough box. There were two buttons on the control panel, one was labelled 'call' and the other, 'second floor'. He sent the lift up to the second floor of the precinct, where it would stay at the back of an empty shop unit, and high above the city carrying its deadly cargo.

Chapter Twenty-Three

Holyhead/ the Golan Heights

The Golan was a Syrian mineral tanker. It carried aggregates and minerals mined in the Middle East all over the industrial world. The mining of metal ore and minerals had become a multi-billion dollar business in recent years, due to the incredible surge in demand from India and China. Domestic deposits of metal ore, once deemed unprofitable to mine, were now turning into valuable commodities because of global demand. Holyhead was the site of a massive aluminium foundry, one of the biggest in Europe. The reason was simple. Holyhead has the second deepest harbour in Europe, only Rotterdam, Holland has a deeper port. This allows bigger ships with a larger tonnage on board to dock in the port safely. The economics of scale makes it cheaper to transport larger volumes of the ingredients required in the manufacturing process, than it would be if smaller vessels had to be used. Exporting the finished product is also more profitable because of the foundry's coastal site, literally a mile from the harbour's jetty.

Britain, like many Western countries is very reliant on imported goods. Food supplies, clothing, medicines and petroleum products, to mention just a few, are all imported. Policing the infinite number of foreign ships that enter our waters is a virtually impossible task. The Royal Navy and the Coastguard work three hundred and sixty five days a year, round the clock, trying to stop the smuggling of people, drugs and other contraband onto our shores. International ports like Holyhead keep detailed manifests of foreign traffic entering their harbours. Very few countries have permission for their sailors to disembark onto British soil, and for good reason. The opportunity to remain in the country illegally is a very attractive one to some.

The Golan had broken several major naval protocols during its short visit. It appeared that Middle Eastern extremists had either stowed away, or been given passage onboard. When challenged about the issue and asked to cooperate the Captain had refused to yield. The ship had been boarded by the Terrorist Task Force and local law enforcement agencies in a joint operation. The Captain and his crew had been rounded up and were being held on deck, in the pouring rain, and freezing wind. The crew were becoming more and more agitated as their clothing became saturated. Several of them had begun shouting at the Captain, obviously aware that he was responsible for their current uncomfortable position.

One altercation had to be physically halted by the intervention of two local policemen. The local uniformed policemen were tasked with guarding the sailors, a task that they weren't too enamoured with, especially as several crew members appeared to be ill. Two of them had vomited on deck and a couple were sitting down, weakened by whatever ailed them. The Captain was refusing to answer any questions at all, which meant that the combined taskforce had to search the tanker from bow to stern. The search was laborious and unpleasant. It did however supply some evidence to support the theory that there were a number of covert passengers stowed away in the bowels of the ship, amongst the ship's cargo.

Two local Coastguard men were helping to search the ship, along with a customs officer. The customs men stationed at Holyhead were important members of Britain's security forces. Holyhead was the primary route for transport and tourists, from Europe to Ireland. They had to be experts at spotting smugglers and detecting weapons and explosives. They had found makeshift living quarters deep in the hold. A single ring gas camping stove, and unwashed mess tins, along with thin mattresses, sleeping bags and blankets. The equipment had to be bagged up and taken away as evidence. It was as they were collecting all the items with the Task Force agents, for forensic examination that the customs officer's handheld gadget beeped. Everyone stopped what they were doing as they were surprised by the unusual noise.

"What's that for?" asked a coastguard curiously. He was wishing that they were issued with computerised gadgets that beeped or buzzed, it'd be exciting.

The custom's man knocked the gadget gently with his torch and then placed it close to where it had made the noise. It beeped louder this time. A Task Force agent recognised the gadget as an explosives detector.

"Is it reading positive for explosives?"

"Worse than that, it's reading positive for radioactive material."

The Terrorist Task Force agent switched of the electric lights in the hold and it plunged into blackness. There were no portholes in the hull this deep in the ship, so it was completely black, except for an area of the steel deck about three yards square that had a luminous blue glow.

Chapter Twenty-Four

Abdul/ News

Abdul was a young boy when the Second World War ended, and the armies of the Third Reich had been defeated and driven out of the Middle East. Egypt, Syria, Transjordan, Iraq and Iran, all tried to take advantage of the situation by invading the new Jewish state of Israel in an attempt to acquire more land. They suffered a humiliating defeat. Israel, supplied by Western allies literally drove the Palestinians out of their own country. There were many accusations of terrible war crimes being committed by Israeli troops. Arab eyewitnesses recounted dozens of stories of massacres, wiping out whole villages of men, women and children. The news of alleged atrocities spread like wild fire through the Palestinian population, prompting them to leave their homes before Israeli soldiers arrived. The majority of those that fled their homes were never allowed to return. They became refugees.

The future brought more bitter failures in further wars with Israel in, 1948, 1956 and 1967. The war of 1956 angered young Egyptians because Israel was joined by British and French forces, in an alliance to win control of the Suez Canal. It was seen as modern day crusader alliance. The Israeli armed forces became the superpower of the Middle East, but they were hated and despised by their Arab neighbours. Western governments provided them with the ingredients and scientific knowhow to develop nuclear missiles, much to the detriment of their more extreme neighbours, Syria, Iran and Saudi Arabia. Abdul financed several extremists groups to carry out a variety of missions against Israel and the West, including the current mission to assassinate senior agents in the UK`s security services.

The Egyptian president Mubarak faced a growing number of Islamic extremist groups from within his own borders, such as those sponsored by Abdul. The indigenous Bedouin tribes that once roamed the Sinai Peninsula freely felt that tourism had robbed them of their traditional grazing and fishing grounds. As a result, Egypt and especially the Sinai has been the site of several recent terrorist attacks, targeted at Israeli,

Western and Egyptian tourists. Abdul desperately wanted to return his nation to Islamic rule; his priority was the destruction of the state of Israel.

Abdul's millions were also being used to monitor the movements of Western prisoners from eastern European countries that participated in extraordinary rendition. He had rogue radar operators in half a dozen countries tracking the movement of aircraft from designated prison facilities. There had been a few false alarms raised, but nothing concrete had ever come to fruition. The chances were that Yasser Ahmed had been tortured and then executed, but Abdul wouldn't give up on his project to find him. His persistence and faith in Allah was about to pay dividends.

Chapter Twenty-Five

MI5

Donna Bangor-Jones stood at her bedroom window in her fluffy dressing gown, watching as her husband Donald climbed into a black Jaguar. The back door closed and the Jaguar's wheels span in the gravel as it found purchase and sped away down their long driveway. It was supposed to be his week off work but he'd been called in again. She would have to break the news to her children that their father would not be going into London with them today. They had promised to take them into the city for a trip to the London Eye, a giant Ferris wheel on the banks of the River Thames, and then on for a family meal somewhere. It wasn't the first time they had been let down and it wouldn't be the last, either.

They lived in a huge five-bedroom mansion on the outskirts of Brighton, which is situated on the south coast of England. The town was popular with highly paid executives, because of its proximity to the country's capital city, London. Her husband's wages supported an extravagant lifestyle, and they wanted for nothing. Donna Bangor-Jones didn't even know what her credit card limit was she was so well off. She holidayed with the kids three times a year, skiing in the Rockies every March, a week in the Swiss villa every June and a beach holiday in August. Donald never joined them as he was always too busy at work. Although she lived a very privileged life, she was incredibly unhappy. Her life was regimented and organised to run like clockwork. Donald had spent twenty-two years in the army, and he liked things to be just so.

He awoke every morning at six o'clock, drank orange juice and tea with his breakfast of two boiled eggs on sliced toast. He ate in complete silence, which no one dared to breach. Then he read the Times newspaper from cover to cover, before he spoke a word to his family. He expected his shirts to be washed, starched and ironed daily. His bedding needed to be changed every day, and he required sex in the missionary position every Sunday morning, except when it clashed with his wife's menstrual cycle; in which case oral sex would suffice. Donna had plotted and planned for hours on end, often colluding with her sisters to avoid being at home on a

Sunday morning. The ordeal of closing her eyes and thinking of England, while her husband puffed and panted his way to an orgasm had become unbearable.

She had a brief affair once with a horny young builder who had carried out some work on their house. It was partly to break the pampered monotony of her life, and partly to see if she could enjoy sex with someone else. She certainly didn't enjoy it with her husband. Donna was a very attractive woman despite her age, and the young builder thought all his birthdays had come at once when he turned up at the house to collect his check. Donna had given her cleaner the morning off, and opened the door in a lacy camisole, which she had bought especially for the occasion. The young builder's eyes nearly popped out of his head, and he couldn't stop staring at her firm tanned thighs. Donna enjoyed the look of uncertainty in his eyes. He wasn't sure if she was just teasing him or not. After a while, she realised that he was too unsure of her to make a move, so she'd let her camisole fall open, accidently on purpose. Exactly ten minutes later, she decided that sex was completely overrated. The young builder had nearly choked her by thrusting his penis too deep into her mouth. It was the first time she'd tried oral sex as foreplay and she certainly wouldn't be trying it again. They had ended up on the dining room floor, rolling round on a sheepskin rug. The floor was hard and uncomfortable and she'd scraped the skin off her elbows and knees. Despite the young stud's enthusiasm, she was not impressed. Life returned to its rich, mundane, ordered existence. She put her energy into making her children happy, and shopping. Sunday mornings didn't seem so bad anymore.

Donna Bangor-Jones turned away from the window and walked into the en-suite bathroom. The cream carpet was one hundred percent wool and felt reassuringly soft beneath her feet. She liked it so much they'd had it fitted all the way through the house. No one dared walk beyond the porch before removing their shoes.

"Mummy, where's daddy going?" shouted her eldest daughter Catherine, who'd watched her father being chauffeured away. She was fourteen going on thirty, already aware that men were looking at her, incredibly fashion conscious, but still fond of her cuddly toys.

"He's had to go to work girls, sorry."

"Oh mummy, he promised to take us to the London Eye, he's always at work, he's just so bloody selfish," said Elizabeth. Elizabeth or Libby, as she was called was twelve, incredibly fashion conscious, but still hated boys.

"Elizabeth Bangor-Jones, don't you dare use that language in this house young lady," her mother shouted, trying to sound annoyed, but stifling a laugh behind her hand.

"Yes, Elizabeth Bangor-Jones, don't use that language in this house," Catherine mocked and pulled her younger sister's pigtails.

"Shut up big bum, anyway I heard you talking to Pamela on the telephone, and I heard you say that you'd touched Jeremy Edward's dick," Libby pulled her tongue out. She had been waiting two whole days for the right moment to drop that bombshell.

"Shut up you little sneak, I did not say that and you shouldn't be listening anyway, big ears," Catherine counter attacked but she was crimson with embarrassment. She hadn't even kissed Jeremy Edwards never mind touching his thingy. He tried to kiss her but his breath smelled so she'd pulled away. All the girls at school fancied Jeremy Edwards and they had bombarded her with text messages trying to get the gory details of their date. Did he feel your boobs? Did he kiss with his tongue? And so on, and so on. Catherine wouldn't be seeing him again but she just wanted to keep up with her peers, who all seemed to be bonking everyone, so she lied.

"I'm not big ears and you're a disgusting slagbag for touching a boy on the dick, I'm telling mummy what you've done," Libby ran toward the bedroom door as if she were about to run to her mother when her mother appeared in the doorway. Libby screeched to halt inches short of a collision.

"What are you going to tell me then exactly?" Donna asked her startled daughter. Libby flushed redder than her sister had already gone.

"Nothing mummy, I was so looking forward to the London Eye, everyone at school has been already, it's just so unfair," Libby pulled her bottom lip over sulkily.

"Well your daddy works very hard so that we can live in this house, and so that you can go to your school. Let's go shopping instead, my treat," Donna Bangor-Jones knew that her materialistic fashion conscious daughters would sooner be buying designer shoes, than spending time with their father. Retail therapy was all they needed.

"Great, I really want some Versace shoes mummy, Jeanette Stockton has the most fabulous shoes, I'm so jealous."

"I need some too mummy, she can't have them if I can't mummy, that's not fair."

"Shut up and stop arguing, the pair of you drive me bananas. Get showered and dressed, the last one to get ready gets the cheapest shoes," Donna said running back to her bedroom. Her daughters sprang into action, laughing and giggling as they went.

"Big bum slagbag."

"Big ears, sneaky pants."

Fifteen minutes later they were climbing into their father's Porsche Cayenne. He'd been picked up by a driver today because there was no parking at the venue where he'd be working. Donald Bangor-Jones was the Director of Britain's MI5, military intelligence agency.

"Ok girls, put your seatbelts on and behave, or we're going straight back home, no shoes and no shopping," Donna knew that the threat would keep the peace in the backseat for about three seconds. She looked in the rear view mirror and watched Catherine pinch Libby's thigh. Libby yelped and scratched her older sister on the forearm in retaliation. Donna Bangor-Jones turned the ignition key and was about to chastise her daughters when the vehicle exploded, blowing every female member of the Bangor-Jones family to bits.

Chapter Twenty-Six

Terrorist Task Force/ Briefing

Tank was standing by the window of the Task Force meeting room. Normally he'd be looking at the ferries coming and going from the Pierhead but today the protective shutters were down. The Task Force was under attack from enemies unknown. The room was filling up with unit leaders, each of them looked after a six-man team. Chen was on the telephone swapping from one held call to the next, gathering up to date information. He was talking quickly, too quickly. He had to repeat everything he was saying slowly because the callers couldn't understand him. Chen was slightly built, but strong and lean. His oriental eyes were more rounded than most men of Chinese origin, but his hair was standard issue, jet black and shiny. He had an infectious toothy smile. Tank watched as the smile disappeared from Chen's face. Chen frowned and grabbed a pen from the desk to make a note. He scribbled a few words before he realised that the pen wasn't working. Chen clicked the nib into place then tried again. Tank tried to see what he was writing but Chen was using his native Cantonese language and writing right to left.

The meeting room door slammed attracting Tank's attention. David Bell had entered the room with an arm full of folders and loose sheets of paper. He'd pushed the door closed with his heel and then leaned his back against it to catch his breath. He was overweight and sweating from the excursion of rushing to the meeting. There was an empty chair four places to his right and he headed for it, letting out a dramatic sigh as reached it. He dropped his files with a clatter onto the desk, much to the amusement of the Task Force agents. The team nicknamed him the fat controller, a character from the Thomas the Tank Engine series, because of his portly figure and superior ambiance. He had a habit of wearing his trousers pulled up to his bellybutton, fastened with a belt, to mask his ample waistline. Although a character of mirth to the team, he was also extremely well respected for his analytical prowess. There was nothing that David Bell didn't know about terrorist organisations their members or their modus operandi. From the pile of information he'd brought with him, it looked like he'd been busy.

"I've got everything we need so far," Chen said.

"When you're ready ladies and gentlemen," Tank wrapped his massive knuckles on the table. They looked like they belonged on an old oak tree, knobbly and gnarled, covered in scar tissue. The table had been laid out in an elongated U shape. Chen used a remote control to bring the digital screen to life. There were police identity mug shots on the screen.

"We've got to take things in the order that we became aware of them, not the order that they happened necessarily," Tank began.

"The two men at the top of the screen were disabled and arrested at Eccleston church this morning. They were armed with a CheyTac sniper rifle. They were positioned outside a funeral that I was attending. They are currently being treated for first-degree burns, and they're not talking yet. The Israeli specials and Mossad are convinced that they're Palestinian guerrillas from the West Bank, but we're not one hundred percent yet."

The screen changed and the burnt out shell of Chen's Jeep appeared on the screen. It was being loaded onto a low loader by a crane arm on the Holyhead breakwater.

"At roughly the same time my Jeep was booby trapped," Chen took over. "The device used was a mercury motion switch, plus timer attached to enough Semtex to send me back to China in a hurry." Chen smiled his infectious smile, and the Task Force men round the table laughed.

"Grace Farrington was attacked at the Royal Liverpool hospital two hours later, but the killer got the wrong target. We're waiting for the Israelis to confirm the dead man's identity, but we're sure that he is also a Palestinian terrorist." Tank paused as a picture of the Major's blood stained office was flashed onto the screen.

"The Major is in a critical condition, undergoing surgery as we speak."

"Who was shot at the hospital?" asked David Bell.

"Her name is Caroline Cambell, we've run her details through the system and there is no evidence pointing to her being a legitimate target. She was killed by mistake because she was a black female," Chen answered.

"Okay, who knew you were going to a funeral today?" the fat controller turned to Tank.

Tank thought hard for a moment, but there were too many possibilities, it would waste valuable time going down that road, but they had to discuss every question openly as a team. He couldn't just dismiss the question as irrelevant.

"Anyone who bought the St. Helens Star last week could have read the obituary columns. Tankersley isn't a common name; they could have put two and two together. Then you've got everyone in this office, all my immediate family, their in-laws and their families, and then anyone that they might have talked to inadvertently." Tank shrugged, it was a waste of time.

The fat controller took off his glasses and cleaned them with his tie while he digested the information. He held them up to his mouth and breathed on the lenses, before clearing the mist with the tie again.

"Who knew that Chen was dispatched to Holyhead today?" he asked without looking up from his spectacle cleaning.

"Only Major Timms," Chen answered.

The fat controller raised his eyebrows in surprise and opened his mouth a little to dramatise the expression he'd made.

"Why does that surprise you so much?" Chen responded defensively.

"It just seems odd that only your commanding officer would know where you are," David Bell shrugged.

"Normally Tank would know too but he wasn't here this morning," Chen explained. "The investigation hadn't even begun when I left for Holyhead this morning. I was sent to confirm if there was anything to actually investigate."

"Therefore someone either followed you, or Major Timms told them where you were going," The fat controller speculated. It was all still guesswork but he was right. There were only a few scenarios that could work.

"I don't like what your insinuating Bell," Chen said, his face reddened and all signs of his smile had gone.

"I thought you wanted me here to analyse the information you have, I'm doing just that," the fat controller put his glasses back on, and he secured them by pushing them to the top of the bridge of his fat round nose with his middle finger. He looked like he'd given Chen the bird across the table.

"I think we should calm down and study what we have here, every one of us in this room is hurting right now, but the facts are the facts."

There was a tense silence in the room. So far, two questions had been asked and there was already conflict in the air. Tank focused his blue eyes on the fat controller and nodded for him to proceed.

"Okay, to summarise then, the firearm captured at the churchyard is a foreign CheyTac Bushmaster sniper rifle. The same model used by Palestinian militias."

Everyone nodded in agreement. The CheyTac was cheap and efficient. It fired a high-powered large bore bullet capable of dropping a horse at fifteen hundred yards, if the shooter was good enough to hit it. It also came with a built in suppressor, which made it silent and deadly at long ranges.

"There were sixteen bullets fired at the Major. Fourteen were removed from the drawers of the filing cabinets and are too badly damaged to analyse. Two were removed from his body and are being analysed now by ballistics, however on first inspection they appear to be similar calibre to the bullets that the snipers were carrying at the church."

"Are they similar or the same?" Chen asked.

"Similar, not the same because the bullets were not carrying out the same job, one was a long distance shot which required more sophisticated aerodynamics, and the other was a close distance assassination attempt. The bullets have the same manufacturer and are the same calibre, but one was made for its destructive qualities, and the other for its accuracy." Tank pointed out the difference.

"If we combine the ballistic evidence with the information we gleaned from Chen's Jeep then we're dealing with experts," the fat controller interrupted. Everyone turned to listen to him. It was obvious that he'd already noticed the attackers' methodology.

"The equipment they are using is state of the art, as is their technical ability to use it."

"They're also well financed, passage aboard a tanker from the Middle East doesn't come cheap, especially if you're carrying weapons," said Tank, "I can't believe that they came all this way to attack the Task Force, it doesn't add up. Even if they'd managed to kill us all, what could they achieve?"

Blank faces stared back at Tank. He was right. Dead agents would be replaced the next day by new agents, who were just as well trained and equally as deadly. The public would never be aware of the assassinations because the Task Force didn't exist, in the public realm there was no such agency. The phone rang and Tank picked it up.

"If you're right, then there must be an alternative motive behind the attacks. They could be a red herring, a smoke screen to stop us seeing what they're here to do. We may not find out until it's too late," the fat controller thought aloud. He looked at Tank's face and realised that whoever was on the line had given him bad news.

"Chen we need all the forensic evidence from the St. John's Tower examined immediately," Tank held the phone on his shoulder while he barked a succession of orders, keeping the caller on the line.

"You recovered a palm print from the shopping centre, didn't you? Have we had the results back yet?"

"Yes, but it's come out negative. We don't have him on file and the Israelis are checking theirs along with the others," Chen answered. "What's the problem?"

"The team on the Syrian tanker have found traces of radioactive material on board the ship."

The room descended into a stunned silence, which was disturbed by a second telephone ringing. It was the line, which linked them directly to government headquarters.

Chapter Twenty-Seven

Grace Farrington

Grace knew that she'd been moved, she sensed the motion of the gurney being pushed and it had made her feel sick. Felling sick was a revelation because she hadn't felt anything for such a long time. There had been people around her, many people. She sensed being lifted and then a strange glowing feeling in her veins, as if they'd injected a different kind of drug into her system. At one point, she thought she'd heard her mother crying but it could have been a distant memory. Her mother cried a lot, when she was happy and when she was sad, and sometimes when she was in between. She was sure she hadn't heard Tank's voice for a while, not today anyway. Grace wondered where he was, she wondered where she was too.

Then she heard shooting far away in the distance. She was sure it was gunfire, but she wasn't sure why she was sure. She just was. It sounded far enough away not to be too concerned for the moment. Then there had been more fuss, more noise, men shouting and barking orders, and her mother crying again. Grace wondered why Tank didn't just come and sort it out; he was good at sorting things out, especially trouble. Although she'd thought about him she couldn't remember what he looked like, in fact she couldn't remember what anyone looked like. She tried hard to focus on his face. It seemed to be very important that she could remember him.

A shadowy shape entered her mind's eye; it was the silhouette of a man. The shape was thick and bulky, muscular around the chest and shoulders. The picture sharpened and she saw his shaved head, just a hint of darker shadow over the ears and above the neckline where his hair root was thicker and still showed. His skin was tanned and rough; there was scar tissue above the eyes left behind by years of competing in the ring. His eyes were creased at the edges, laughter lines or wrinkles depending on what mood he was in. Then the eyes came into focus and they were sky blue. The man smiled at her, white teeth set in a Desperate Dan jaw. It was Tank, that's what he looked like. She remembered and it made her feel like smiling, but she couldn't of course.

The face wavered in her memory and the man's eyes filled with tears. Teardrops ran freely down his face and she could feel herself being carried off the floor. There was the sound of gunfire again but this time it was in her dream, and there was wind, lots of wind, like a helicopter nearby. There was sand and it was hot, like a desert somewhere. She wasn't sure how she knew it was a desert, but she did. Then she saw the face above her; he leaned close and kissed her cheek. He whispered something to her as the engine noise got louder and the wind blew stronger. The helicopter lifted gently in her dream and it carried her up and away from him. She could still see him. Tears stained his dusty face as they traced a path down his cheeks. Grace didn't want to leave him again. She felt pain in her arm. Her bicep felt sore, so did her shoulder, and her back ached. Her nervous system was communicating with her brain again, telling her that it had suffered severe trauma and was in pain. Grace Farrington sensed the daylight beyond her eyelids. They flickered nervously and then she opened her eyes and woke up.

Chapter Twenty-Eight

Boris McGuiness

Boris McGuiness was forty-three years old, but he was much fitter than most men of his age, which he was proud of. He stood six feet tall and weighed around twelve stones in his underwear. His hair was platinum blond and completely untameable. It stuck up, curled up and stuck out at will, he'd long since given up trying to control it. It was just a curly blond mop, but it characterised him. Boris had two teenage sons, Kenneth was thirteen, and Fernando was fifteen. They both inherited their hair from their father and when the three of them were together, they looked like three peas in a pod. Boris tried to spend as much time as he could with his sons, but the pressures of work didn't always allow it as often as he would have liked. They'd lost their mother five years earlier in a tragic suicide, and Boris had felt guilty ever since.

Chandelle was ten years younger than Boris when they'd married. She had been a career woman since leaving school and aspired to continue in her chosen profession after getting married. Unfortunately, things didn't work out as planned. She became pregnant almost immediately and lost her position at work as a result. The pregnancy was a nightmare. She not only suffered from morning sickness but afternoon, evening and nighttime sickness too. Her blood pressure sharply increased and she had to spend extended periods lying on the sofa, resting with her feet up. Chandelle was an energetic, active young woman, and the long periods of inactivity made her feel trapped and resentful. Things didn't get any better once Kenneth was born. She suffered from terrible postnatal depression, and lost her enthusiasm for sex, her child and life in general. Her husband was constantly at work and was no help or support to her. Boris always seemed to be frustrated by her apathy, disappointed in her generally. Chandelle hid her sadness well, not wanting to be seen as a bad mother by her family and friends, and she began to eat. By the time she fell pregnant the second time she had ballooned from a fit size twelve to a tight size eighteen. Being fat made her even unhappier, and being unhappy made her eat more. Her mental health spiralled out of control and she was prescribed a cocktail of anti depressants, which turned her into a fat zombie in a space of two months.

Boris couldn't cope with the pressures of work and the constant battle to keep the children well looked after at home. Chandelle just couldn't cope with the housework and her depression. He had noticed that his wife was feeding their children nothing but frozen ready meals, fish fingers and chicken nuggets, which according to the packaging had never seen either a fish or a chicken during production. The final straw occurred when he arrived home late one evening to find his wife in bed and his sons alone in the kitchen, arguing over the last remaining beef and tomato pot noodle. The cupboards were empty. In the end, Boris put his sons into boarding school, explaining to the family that it was for the best. Privately educated children were a fashion accessory in the circles that Boris and his family moved in. It didn't seem out of the ordinary to pack them off to school, in fact it was seen as the, done thing.

Losing her children was the last straw, instead of just eating for comfort she started drinking for comfort too. The atmosphere at home became unbearable, as Boris arrived home late from work, he'd find his wife lying in her own vomit and faeces, comatose from the cocktail of drink and drugs that she swallowed every day. By the time, she woke from her drunken stupor Boris had left for work, and the cycle started again. He started spending more time at work, staying overnight more than he needed to, just to avoid going home. He became desensitised to her feelings and she became fatter and more depressed. She felt that she had lost her career, her identity, her looks, her figure, her children, her husband and finally her dignity. Eventually, she'd thrown herself from the platform of her local railway station, and Chandelle was cut in half underneath the nine fifteen from Euston to Manchester.

Boris waited three months before telling his sons that she'd died from a heart attack. They were devastated by the news and Boris was destroyed by their grief in turn. When they returned to school, the other pupils got wind of what had happened. The truth soon came out and they were taunted by school bullies about their mother committing suicide. Boris then had to tell them the truth, which just compounded the situation tenfold. He'd taken them from their boarding school and found them another, which was situated hundreds of miles away in the north of

Scotland. The boys felt isolated and alone, and Boris was racked with guilt. He made a pact with them that every holiday they would go away for a few days. Kenneth and Fernando settled into school life, the discipline and work ethic was exactly what they needed to carry them through their troubled teenage years. They joined the schoolboy scout troop and developed a liking for camping and mountain walking. Boris kept his word, and every holiday they headed for the Cumbrian Lake District or the Welsh Snowden range.

On the day of the first attacks, Boris woke at four in the morning. The dawn chorus was in full swing and it sounded like every bird in Snowdonia was perched on their tent. Dawn had broken but the rain was still pouring down. Their tent was holding firm against the deluge for now, but if it wasn't for his promise, he would be at home now safely tucked up in bed with a milky coffee and a good book. The indigenous Welsh mountain sheep joined the birds announcing that another day had dawned and he heard his sons rousing from their sleep, rustling around inside their sleeping bags. He climbed out of his pit and switched on a single gas ring to boil a kettle full of water. His boys would want their morning pint mugs of tea when they woke up.

A Honda motorbike turned into the campsite slowly, the rider spotted the number plate that he was looking for, and then he revved the machine, parked up and waited.

Chapter Twenty-Nine

Abdul

Abdul groaned loudly as he climaxed, his brains clouded over for a precious few seconds then the sensation was gone along with his lust. He pushed the Egyptian woman off him and reached into his bedside cabinet drawer for his money, he paid her the equivalent of her full week's wages, farted and climbed out of the huge bed. There was a full-length mirror fixed to the wall at the edge of the bed, it was framed with an ornate brass frame. Abdul turned sideways and breathed in, making his fat potbelly disappear for as long as he could hold the breath, which wasn't very long. He breathed out and his potbelly swelled to its normal size.

"You are still very sexy Mr Ahmed," the woman said as she gathered her clothes from the floor next to the bed.

"Are you still here? Shut up and get out, hurry up," he barked at her. She scurried around trying to pull her knickers up and run at the same time. Abdul made a mental note that her arse wobbled as she rushed around, he wouldn't be using her again, and they needed to be slimmer than that.

He walked into the bathroom, lifted the toilet lid and peed. He bent his knees a little and forced out another fart as he emptied his bladder, the smell of the woman permeated up to his nostrils. Abdul stepped into a marble tiled shower cubicle. It was big enough to accommodate a small family saloon car. He turned on the shower and let the warm water wash the smells of the previous evening off his body. The water jetted into his face and he opened his mouth to allow it in, letting it dribble from his chin. The water gushed noisily all over him, and he only just managed to hear his phone when it rang. He turned off the water to be sure that it was ringing. Abdul grabbed a thick towelling robe and picked up the bathroom extension hand set. He caught his reflection in the mirror, and he smoothed his thick black moustache with his thumb and forefinger.

"Sabaah Al-Khair Abdul," the voice greeted him in Arabic.

"Sabaah An-Noor," Abdul returned the traditional response.

"I think that we have found your friend," the voice said. Abdul remained silent. He wasn't completely sure if the caller was genuine.

"Who is this?"

"Who I am shouldn't concern you, however the information that I have for sale does. You have been tracking certain illegal flights from Eastern Europe, have you not?"

"Yes, I'm interested in the whereabouts of Islamic prisoners of war, who are being held illegally by the West," Abdul replied coyly.

"I really don't care what your reasons are Mr Ahmed, I have information which indicates that your real target is being moved."

"My real target?"

"Yes, Abdul your real target, please don't insult my intelligence, you've been searching rendition flights out of Eastern Europe, looking for Yasser Ahmed."

Abdul remained silent. His stomach felt like it had butterflies in it, excitement was growing at the thought of his inspirational leader being found alive. He had to be careful that it wasn't a set up.

"I'm not one hundred percent sure who you are talking about, but you have my attention," Abdul replied cautiously.

"Check your e-mail Mr Ahmed. There is flight information attached to a word document, which contains the details of a bank account in Zurich. Transfer one million American dollars into the account and I will send you the rest of the flight plan. Be quick Mr Ahmed they will not hang around, it's a once in a life time opportunity."

The line went dead and Abdul ran into the bedroom to retrieve his laptop.

Chapter Thirty

Terrorist Task Force

The information that was now streaming into the Task Force from forensics was causing growing concern. Tank called the team back into the meeting room for an immediate update.

"The preliminary results from the Golan are in, there are two radioactive substances, that have been positively identified, cobalt and strontium 90," Tank paused as some of the team whistled and shook their heads, shocked at the possible connotations.

"So are we looking for a nuclear bomb?" asked a team leader.

"No, definitely not," the fat controller interrupted. This was his field of expertise. "Cobalt has been used before in the manufacture of what's called a salted bomb. Cobalt is highly radioactive. It is in a constant state of decay, and as it decays it emits powerful gamma radiation, to a degree that it would make unprotected humans sick, just by being in close proximity to it, but it can't be used to create a nuclear explosion."

"That adds up, the report mentions the condition of the sailors on board the Golan, some of them were displaying the symptoms of radiation sickness, vomiting, weakness, diarrhoea, it all fits." Chen was reading from the report.

"Anyone that has been close to cobalt, without protective clothing will display those symptoms within a seventy two hour window. The seriousness of the illness is dependent on the length of time the subject has been exposed to the substance," the fat controller explained.

"So what's the prognosis if we are dealing with a salted bomb?"

"Well most people know them as, dirt bombs. The fact that they contain radioactive materials causes panic. In reality it is a standard explosive material such as Semtex or C4, even artillery ordinance can be used, packed around a radioactive substance. The subsequent explosion disperses the radiation into the atmosphere and contaminates the area," Bell continued.

"So the actual explosion isn't as catastrophic as a nuclear bomb?"

"Nowhere near as bad, it's a propaganda weapon, the idea of a radioactive bomb exploding causes hysteria," Bell said. He stood up and removed his glasses again, and then he put one of the arms in his mouth. "Imagine a dirty bomb being exploded in a city. The initial explosion would cause physical damage around the detonation site, and then a much wider area would have to be evacuated while the radius of contamination is calculated. Shops, houses, businesses, roads, everything would have to be decontaminated over an extended period of time, during which there could be absolutely no access whatsoever allowed."

"How long is an extended period of time, as you put it?" Tank asked.

"Fifteen to twenty years, maybe more. The half-life of strontium-90 is around twenty-eight years. That would be how long the physical damage would take to clean up, but then if you think about it logically, who in their right mind would go back into the area to live or work?" The room remained silent while they thought about it.

"Would any of you work there, send your children to school there, drink water from a tap there?" the fat controller had studied the after effects of the nuclear disaster that affected Chernobyl, and the surrounding populations, most of them remained void of human life for years .

"You would literally have to bulldoze the entire area and leave it for a generation, until people forgot." David Bell pulled his trousers up at the waist and sat down again, putting his glasses back on and looking at everyman in the room one at a time.

"Then multiply that by two or three cities simultaneously, it would bring this country to its knees," Chen added. The financial ramifications of huge areas of the country's biggest cities being turned into radioactive wasteland would decimate the economy.

"What about the other compound, strontium 90?" Tank asked.

"Well I'm glad you asked that, because it is still a radioactive isotope, but this one emits beta radiation, and it's very nasty. It would have the same effect as cobalt, except the cleanup would take decades rather than years," the fat controller smiled.

"How easy is it going to be to find it?" Tank asked.

"It should be relatively simple in theory, because both substances radiate a field of charged electrons, which should be visible on your heat sensors."

"How big would the device be?"

"How long is a piece of string? It really wouldn't need to be big, I should guess that a suitcase device would be enough to contaminate about five square miles," the fat controller made a triangle with his fingers.

The door opened and a female face appeared round the door,

"Tank, the Prime Minister's secretary is on the line, she says it's a matter of national security."

"Put her through on the speaker," Tank said.

"Agent Tankersley I must apologise for the interruption, but I have some bad news I`m afraid," Janet Walsh said. She'd been the legal secretary at number ten to a succession of Prime Ministers. Her professional demeanour and no nonsense attitude made her an asset that an incoming government did not want to lose. She was the type of woman that looked both professional and attractive in a business suit.

"It's not a problem Janet, please go on," Tank said.

"There's been an attempt to assassinate General Bangor-Jones, We thought it too much of a coincidence for it not to be connected to Major Timms being shot," Janet Walsh was the first point of call for all the security services, she'd analyse incoming status reports, and then filter the information to whoever needed to know.

"Attempt?" Tank asked.

"Yes, an attempt. His car was blown up outside his home; he'd just left for work with a driver. There are three fatalities, I'm afraid that identification is proving to be difficult, but we think they're his wife and children."

The room stayed silent, most of the agents looked at the table or the floor, avoiding eye contact with each other. They worked in a violent cynical world, every single one of them was a trained killer, but every one of them had an Achilles heel, their families. Their thoughts went to Donald Bangor-Jones, the military director of MI5 and how terribly aggrieved he must be by the loss of his children. The guilt would be unbearable.

"They're connected, they must be. The problem I have Janet is that someone has access to not only Task Force personnel files, but also MI5 information too. They're both encrypted, password protected and agency specific," Tank said.

"I'm not sure I follow, agent Tankersley."

"MI5 have security access to other agency files, but we don't have access to anyone else's information, it's safer that way," Tank explained.

"I'm still not with you, agent Tankersley, what are you saying?"

"Whoever got Task Force information must have accessed the information from MI5 computers, not vice versa, there's a leak Janet, and the leak is in that agency," Tank couldn't be any more specific.

"Ah, I see where you're coming from now. We may have a problem there," Janet Walsh obviously knew more than she was letting on.

"Would you care to elaborate Janet?"

"We seem to have lost one of our agents. Well one of our ex-agents to be more precise," she explained. "Do you remember agent Garden?"

"Yes, small weasel type man wasn't he?"

"That's him to a tee, well he's disappeared. We like to wipe the slate clean when someone leaves the service, but it appears Garden took a trip to Egypt a couple of months ago and never came back," she said.

"There are only two possibilities then, either he's gone over to the other side and sold information, or someone's extracted it from him forcefully. What level was he?" Tank asked. The higher up the food chain he'd been the more valuable the information he had. Over two hundred Western secret service agents have simply disappeared since the early nineties. No one will ever know if they defected for financial gain, or spent the last painful days of their lives in a foreign torture chamber.

"He was a grade one; I'm afraid, top of the tree."

"If he's been gone for months then we must assume that all his information has been gleaned. Has everyone been accounted for at the agency?" Tank asked. It appeared that there was more than one agency under attack.

"No, not yet, we've alerted all our government agencies and the security staff from Westminster, but there are several members of staff unaccounted for. I'll contact you if there is any more information. Have you made any headway in the investigation?" Janet Walsh changed tack.

"We are communicating with Israeli Mossad, so far we think the attacks are coming from a West Bank terrorist cell, Palestinians, but we are waiting for definite confirmation from them," Tank took a deep breath and carried on, "we've found evidence that they gained passage from a Syrian tanker named The Golan Heights, and jumped ship when it docked in Holyhead."

"So you know who they are, where they're from, all we need to know now is where they are and what they're going to do next," she said.

"We think that we have an idea of what they're planning, and it's not good news I'm afraid," Tank said.

"Okay, let's get all the cards on the table agent Tankersley, don't beat around the bush," she said in a manner that made it obvious why she was in the position that she was.

"We've found traces of radioactive substances on board the tanker, cobalt and strontium, they can be used to make a dirty bomb," Tank explained.

The line remained silent and Tank signalled to David Bell to explain in layman's terms, what the worst-case scenario would be.

"Secretary Walsh, the initial explosion of a terrorist dirty bomb, is unlikely to result in many deaths, relatively speaking." The Fat controller shrugged the last two words to emphasise their importance.

"What do you mean, relatively speaking?" Janet Walsh asked, sounding a little irritated by the flippant use of the phrase.

"Technically a dirty bomb is not a weapon of mass destruction. It is however a weapon of mass disruption. Its purpose would be to create psychological panic, mass hysteria, and terror, through ignorance. The containment and decontamination of thousands of displaced, panic-stricken people would be extremely expensive, and a logistical nightmare. Add to that the rendering of the affected area unusable and you have an economic disaster," he finished with a smile, removed his glasses and cleaned them again on his tie.

"Fucking hell," the Prime Minister's secretary swore for the first time in ten years.

Chapter Thirty-One

Boris/ Kenneth/ Fernando

Boris filled a small tin kettle with bottled water, and then put it on to a gas stove to boil. He took three paper cups from a sleeve and put a pyramid tea bag into each one, along with a splash of milk, and one teaspoon full of sugar. His sons took their tea the same way he did, white with one sugar. They parted their unkempt blonde hair the same way he did, pulled the same faces when they talked, and used all the same facial expressions. Both of them supported the same football team, Liverpool, the same cricket team, Lancashire, the same rugby league team, St Helens, as their sport mad dad. They were two chips off the old block.

The boys had become clingy after their mother's suicide; they rang him every evening from boarding school before they went to their dormitory. The time they spent together during school holidays was incredibly precious to them. Boris took them to watch football matches as often as they could get tickets, but their real passion was wrestling. They couldn't get enough of the American entertainment sport, the character names, the incredible athleticism of the competitors and the razzmatazz captured their young imaginations. They were forever rehearsing wrestling moves and re-enacting classic match ups, providing their own running commentary for an imaginary crowd of thousands, usually ending up with one or both of them in tears.

Boris heard his youngest son, Fernando rummaging around, the zip on his sleeping bag opened noisily. Then the zip on the compartment flysheet opened and Fernando's scruffy head appeared.

"What time is it dad?" he asked.

"It's time to get up lazy bones," Boris said ruffling his son's hair.

"What time is it really?"

"Tea time," Boris said pouring hot water into the three paper cups.

"Dad, what's the real time, stop messing about," Fernando said and he play punched his dad on the shoulder.

"I don't know, my watch is in the car son," Boris said.

"Well I know what time it is any way," Fernando said unzipping the flysheet to his brother's bedroom compartment. "It's show time!" he said as he launched himself on top of his sleeping brother.

"Stone Cold drops in the people's elbow, followed by a Hulkster leg drop," Fernando commentated for the imaginary crowd. He dropped onto his brother and struck him with the back of his elbow. The he stood up and jumped on him again, this time striking with the heel of his foot.

"Get off me you little knobhead!" Kenneth shouted at his younger brother, but he couldn't move because he was pinned inside his sleeping bag. Fernando made the most of his brother's inability to strike back. He stood up quickly and then jumped on him again knees first.

"He delivers the Tombstone, it's got to be over now, and the crowd are on their feet, they're going mad," Fernando shouted as he knocked the wind out of his brother.

"Aaah! You little git," Kenneth moaned.

"Kenneth stop swearing at your brother, I hope you don't use language like that at school young man," Boris said, "and get off your brother Fernando, this is a tent not Madison Square Garden."

Fernando climbed off his brother and grabbed his tea. He sat next to his dad, who ruffled his hair again.

"You could cause trouble in an empty room, young man," Boris said laughing, "come and get your tea Kenneth."

Kenneth lumbered out of his pit and sat down on the opposite side of his father. Boris handed him the cup of hot tea, which he took with one hand, while his other hand reached behind his father and pushed Fernando's head forward, just as he was about to sip his drink. Fernando burnt his lip on the scalding liquid, and spilt it down his top.

"Dad, look what he made me do, you little knobhead," Fernando shouted at his brother.

"You asked for that, and you're the knobhead not me," Kenneth said.

"Will you two stop saying that terrible word; I will not tolerate you swearing at each other, what would your mother think?" Boris used his last resort. Mentioning her name always shut them up for a minute or two. The boys were silent while they finished their tea, and Boris started to feel guilty again. He shouldn't have said that. The boys sat either side of him in silence, holding their cups of tea to their lips. He decided to lighten the mood. He timed it perfectly, placing his own tea on the groundsheet unnoticed, and then play slapping the boys on the back of the head simultaneously, spilling their hot tea.

"No way dad, that's just not cricket!" cried Kenneth wiping tea from his jumper.

"Get him! Let's tag team him," said Fernando as he pounced on his father knocking him backwards off his little camping stool.

"I'm doing a choke slam," Kenneth shouted and he tried to grab his dad round the neck.

"I'm doing the three amigos," Fernando said as he began a series of three star jumps around the tent, before finally pouncing on his hysterical father. The three of them ended up in twisted melee of arms and legs, chuckling until they thought they would cry.

"Boris stopped laughing first. He'd turned slightly to catch his breath. Then Fernando and Kenneth followed their father's gaze, confused at why he had stopped laughing. The three of them sat silently staring at a man dressed in motorcycle leathers, and still wearing a full-face helmet. He was pointing a huge ugly Bulldog revolver at them, fitted with a suppressor.

Boris died first as two fat dumdum bullets smashed into his chest. Fernando and Kenneth followed immediately after. Their bodies were found two days later when the campsite manger received complaints about the smell coming from the tent, and the audible buzzing of a million blowflies.

Chapter Thirty-Two

Yasser Ahmed

Yasser was sat in his cage with his back against the mesh. The sun was just coming up over the desert from the east behind the long low mountains in the distance. The rising sun cast them in dark shadows giving them a forbidding appearance. It was the third sunrise he had witnessed from the wire compound that had become his home, and he relished the time he'd spent there. It seemed like a lifetime since he had been in the open air with the blazing sun on his skin. Even his festering shoulder had displayed signs of drying up slightly. Scabs were starting to harden where running sores had been days before, as the healing power of the sunshine and fresh air worked its magic.

The same three Eygptian men had guarded him since he'd arrived. The pilot was also still on site along with the helicopter engineer that had stamped on his shoulder, making five of them. Yasser dreamed of spending some quality time alone with engineer. He needed to learn the meaning of respect. The man had hurt Yasser for no other reason than the fact that he could do so, with no consequences. Yasser had killed and maimed hundreds, but he had a cause. He was a general fighting a war that had raged since Islam`s conception. The engineer had no such cause, and he needed a lesson in humility.

The Egyptian guards were all inside the small felt roofed building that adjoined his cage. Yasser could hear them talking, laughing, and even squabbling over a game of cards every now and again. The smell of spicy food drifted from the open windows making his mouth water, he hadn't eaten for three days now. One of the guards with a non-descriptive olive green uniform and high leather jackboots had come outside every two hours on the dot, to give him water. Yasser decided that when the time came he would give the man water, in return for the compassion that he had shown. No one forced him to bring water out to Yasser. The guard refused to speak, just nodding when Yasser thanked him for his kindness, but conversation was not what Yasser needed right now. He needed the opportunity to slit the guard's throat, steal his weapon, slaughter the others and escape. He'd kill them all except the guard that had stamped on his ruined shoulder, he'd spend some time alone with him before he left this remote airfield.

As the sun climbed higher, the structure of the distant aircraft hangar became visible. The three bright yellow airplanes still hadn't moved, and they shimmered in the morning light as the heat haze rose from the runway tarmac. The sky above him was the most incredible blue colour, and yet the horizon was still dark.

He wasn't sure at first because the distant skyline was still just a strip of dark blue, speckled with fading stars, but there was movement on the horizon. As the fading strip of night sky shrunk below the distant horizon, tiny shapes appeared far away across the desert. Some of the shapes were small, some much taller swaying slightly. As time went by, he realised that the taller shapes were Camels. He could hardly believe that there were men walking, and men riding camels across the barren wasteland toward him.

Bedouin tribes had crisscrossed the deserts of Africa and the Middle East for centuries. They were traditionally extended every courtesy by anyone they met. They were given fresh water and traded food supplies with the small communities that they stumbled across. It was seen as bad luck to refuse the Bedouin the opportunity to replenish their water supplies. Yasser watched for hours as the caravan approached the airfield, a dust cloud created by the camels followed their progress. He didn't know if they would continue on their travels without stopping for water, or if they would ask the guards for supplies. He could only sit and wait, and pray.

Chapter Thirty-Three

Terrorist Task Force

Graham Libby was the Task Force scientific advisor, forensic and ballistic expert, coroner and all round brain box. He was sifting through the mountain of information that had been gathered from the St John's incident. His laboratory was a long rectangular shaped room lined with metal racking, designed for separating and storing evidence during analysis. The main body of the lab was dissected by three workbenches, each of which could be utilised from both sides, simultaneously. The benches held a line of implements and medical appliances positioned along the middle of the work surface, allowing several technicians to work simultaneously from opposite sides of the table. The evidence racks were already full to bursting point, packed with labelled brown paper bags. Uniformed policemen continued to bring more and more items in for analyses, which were now being lined up on the laboratory floor.

Tank entered the lab and made a beeline for the scientist.

"I've got your message, anything new to report Graham?"

"Come and look at this," the scientist said excitedly.

He led Tank to a workbench that had the tattered remains of a bloodstained suit spread out on it. He switched off the desk lamps and turned on an ultraviolet torch. The material at the back of the jacket had a patchy glow, as if luminous talcum powder had been sprinkled on it. Tank looked at Graham Libby for an explanation.

"This is the suit worn by the booby trapped body in the lift at the bottom of the tower. Since we received the information about the radioactive substances from the Syrian vessel, we've scanned everything with a Geiger counter, the suit is contaminated."

"So was it in contact with the same radioactive substances that we found on the ship?" Tank quizzed.

"Oh, I can't tell you that I'm afraid, only that it was in close proximity to a radioactive field recently," the scientist explained.

"I can tell you that the levels displayed by this material are mirrored by contamination readings that we took from the lift itself. The most convincing evidence however is that it is emitting both beta and gamma radiation." He went along the bench to a set of black and white negatives, which pictured a badly buckled, blood stained lift car. There was a square smudge on the floor, highlighted by ultraviolet light, about three feet square.

"Beta and gamma radiation, and that matches with the profiles for cobalt and strontium. Is that the imprint of a device?" Tank asked remembering what the fat controller had said about how much damage a suitcase dirty bomb could cause. Worse still, he was thinking that it was evidence that the radioactive material was actually in Liverpool city centre somewhere.

"Not necessarily no, it tells us that a container was placed into that lift car that was either radioactive itself, or contained radioactive materials, but look at this, I haven't even started yet."

The scientist rubbed his hands together. He stepped sideways further down the bench, obviously following a scientific trail of analysed evidence. Tank rubbed his blue eyes as he tried to follow the doctor through the vagueness and speculation of a scientific investigation. It was probably very interesting if you're a scientist, but just plain frustrating as the investigating team looking for concrete answers. There didn't seem to be anything specific yet and he didn't have time for indicators, might be and possibly, maybe and could be. He needed solid leads to follow.

The next set of negatives showed the incinerated remains of the old restaurant. The charred skeleton of a human being, grinned a macabre toothy smile. On the floor to the left of the remains was another rectangular smudge that glowed blue. Tank nodded, whoever put the container in the lift also removed it at the top of the tower.

"The explosion in the tower, it wasn't what you're insinuating was it?" Tank asked confused. The fat controller had told them that the actual explosion of a dirty bomb would be no different to any other detonation in character. There would be no terrifying black mushroom cloud collapsing in on itself, identifying it as containing nuclear isotopes. There would be a big bang and then people would start getting sick.

"What? Oh no, it wasn't a dirty bomb. I'm sorry if I gave you that impression, although it would have been the ideal place to explode one, being so far above the city, prevailing winds and so on, it could contaminate most of the North West," Graham Libby explained matter of factly.

"The tower has been checked for anything that could have been left there, and the area is clear, so where did the container go?" Tank said. Graham Libby picked up a stack of negatives. He placed the first one on the desk and then stacked the others one at a time on top of the first one. They showed the wide arcing stairwell that led from the top of the tower to the shopping centre below. The stairs showed the same patchy blue smudges on random steps, as if someone had carried the container a distance, and then placed it down to rest. The further down the stairwell the photos pictured, the more frequent the smudges could be seen, as if the fugitive was becoming increasingly tired.

"Where does this trail lead to," Tank asked the obvious question, growing bored of the scientist's enthusiasm for his work. He needed answers, how the science lab arrived at the answer didn't matter right now.

"I'm just getting to that," the doctor replied stiffly, a little disappointed that Tank wasn't incredibly impressed with how clever he was.

"Please get to the point Graham, there could be a device out there somewhere heading for god knows where, about to be detonated," Tank spoke quietly and kept his voice at an even pitch. The tech boys had obviously done a great job but Tank had terrorists to catch. The pictures followed a luminous trail down the stairwell, into the shopping mall and out onto an exterior balcony. There it seemed to disappear.

"The trail ends here at this balcony," the scientist said gruffly.

Tank remained silent and folded his arms waiting for Graham Libby to proceed. He was testing his patience now. The last thing that Tank needed right now was a sulky science officer. He knew the doctor was gagging to explain his theory, so he waited for him to crack first. It took just a few seconds. Graham Libby cleared his throat and continued.

"There are no more contact readings in the area, it appears as if the container was then either carried off, or put onto wheels and dragged."

Tank nodded in agreement, because it made perfect sense. The device could be anywhere by now, London, Manchester or any other big city.

"So there you are, you've got less than a mile square to search then, it's not brilliant, but it`s the best we can do for now," Graham Libby folded his arms looking a little deflated. Tank looked completely baffled.

"What do you mean a square mile, I don't follow you Graham," Tank unfolded his arms and leaned over the negatives again looking for a solution to a conundrum that he didn't understand.

"Well if you'd let me finish what I was saying then you would understand perfectly," the scientist said patronisingly coking his head to the side as he spoke.

"Tank's face flushed red and he could feel the anger rising. He didn't like being messed about, especially by his own team, he couldn't tolerate office politics, and he'd rather someone tell him that they were pissed off, than pretend that they're okay. If the problem was out in the open then he could deal with it, and then move on to the next issue. Graham Libby realised from the look in Tank's eyes that he had overstepped the mark. He coughed nervously then continued in a hurried fashion.

"I was trying to explain that the whole area was sealed off, and the area was being monitored and scanned by police helicopters, packed with body heat sensors."

Tank was starting to get the picture, and it wasn't a pretty one either. Graham Libby continued, regaining his enthusiasm.

"The amount of radiation this container is giving off would have registered like a small supernova on their screens; if it had left that area then it would have been reported. We would definitely not have missed a reading like that. I'm absolutely convinced that the container never left the city centre, Tank," the scientist rubbed his hands together as if he'd just discovered the cure for the common cold.

"If there is a radiological dispersal device in the city centre then you have a problem," Graham Libby shook his head, worried by the thought.

"Now if you can give me five more minutes of your time, I'd like to show you this," the scientist continued. He picked up a test tube, which contained a thick viscous material. He turned off the desk lamp again. The substance glowed blue in the dark.

"What is it?" Tank asked.

"Vomit, it was recovered from the lower balcony of the shopping precinct, close to the entrance of the delivery basement. Whoever secreted this is very ill indeed, so I'd assume that they carried your radioactive materials for an extended period of time, without any protective clothing."

"What would be his prognosis?"

"He's terminal, there is no treatment for this level of exposure. If he isn't already dead, then he soon will be. I don't think that he left that area because his heat profile would have been spotted. There is some good news however, the DNA matches the hand print found on the mirror at the tower's fire exit, plus he'll be glowing like a Christmas tree on your heat sensors."

"So it looks like we're heading for that basement."

Chapter Thirty-Four

Yasser

Yasser was still watching the approaching Bedouin caravan in the distance. The dust cloud they created was shimmering in the early morning heat. He heard the door of the felt roofed guard shack creaking open. The door hinges were full of desert sand, which made them screech and groan. The same guard as usual walked toward his cage carrying a canvas water flask, the personnel never changed. Always the same Egyptian soldier brought him water. Yasser stood up and walked to the cage door. He greeted the guard in Arabic. The guard ignored him as usual, slid open the meal hatch and passed the water bottle through. Yasser swapped it for the empty container that he'd used through the night. The guard nodded, and then he took the empty flask from Yasser and closed the hatch again. The guard turned away from the cage and rubbed his sleepy eyes. When he opened them, again he was facing the hangar in the distance. He straightened up surprised by the sight of the Bedouin caravan approaching the airfield. He hadn't noticed them earlier when he left the shack. The guard started shouting his colleagues as he rushed back into the felt roofed building in a panic.

Yasser heard muffled voices, expressing alarm, and the dull thud of army boots being pulled on in a hurry. The door squealed open again and Yasser's five captors emerged from their shack, carrying ancient Enfield 303 rifles. He was surprised to see the Second World War rifles. They had wooden stocks and a small magazine that held just three bullets. Whoever supplied this outpost with its ancient British weapons didn't expect them to be needed. Yasser was dismayed. The rifles fired one bullet at a time, and the next bullet had to be chambered into the breach manually. A one armed man couldn't fire more than one bullet. Even if Yasser managed to steal a rifle it was no use to him, he needed an automatic weapon.

One of the Saddam Hussein lookalikes was watching the approaching caravan through a huge pair of field glasses, and again they were British standard army issue from the last century. The helicopter pilot ran to his aircraft and opened the cockpit door. He reached inside and removed a nine-millimetre Tokagypt automatic pistol. It was by far the most efficient weapon that his captors had. It was the weapon that Yasser would need if he was going to kill his guards quickly. The guards started bickering between themselves in Arabic, apart from the helicopter pilot and his mate, who were struggling to keep up with the conversation. Yasser could hear that the general crux of the argument was whether to accommodate the Bedouin if they requested water and supplies. One of the guards was adamant that they should, and one was adamant that no one should be allowed to approach the airfield. The third soldier didn't really care and he leaned against the wall smoking a cigarette, enjoying the morning sunshine.

The Bedouin caravan took a diagonal path across the airfield heading directly for the guardhouse. Yasser could hear their pots and pans clanking as the camels swayed and plodded across the desert runway. The females of the tribe walked behind or alongside their husband's camel, herding the family goats and sheep as they went. Their incessant chattering mingled with the other sounds from the approaching tribe. The wind blew and the sound of the animals bleating, drifted to Yasser on the breeze, goat bells tinkled, camels bayed and children laughed. The cacophony of desert life made Yasser feel very sad, longing for a life that was lost many years ago, when Iraq belonged to Iraqis, and Christian soldiers fought each other, not Islam.

The camels stopped one hundred yards from the five guards and their hut. The women and children peeled away from the adult males, and herded sixty or so sheep and goats to a separate area. Without any instruction, the women broke camp, pots rattled and a small fire was being prepared ready to cook a Bedouin breakfast on Yasser watched the well-rehearsed process with delight. The Bedouin tribes always travelled at night, using the stars to navigate across the endless sand dunes, maps were of no benefit in the desert. When the sun rose and the adult men stopped their camels, then the women and children set up camp, watered the animals, fed the tribe and then slept. It was obvious that the Bedouin were bedding down adjacent to the airbase, whether the Egyptian soldiers liked it or not. The tribe was eighty men strong. The Bedouin never count the number of women and children in the caravan. Only adult men capable of working and fighting are counted. The more adult males the tribe has, the greater its kudos with other tribes.

Three of the camel riders broke away from the tribe and plodded casually toward the guardhouse, flanked by half a dozen tribesmen on foot. The Bedouin were all armed with Soviet built Kalashnikov assault rifles. They were old clumsy weapons, but extremely reliable and easy to maintain, which is essential when you live in a world where sand pervades every tiny crack and orifice.

"As-Salaama Alaykum," greetings peace be with you, the first Bedouin tribesman shouted as he approached. His face was covered from the dust and the sun with his head wrap. He touched his head, his mouth and his chest as he greeted them.

"Wa Alaykum As-Salaam," the Eygptian soldiers replied in unison.

The helicopter pilot and his mate just nodded a silent greeting. The Bedouin men eyed them suspiciously, as they had not offered the traditional Arabic greeting in response to theirs. The Bedouin spoke the same Arabic language as other people from the Middle East, but their accent can be very different. Accents can vary dramatically from one tribe to the next. Yasser tried to follow what was being said between the two parties but they were too far away from him, and the Bedouin spoke quickly in an unfamiliar dialect. He heard a request for water being made and then some discussion following it between the Eygptian soldiers. They were bickering again.

One of the guards seemed to take control of the situation and he pointed to an area that Yasser could not see, because it was obscured by the felt roof guardhouse. He could only assume that there was a water storage tank somewhere, and an outside tap. The guard was indicating that they could use that supply. If the Bedouin caravan used the water at the other side of the guardhouse, it would keep them away from Yasser. More to the point, they wouldn't even see him from where they were.

It appeared that a compromise had been reached and the three camel riders moved their animals out of Yasser's line of sight, behind the guardhouse. The helicopter pilot relaxed and placed his black automatic weapon into his waistband. He slapped his mate between the shoulder blades and they went back into the shack out of the burning sunshine. As they entered the guardhouse, Yasser heard the polyphonic ringtone of a mobile phone. The helicopter pilot answered and spoke quickly in a language Yasser still couldn't identify with, Greek maybe, Albanian possibly, Macedonian probably, he couldn't be sure. The pilot came back out of the shack and swaggered toward Yasser`s cage, still talking into his cell phone. He was grinning at Yasser, not a nice grin, a sick malicious grin, a sadistic grin. Yasser stared back at the pilot and realised that his time here had run out. Orders were coming through to move him to another hellhole of a prison. Another team of Christians would torture him to the point of death, trying to extract as much information from him as they could before he died.

It was obvious from the look on the pilot's face that he enjoyed his job. Being stuck in a sweltering shack in the middle of the desert somewhere was not the part of the job, which he enjoyed. He had been waiting for the order to take Yasser to his final destination since the moment that they arrived. Yasser had made the mistake of building his hopes up. It's what desperate men do, but now his heart sank and his glimmer of hope started to fade away.

The pilot ended his call and approached the cage, still grinning. Yasser's facial expression never changed, he just stared into the pilots eyes. The pilot returned the stare but his eyes flickered. There was something beyond Yasser's eyes that frightened him. They were deep and milky, like a shark. The pilot sneered, coughed up phlegm from the back of his throat and spat it at Yasser. The green globule landed on Yasser's leg but he ignored it, and continued to stare at the pilot with his ice-cold eyes. The pilot let off a tirade of abuse that Yasser didn't understand. He picked up a stone and threw it between the bars, hitting Yasser above the left eye. A small trickle of blood ran from a little nick on his forehead, but he still didn't overt his gaze.

The pilot tired of his unresponsive prisoner and turned back toward the guardhouse. He was disturbed by the aura of menace that he'd sensed from Yasser. The slightly built, one-armed Iraqi man had an air of evil all around him. Yasser heard the guardhouse door slam closed, only then did he wipe the blood from his face and the phlegm from his leg.

"Do not turn round Caliph. I bring good news from an old friend of yours. Today Allah will release you from your captivity, be patient, when the sun goes down we will strike."

The voice was behind him. Yasser heard someone scurrying off behind him into the shadows of the guardhouse. He didn't turn around. He didn't want to really, because he was holding his breath, excited that help had arrived. The Bedouin had herded their animals around the water supply beyond Yasser's range of vision. They were bleating noisily and the constant chatter of the women and children drifted across the felt roof to him. It was a comforting sound, a normal sound from his past and it reassured him that all would be well.

Chapter Thirty-Five

Nasik

Nasik could hear the sound of diesel engines coming and going on the other side of the metal roller shutter. The shopping precinct must have been given the all clear to reopen. Deliveries had been arriving for at least half an hour or so. At least that is what his befuddled brain was telling him. In fact, he had been asleep for nearly eight hours. After sending the radioactive toolbox up in the goods lift, he had sat down to rest and lost consciousness almost immediately. He was cold, very cold.

The storage unit that he'd woken up in was built from bare breezeblocks. The floor was concrete. Decades of usage had left the surface marked from the rubber wheels of a thousand forklift trucks that had trundled from the loading bay to the goods lift and back. He shivered from the cold. Nasik rubbed his hands together for warmth and then recoiled from the pain in his right hand. He didn't remember hurting himself, but his hand felt like he had burnt it, or scalded it. The light in the storage unit was hurting his eyes, so he squeezed them shut to rest them. They felt like he had grit beneath his eyelids. Nasik rubbed his eyes with his hands and the pain in his right hand shot through him again. He cried out in pain this time. He looked at the offending hand, turning it slowly and trying to open and close his fingers at the same time. His hand had swelled to twice its normal size and had turned an angry purple colour, like a deep-seated bruise. The index finger looked like it was about to burst, he could no longer distinguish where the knuckles should be. As he rotated the hand and studied it, tears ran down his cheeks. Nasik ran his left hand through his tussled hair and huge clumps came away between his fingers. He stared from the swollen hand, to the hand full of hair and then back to the swollen one again.

He knew now that they had been betrayed. His mission was to shoot a senior member of the British counter terrorist services, leave the explosive device in the lift, and then escape in the van that he'd arrived in. The rendezvous point was already arranged. Once they had all completed their separate missions they were supposed to meet up on the car park of a pub called the Bay Leaf, in Treaddur Bay, on the outskirts of Holyhead. From there they were to return to the Syrian tanker, which had brought them and then rest on the voyage back to the Middle East where the never-ending battle for Palestine beckoned them.

He leaned on one elbow and wretched. He vomited thick yellow bile, flecked with blood; an acidic taste clung to the back of his throat. Nasik wiped saliva and yellow drool from his chin with the back of his hand, and tufts of his hair stuck to his face. There was something in the box that had made him sick, something powerful enough to burn his skin and make his hair fall out. He felt so tired and his eyes were becoming more painful and gritty. Nasik wasn't sure what time it was but he needed to get back to the van, and then drive one hundred and five miles to the rendezvous point. The Syrian tanker had a sickbay and a medic. He just had to get there, take some medicine and then he'd be fine. Nasik closed his gritty eyes again; he thought that if he just slept for a short time he could regain some of his energy and then drive to Holyhead. He placed his painfully swollen hand gently on his chest, out of harm's way and drifted off into a troubled slumber that was plagued with nightmares.

Chapter Thirty-Six

Tank stood on the roof of Canning Place. He looked east toward the St. John's tower. The huge concrete structure was the colour of sand except for the disc shaped section at the top, once a restaurant, more recently the home of Radio City, now a blackened shell. A shiver ran down his spine as he thought about the hapless policemen that had breached the skyscraper's windows, only to be blown back through them by the gas explosion. Tank had no doubt in his mind that the Kevlar body armour worn by Britain's security services would have protected them from most of the blast. They would have been alive until they hit the pavement hundreds of feet below.

He turned as he heard a helicopter approaching. A huge twin rotor Chinook was flying across the River Mersey toward the helicopter pad at the top of the police headquarters. Tank watched a wooden sailing galleon unfurling white canvas sails on three masts that were as tall as pine trees. The canvas billowed and flapped as the wind filled it, sailors rushed about on the decks tying off rigging and harnessing the wind. The river looked a deep blue colour today, and the wakes left by various different sailing vessels were pure white in comparison. It was a scene of calm and serenity. It was a scene of complete contrast to the turmoil John Tankersley was feeling right now. Grace had apparently shown signs of life and he wanted to be with her. Major Stanley Timms was fighting for his life on an operating table. Attempts had been made to behead the Terrorist Task Force by taking out its key personnel, and somewhere in the city, there was a radioactive dispersal device. It seemed like hoisting the main brace and sailing off into the blue ocean was a far more attractive option at this moment in time.

The Chinook neared, blasting dust up with the downdraft from its twin rotors. It seemed to hang in the air six feet from the landing pad before finally bumping down on the reinforced roof of the police headquarters. Tank ducked as he ran to the helicopter and slid open the passenger compartment door. Janet Walsh, the Prime Minister's secretary, shook his hand quickly in greeting and then stepped down from the aircraft. She was followed by the Home Secretary and the Minister of Defence. Tank shook hands with them and then ushered them away from the helicopter to the roof access door. He opened the steel door and then stepped back to allow them to enter the stairwell. There were eight stone steps leading down to the Task Force office.

"How is the Major?" asked the Minister of Defence.

"It's touch and go I'm afraid Minister," Tank replied as they walked down the steps.

"And his wife, are we looking after her too?" Janet Walsh asked concerned. The attackers from the previous days had showed no mercy or compassion for the families of the secret service personnel that had been targeted. Armed police and military personnel had been deployed to bodyguard as many possible targets as they physically could. Some families had been moved to secure locations on military bases to ensure their safety.

"She is with him at the hospital; they're being guarded by our uniformed division."

"And how is Grace?"

"She's safe Minister," Tank said, wishing that he hadn't asked. It just made him remember how badly he wanted to be with her.

The group passed through the open plan office toward the lift, which was at the rear of the building. Task Force agents were assembling ready for action. There was black body armour on every chair and every desk that they walked by. Well-oiled machineguns of various makes, shapes and sizes were being checked and tested ready for battle. Utility belts were being fastened, loaded with smoke grenades, stun grenades, fragmentation grenades, spare magazines, combat knives and shiny handcuffs. The agents nodded to him as Tank led the government officials into the lift. They were nearly ready for action, and all they needed now was the order to move.

The lift door opened, and Tank stepped into the elevator car and pressed an unmarked button, which was situated beneath the button marked basement. He took a bunch of keys from his belt and inserted a skinny silver key into the control panel, and turned it. The key activated authorised access, which allowed the lift to descend to a subbasement, which had been built to service Britain's biggest listening post and crisis centre. The subbasement had been excavated at the same time the three traffic tunnels were built beneath the River Mersey, so that the public wouldn't know what was going on beneath the city centre.

The government used the building of the tunnels as the perfect cover to construct a secret nuclear, biological and chemical proof bunker and command centre, which stretched underneath the city and beyond. The military built an underground service tunnel, which connected the bunker to a state of the art surveillance facility four miles away. The surveillance facility was situated beneath, and inside a derelict preparatory school in a leafy suburb of Liverpool called Woolton. Newborough School was a towering monolith built from dark local sandstone, looking more like a Victorian asylum than a place of learning. The deserted playground, once the setting of epic conker fights, classic games of marbles and mass kiss and chase sessions, was long since overgrown with nettles and weeds. The tall stained glass windows were boarded up and the gigantic rusted metal gates chained and padlocked, disguising one of the most sophisticated spy facilities on the planet. Inside the moss covered old school was a world of computer screens, digital readouts, satellite-tracking units, cipher and deciphers departments, code making and code breaking units, the quickest computers and the sharpest brains that the Western world possessed.

The lift reached the subbasement and the door slid open to reveal a hive of subterranean activity. They stepped onto a solid rock floor, which was as wide as a dual carriageway road. The walls and ceiling were curved as if they were standing inside a massive reddish sandstone pipe. A military jeep was parked waiting for their arrival. Tank opened the rear door and the Prime Minister's secretary climbed into the rear seat. The two government aids climbed in unassisted and Tank took the front passenger seat. The driver saluted loosely and put the vehicle into first gear.

They covered the four miles in less than ten minutes. The conversation was kept to a polite minimum, everyone had their own concerns and undisclosed agendas. The government officials wouldn't show their hands until they'd received all the information that they required to make an informed decision. The snippets of confidential information that each department had received were pointing to a terrifying scenario. All the relative parties needed to communicate with each other, before any concrete plans could be made.

They reached the control centre and entered through a revolving glass door, which was designed to be a barrier to a chemical or biological attack. They passed through the doorway into a large reception area, which was encased by bombproof plate-glass walls. To the right, through the glass wall they could see a control room. Banks of computer terminals were lined up in a semicircular pattern, and the floor was terraced like an amphitheatre, rising toward the back of the room. Tank headed left toward a large rectangular conference room. Through the glass walls, Tank saw over a dozen people milling about in small groups, some were uniformed military officers, some ministers from various home office departments. Inside were some familiar faces, and some not so familiar. Tank scanned the busy room, mentally noting who was who. He spotted Chen and the fat controller already seated at the meeting table. The table was polished dark oak, long and somewhat out of place in its high tech surroundings. At one end of the table was a wall packed with digital screens, the other three walls were floor to ceiling plate-glass, like a huge fish tank.

"Let's get started ladies and gentlemen please," Janet Walsh addressed the room in an assertive voice, which belied her polished appearance. The room became silent and people shuffled around the elongated table, looking for a tab with their name on it. It resembled an adult game of musical chairs. Tank wandered through the melee to where Chen and David Bell were seated. Directly across the table from them were two men that Tank didn't recognise.

They were dark haired, olive skinned, with deep brown eyes and long black eyelashes. One of the men, who were sat on the left hand side of his colleague, had a sharp hooked nose, which Tank associated with a Jewish heritage. He figured that they were Israeli secret service however there were so many Israeli counter terrorist agencies and clandestine military units that he couldn't even begin to guess which one they belonged to. He was glad that they were there; they'd been waiting for them to supply vital information about the Palestinian insurgents that had been captured. The general clatter of chairs being scraped as people took their seats quietened and the room fell into a readied silence.

"I'm not going to waste valuable time introducing everyone; we'll do that as we progress through the agenda," Janet Walsh began taking charge of the situation like it was second nature, "I'd like the Task Force to update us first please, if you don't mind Tank."

Tank remained standing and headed toward a digital screen, which was fixed to a white Formica wall, surrounded by smaller screens. He picked up a pen shaped remote and clicked the screen to life. The faces of two men appeared, looking like they'd come second best to a petrol bomb. He clicked again and a third face appeared next to the first two. This man was clearly dead.

"You're all aware that a series of well planned assassination attempts have been carried out across the British Isles," Tank began.

The faces of Major Stanley Timms, Boris McGuiness, Donald Bangor Jones and Grace Farrington flashed onto the smaller screens in turn, and then disappeared just as quickly.

"Major Timms, the head of the Terrorist Task Force is in a critical condition in hospital. He was shot by a sniper in his office from almost half a mile away. Two bullets hit him in the back, and he's touch and go. Boris McGuiness, a senior officer of Her Majesty's MI6, and his two sons were shot and killed while on a camping trip to Snowdonia. Donald Bangor Jones, MI5, left for work and his wife and two daughters were killed in a car bomb attack."

The room remained deadly silent. Everyone was well aware that whoever had accessed the personal information files of the victims would probably also have their details as well. Every single person in the room was a target, and apparently now so were their families. The single biggest strength of the secret services was that they remained a secret. Their anonymity was their most powerful weapon, and now because of a security breach it had suddenly become their biggest weakness.

"Assassination attempts were made by sophisticated, well trained, highly skilled personnel, probably of Palestinian extraction," Tank looked to the Israelis for further comment. The man with the hooked nose stood up, coughed to clear his throat and then spoke in perfect English, with no discernable accent.

"I am Major Goldstein from the Israeli intelligence department. We can positively identify these two men," he began pointing to the burns victims that Tank had disabled at his grandmother's funeral.

"They are Abdel and Pita Abuhamza, former members of what you would call the Palestine Liberation Organisation. We know that in recent years their focus was not only on the Palestinian situation. They joined a faction of the Axe group, headed up by Yasser Ahmed, involved in Chechnya, Afghanistan and Iraq. They were both students and teachers at a camp sponsored by Yasser Ahmed from June two thousand, until two thousand and four. It was at this time that our agencies lost track of them completely." The Israeli paused as he could see people raising hands to ask questions.

"Were your agencies aware that they were headed here?"

"Absolutely not until they were here already, I can assure you that we have been trying to trace these men for years. Our Sayaret Matkal, or Unit-two six nine, is a highly effective counter terrorist unit, and special operations group, working directly under the command of the Israeli intelligence ministry, not the military. They specialise in locating and removing problem terrorist personnel from their own communities, in the West Bank itself. They have made numerous incursions into Gaza and the West Bank looking for these men, without success, which means that they were not there to find. They'd left the country, as this unit does not make mistakes." The Israeli tapped his pen on his hand to emphasise his point.

Tank knew of the Sayaret Matkal, they were almost as feared as the SAS, and from what he knew about them, the Israeli was correct. If they couldn't find the Abuhamza brothers, then they weren't there to be found. That meant that key terrorist personnel had left the Middle East for an extended period. They did not know why. Where had they been, and more importantly what had they been doing?

Furthermore, Tank knew that the Israelis had an even better unit than the one in question, if that could be possible. The most feared Jewish outfit is a complete unit of Israeli Arabs, known as the Sayaret Duvedevan. They were called the 'mistaravim', or 'becoming Arab'. This unit dedicated their entire lives to mixing with and integrating into Muslim communities, often taking wives and having families. They had personnel deployed in Muslim communities all over the Middle East, Egypt, Jordan, Syria, Iran and Iraq. Israel is a formidable military superpower with a nuclear deterrent. None of its Arab neighbours possesses the military firepower to successfully invade the Jewish state, without risking terrible consequences.

Its biggest threat to security is Islamic insurgency. Years of constant suicide bombings had forced Israel to send men deep undercover to sniff out the leaders of the terrorist groups. The fragile state of Israel depended upon the information that these clandestine units provided for its existence.

"What's known about the other man?" the minister asked.

"His name is Abu Anbar, born in Palestine to a once wealthy family. He joined the insurgency late in his teenage years, and we know that he spent time at Yasser Ahmed's training camps. He wasn't a known associate of the Abuhamza brothers, we wouldn't have connected them if he hadn't been killed during this operation," the Israeli answered.

"And what do we know about their known associates?"

The Israeli looked to Tank for support. The tone of the question coming from the floor indicated that the anger felt by everyone being directed at the Israelis, as if it were their responsibility.

"Who their known associates are really doesn't matter right now," Tank interjected. The man who'd asked the question was sat at the far end of the room dressed in an American military uniform of some description. Tank didn't know who he was or what rank he was, and he didn't really care. His days of being concerned about upsetting someone of senior rank were long gone. He answered straight to the Prime Minister's office, everyone else could whistle.

"I beg to disagree. It's vital that we know who they are," the American blustered defensively.

"It isn't," Tank shot him down quickly, as there was no time for arsing about with the general, no matter what his name was.

"Agent Tankersley is right," Janet Walsh interrupted, "we have much more serious problems to discuss."

"What can possibly be more important than identifying raghead terrorists, who think they can come over here and play merry hell with all and sundry?"

"Well if you'd shut up and listen for a minute then you'll find out," Tank said politely, thinking that if the General didn't shut up, then he would throw him through the revolving door.

"We have found evidence of radioactive materials on board a Syrian tanker that was delivering aggregates to an aluminium plant at the port of Holyhead, Wales," Tank continued. "We think that the terrorists arrived here on board this tanker." A picture of the Syrian vessel appeared on the smaller screens again, and then it was replaced by the black and white image of the lower deck glowing. The riveted steel deck was painted with red metal floor paint, and there was a distinct square smudge in the centre of the picture where the huge toolbox had been. The room fell silent again, the American flushed red with embarrassment as he realised that there was much more to this insurgency than first met the eye.

"We have also found traces of the same materials here in the city centre," Tank changed the pictures again, and the images from the St. John's Tower appeared on the screens. The luminous smudges that left a radioactive trail down the towering stairwell and into the shopping precinct flicked across the screens. The final picture was taken on the first floor balcony of the mall. It showed a pool of vomit next to the underground entrance door.

"We are sure that the secretor of this vomit has been in contact with the same radioactive substances. It has tested positive for both beta, and gamma emitting rays, matching the profile of cobalt and strontium-90. We think that the secretor was exposed to the radiation for an extended period, without any protective clothing. He`s probably dead already. The conundrum we are facing is that we're almost certain that the material never left the city centre. It was completely cordoned off by our uniformed divisions, and there was air support provided above the area, all fitted with heat sensors. There was nothing reported by any of our units that could be related to this material, our best guess is that it's beneath that shopping mall somewhere. We are shutting the town centre down completely, and evacuating all built up residential areas situated downwind of the area," Tank shrugged at the American as he finished, and the man nodded solemnly understanding the severity of the issue.

"What type of radioactive materials are we talking about?" asked the defence minister.

Tank was about to answer but the second Israeli, who had so far remained silent, stood up and waved his hand to indicate that he would answer the question. Tank gestured for him to continue, hoping that the Israelis could shine more light on the subject than they already had.

"I'm Doctor Graff, and I am from the Israeli nuclear science department. Our sources have gathered evidence, which will confirm what the Terrorist Task Force is suspecting. We are positive that Axe are in possession of cobalt-60. They also have at least two Russian made thermoelectric generators," the Israeli explained to a room full of concerned, but confused faces.

"I can see that this has caused some confusion, please let me explain and you will understand."

He walked to the digital screen and removed a computer disk from his jacket pocket, and then slid it into the receiver. The pictures on the screens changed. The image of a remote lighthouse situated in the far northern extremes of the old Soviet Union, surrounded by pack ice appeared. Its revolving light warned shipping that it was approaching the point where the ice flows met the continent. Then a beacon fitted with an aircraft warning light, situated on top of a rocky mountain summit appeared on the screen next to it.

"These are just two examples of thousands of remote Soviet warning beacons. Marine lighthouses, aircraft warning beacons and remote airfields, which are situated hundreds and hundreds of miles away from the nearest source of electricity. The Russians developed, built and deployed thermoelectric power generators to the far reaches of the former Soviet Union. Their theory was that these units would provide a power source that never needs to be refuelled for a thousand years. They made petrol generators and their maintenance staff obsolete." The Israeli went quiet.

"That's very interesting but what is your point?" the defence minister asked.

"I'm sorry that I am not being specific enough for you. These thermoelectric power generators are fuelled by radioactive isotopes. Most of them contain beta emitting strontium-90," he changed the picture again.

This time a series of photographs appeared depicting dead bodies, which had swollen, to unrecognisable proportions. The skin had been burned purple and their facial features were so bloated that they were barely recognisable as human.

"This is a family of woodcutters who lived in a small village Georgia. When the Soviet Union collapsed in 1992, they stole one of these generators from a remote hilltop to provide heat for themselves and their families." He flicked through more autopsy pictures.

"Two days later a local policeman investigating reports of the disappearance of the aircraft beacon found them like this. Apart from the obvious casualties the policeman himself and seventy five other people from the village died within three weeks of becoming contaminated," the Israeli finished his explanation, leaving the people in the room in shocked silence.

"You think that these Palestinian insurgents are in possession of a number of these generators?" the American asked.

"We think that they are in possession of the strontium-90 that was inside them. Many of these generators have simply disappeared. The metal casings and radiation shields are sold for scrap, and the isotopes inside traded for the arms industry. We are sure that they have strontium, and that they have mixed it with cobalt-60. It is a simple operation to surround them with a conventional plastic or liquid explosive to create a salted bomb, or dirty bomb, or a radiological dispersal device."

"How could they have transported such a powerful beta emitting device so far across the world without becoming infected themselves?" Janet Walsh asked.

"They couldn't, quite simply. To transport that type of material safely it would need to be encased in lead, sealed inside a radioactive proof flask. All personnel being exposed to the flask would need several layers of protective clothing, and a thorough decontamination programme afterwards. The method required is so costly and expensive that it is virtually impossible to move it safely. That`s why the Soviets didn't worry about leaving the generators scattered all over the remote areas of the country. There were no populated areas nearby, and if anyone did stumble onto one of them and tried to steal it, then the result is on the screen." The Israeli with the hooked nose finished explaining and he pointed to the screen again. The pictures of radiation burned bodies, twisted and swollen demonstrated the power of radioactive beta rays.

"So whoever constructed this device never intended for the carriers to return?" Chen asked.

"Absolutely not, the carriers could have been oblivious, but the more likely scenario is that they were compliant with the plan. This time the suicide bombers will not die in the explosion, but will die either before it, or soon after. Whatever the motives it's an act of Islamic Jihad," the second Israeli answered.

"We think that when the Abuhamza brothers left the West Bank they'd gone to the old Soviet Union in search of such materials, and that's why our clandestine units couldn't trace them."

"What's our worst case scenario?" asked the fat controller.

"If a device salted with cobalt-60 and strontium-90, the size of the photographic imprint explodes in the city centre, then it will become a contaminated wasteland. It will be economically useless and devoid of human life for decades," the Israeli answered.

David Bell smiled because he'd said almost exactly the same thing, word for word at the Task Force briefing earlier. No one else in the room could understand his apparent glee at the bad news, but he liked being right.

"I assume that the Task Force has a plan of action?" Janet Walsh looked at Tank for a response. The Israelis remained standing, which she thought was a little odd, as if they had more bad news that they hadn't imparted with yet.

"Once our uniformed division has completed the evacuations then we're going into that delivery basement," Tank clicked the remote and architectural plans of the subterranean delivery area appeared on the centre screen. A labyrinth of access roads, shuttered storage areas, lift shafts and stairwells covered over a square mile.

"Why haven't they exploded the device already?" asked the defence minister.

The Israelis looked at each other furtively, and the silent communication was spotted by several people in the room. Janet Walsh shot them both a withering glance, which prompted them to spill the beans.

"We think that the device will have been hidden awaiting detonation by a timer," the hooked nosed Israeli began. He looked to his colleague for support."

"The size of the potential device that you have discovered does not show direct correlation with the amount of strontium-90 contained in the thermoelectric generators. The size of the device means that there is more than one, it's not big enough," his colleague helped him along.

The officials around the table became restless as the implication that there was more than one device became clear.

"Our sources suggest that there is a plan to explode several devices simultaneously. A synchronised attack on Israel and the West," hook nose continued.

"Israel? I don't follow," Tank said.

"We thin

k that there will be a similar attack on Jerusalem and New York," the Israeli intelligence officer dropped a bombshell.

"I think that you'd better tell us exactly what you know Doctor Graff, and I don't mean at Thanks Giving sir, I mean right now!" said the American officer in a slow southern drawl, he was already reaching for his cell phone.

Chapter Thirty-Seven

Yasser Ahmed

Yasser was trying to prepare himself mentally and physically for the escape bid that had been planned by someone. He didn't know who it was or how they'd found him, nor did he know what was planned. All he knew was, that live or die he couldn't go back into the torturous barbaric regime of extraordinary rendition. Yasser had tortured and killed more people than he could remember, and he could recognise the signs of when a human being no longer cared whether they lived or died. He had reached that point months ago. He would escape today or die trying. The infection in his shoulder seemed to be drying up, fresh air and the lack of torturers stabbing at it was allowing massive blackened scabs to form. It even smelled better, which was a good sign.

Yasser stood with his face pressed against the steel bars of his cage, looking at the Bedouin tribesmen that he could see in his line of vision. Most of them were hidden by the single story guardhouse that blocked his view to the east of the airfield. There had been a cacophony of sound earlier as they fed and watered their animals and themselves, but it was much quieter now. The midday sun was scorching down on the desert, pushing temperatures over one hundred and forty degrees. Many of the Bedouin took shelter from the burning heat beneath the canvas gazebos, which they carried across the desert sands, along with all their other possessions.

Two men in particular had attracted Yasser's interest. On first inspection they appeared to be the same as the other Bedouin, but if you looked in detail there was a number of tell tale signs which indicated that they were not who they pretended to be. Their skin was smooth, unlike the sundried, wind-parched skin of their companions. The outdoor life of the Bedouin took its toll on the facial skin of the men and women. Constant sunshine, wind and dehydration made the Bedouin look much older than their actual years.

These two men were in their twenties Yasser guessed, but there was no sign of the wrinkled skin of the genuine Bedouin. Their garments weren't right either. Although authentic, the colours were too bright, too new, not yet faded by the burning Eygptian sun. They simply weren't dusty enough. The two men had arrived on camels with the caravan, but they'd stayed at the western edge of the community, always keeping Yasser in view. They had even discretely approached the guardhouse, speaking to two of the guards and shared cigarettes with them, before wandering back to their camels.

Yasser wondered how many of the caravan were involved in the escape plan. The Bedouin chief would certainly be aware that they were concealing Islamic combatants, and if the rest of the tribe were sympathetic to Yasser's cause then they were a formidable force. The Bedouin tribes of Egypt were nomadic people that had travelled around the deserts of the Middle East for centuries unhindered. The expansion of tourism and capitalist ventures robbed them of their ancestral hunting and fishing grounds. Few insurgents came from the Bedouin tribes, but hundreds had been hidden by them. The three Eygptian guards were too few and too poorly armed to resist the Bedouin caravan if it became hostile. They were also too far away from anywhere to call reinforcements. Yasser was becoming more and more confident as the day past.

He heard muffled sounds from the guard hut, and the piercing polyphonic ringtone of the pilots mobile. Then his hopes were shattered when the door to the guard hut opened, and the pilot and his mate ambled over to the helicopter. They were both carrying kit bags, which Yasser guessed contained their travelling gear. They climbed into their aircraft and began pre-flight checks. Yasser's heart sank and he looked pleadingly toward the Bedouin in the distance.

Chapter Thirty-Eight

The Bedouin

Megdah and Melad sat up straight when they saw the helicopter pilot and his mate climbing into the aircraft. Megdah whistled toward a group of Bedouin tribesmen who were dozing beneath one of the larger canvas gazebos. They looked toward the helicopter and realised that it was being prepared for takeoff. They had been sent here to rescue their inspirational leader Yasser Ahmed, and it would be more than their lives were worth to fail. Megdah jumped to his feet and ran over to the chief's gazebo. The chief was a wizened old man in his mid forties. There was a line for every month he'd lived outside in the sun carved deeply into his face, significantly aging him. His dark beard was peppered with grey hair, which was slowly winning the war for chin space, against the black hair. He was drawing heavily on a Marlborough cigarette, as western tobacco was now cheaper than their own, and easier to come by.

Megdah pointed to the helicopter and spoke quickly to the chief. The chief nodded slowly and pulled on the cigarette again. He turned toward a group of Bedouin children and shouted instructions to them in a dialect that Megdah could barely follow. The children ran away laughing and chattering in their guttural tones. The chief turned to the agitated Megdah and gently waved his hands, palms down facing the floor, in a calming motion. The elders of the Bedouin tribe started laughing at Megdah, which only served to rile him even more. He couldn't allow them to take Yasser Ahmed away at any cost. The Bedouin tribesmen had been chosen to help them with this mission because it was well known that this particular chief was sympathetic to the Islamic extremist cause. He hated Egypt's president Mubarak because he'd traded Bedouin fishing grounds for Western money and arms. The Bedouin tribe had also been paid well by their sponsor to take Megdah and Melad along, to identify Yasser Ahmed, and to provide the firepower to rescue him. It had all gone well until now. Now that their target was in sight, all the Bedouin tribesmen could do was laugh at Megdah.

"Do not panic my young friend," the chief said gently, sensing that the Arab was becoming annoyed. "Sit down and share a cigarette with me."

The chief took a packet of red Marlborough from his dusty white cotton robe and offered one to Megdah. Melad approached, and he was uncertain of what was happening, and the chief gestured for them both to be seated, and gave them cigarettes. The chief spoke to his elders who were all sitting or lying on straw filled cushions around the perimeter of the open gazebo. The gathering burst into laughter again, much to the distain of Megdah and Melad. None of the Bedouin had even retrieved their Kalashnikov rifles yet.

Megdah didn't want to offend the chief but this was becoming unbearable. He looked to his colleague but he looked as if he was more concerned for their own safety than what was happening with the mission. They were heavily outnumbered and hundreds of miles away from anywhere. If the chief said, they should smoke a cigarette first then they would have to do just that.

Two things happened at the same time. The children that the chief had spoken to earlier appeared at the western edge of the Bedouin camp, where Megdah and Melad had been sitting. They were running along with their hooked sheep crooks, herding the sheep and goats into a mini stampede toward the guardhouse. They were creating a ridiculous amount of noise, frightening the animals into flight, running and bleating loudly across the sandy runway. At the same time, one of the Bedouin women carried a black silk wrapped parcel into the gathering of elders, and she placed it at the feet of the chief. The elders burst into laughter again.

The chief stubbed out his cigarette and unwrapped the black silk material from the prize inside. Megdah stared in disbelief as the chief picked up a shiny well-oiled American M16 rifle. The rifle was fitted with a brand new state of the art, image intensifying digital scope, which looked like a black video camera from the nineteen eighties. The chief picked it up quickly and pointed the weapon around the room aiming at the gathering, at the same time as making a mock machinegun noise with his mouth.

"Da-da-da-da-da-da-da-da-da," he simulated shooting everyone down, much to the amusement of the Bedouin tribesmen who rocked backward and forward laughing at their chief's mischief making. Some of them grasped imaginary bullet wounds and made gagging noises as they pretended to be shot, adding to the chief's pantomime. Megdah and Melad swapped glances, not knowing whether to humour the wrinkly Bedouin or not. The chief reached into the black silk parcel again and retrieved a thick black metal suppressor. He displayed it to the crowd like a magician who'd just pulled a rabbit from his hat. The Bedouin tribesmen rolled with laughter again and clapped their hands in applause. The chief screwed the silencer into the business end of the M16, and then pretended to shoot everyone again. His audience responded on cue with exaggerated laughter and more imaginary bullet wounds.

The chief removed the bullet clip, he checked the magazine and snapped it into position, suddenly the smile on his face was gone, the muscles along his jaw line tensed visibly. The M16 was pulled tight into his shoulder, his right eye just millimetres away from the telescopic sights; the index finger of his right hand was positioned firmly against the trigger, while his right thumb slid off the safety catch.

The Bedouin gathering became silent as they watched their chief tuning from a clown into well-practised marksman. They had seen it many times before. The rifle was his pride and joy and using it with the precision of a sniper was the chief's party piece. There was very little to shoot at in the desert. The chief moved his jaw slowly as he concentrated, grinding his back teeth against each other, waiting for that moment when the body was perfectly poised and balanced to make a long range shot. The perfect moment when the trigger should be squeezed can't be taught to anyone, it has to be felt, a complete merging of mind body and machine. The perfect camouflaged killing machine.

Chapter Thirty-Nine

The Jerusalem plot/ Armageddon

"The Bible says in the Book of Revelations that the end of the world will begin and end around the land where Jesus was born," Doctor Graff said very slowly, "religious or not, what we are about to tell you could indeed be the beginning of the end."

The room had settled back down to business following the Israelis shocking disclosure of information. Urgent calls had been made to various communication hubs in America, warning that a synchronised attack could be imminent, and that once again New York was a possible target. After a brief five-minute break, all the original government and military officials were ready to discuss the options. A satellite link had been patched through to the big screen, and the American Secretary of State was party to the meeting first hand via a conference call. She looked like she had just been dragged out of bed in the middle of the night and given terrible news, which was about right.

"Whatever your religious beliefs you must understand what significance Jerusalem holds for those that are religious. For Christians the world over it is without a doubt the centre of the universe. Likewise for those of Jewish descent, whatever type of Jew, the Western Wall, or Wailing Wall as you know it, is the focus of our religion," the Doctor paused for effect.

"For Muslims it is home to the oldest building in Islamic history, they used to turn their prayer mats to face Jerusalem before Mecca become their holiest city. An attack by Muslim extremists, turning the old city into a radioactive no go zone would cause an irreversible religious melt down."

"This information is so sensitive that we haven't even shared it with our own military chiefs. If the plot leaked out we think that there would be reprisals that would escalate out of control, dragging the Muslim countries around us into a nuclear conflict," the Israelis Major explained further.

Tank had visited the city several times and remembered its deep religious history and significance. People have lived in the area between the Mount of Olives and the Judean hills for over five thousand years. King David, the ancestor of today's Jewish peoples, captured Jerusalem at the beginning of the first century BC. He built an altar for worship on the summit of Mount Moriah, where Abraham had prepared to sacrifice his son, Isaac on a rock. This rock became the place where Solomon, David's son, built his temple, which housed the Ark of the Covenant. The remains of the base of this temple form the Wailing Wall, and the centre of the Jewish faith.

Millions of Jews from all over the world make the pilgrimage to the wall every year, bringing with them billions of dollars for tourism. Tank had visited the wall, huge sand coloured blocks hinted at how massive the original temple must have been. Between the blocks, were millions of tiny scrolls of paper, containing personal prayers written by pilgrims and then rolled up tightly and stuffed between the huge ancient building blocks.

Close by, and built above the temple ruins, is the Muslim mosque, the Dome of the Rock. It was built to mark the spot where the great prophet Muhammad ascended to receive the Islamic commandments from Allah. One of Islam's holiest shrines, it is the world's oldest, and possibly the most stunning Islamic building in the world. It towers above the old city. A huge golden dome one hundred and ten feet high and sixty-five feet in diameter is supported by octagonal shaped walls decorated by some of the most ornate blue mosaic murals in the world. Tank could see what a devastating impact sealing of these religious wonders for decades would have. Resentment would spread across the planet, Christians blaming the Jews for allowing their religious epicentre to be desecrated. The Jews would retaliate against the surrounding Muslim states, probably backed by America. Armageddon would be just around the corner.

"Where has the information about this plot come from exactly?" Tank asked. Everyone had the religious message for now, and it was time to move the discussion on.

"Our intelligence sources must remain confidential, but we can tell you that the information was first viewed with extreme speculation on our part. We didn't believe that the Palestinians could carry out such a complex plan alone, even with the help of the Axe organisation. They certainly could not have attacked your security personnel without a significant amount of inside information," the Israeli Major answered and looked directly at Janet Walsh.

She understood the silent communication. There was blame and accusation in the look. She breathed deeply before responding.

"We lost track of one of our most senior estranged MI5 agents several months ago, he was dismissed from his position, and we now believe that he may have copied several encrypted files to disk format before he left. A financial motive, probably, he was last seen on vacation in the Egyptian resort of Taba, situated on the Israeli border," she stared back at the Israeli allowing the returned accusation to sink in.

Espionage and counter espionage, Western agents disappeared all the time, with no one ever really knowing where they went, kidnap or defection. The Israelis had been found guilty of harbouring several key Western spies, offering them a haven in the sunshine in exchange for secret information.

"Touché, Secretary Walsh," said the Israeli. "Unfortunately he didn't fall into our hands, however some of our deep cover agents heard rumours that a British agent was being interrogated, and that the information he was imparting was of unprecedented quality."

"We believe that he had access to top secret information, is that true?" interrupted the American officer. Everyone turned to look at him, and he realised that the question he'd asked hinted that he had information that he shouldn't have. He blushed for the second time that day.

"Yes, he was a tier one agent. He had access to most of our encrypted information files, and the override codes that they require to work," Janet Walsh knew that there was no point in beating about the bush now. The leak was from British Secret Services, and now they had to deal with the fallout. She continued.

"We categorically do not have access to foreign personnel files, however we suggest that you delete all your details, change your encryption codes and protect your key agency personnel."

The room remained silent again. Tank stared at the floor in embarrassment, and then he looked at the American, who had flushed purple in rage. Chen stared wide eyed at Tank, surprised by the implication. The Prime Minister's Secretary had admitted that British intelligence agencies had been spying on its allies, and then lost vital information to the worst possible enemies that it could. The American politician on the satellite link was receiving her information via an encoded link, which took the information, scrambled it, and then translated it again for her to understand. The process delayed the dialogue by four seconds, compared to real time.

"I take it then that your agent could have compromised our national security as well as your own?" the question came over the speaker system, beamed in from across the Atlantic.

"We wouldn't rule anything out right now," the Prime Minister's Secretary, replied diplomatically, "as I said earlier, we categorically do not possess access to foreign personnel files; however we'd advise that you take every precaution to protect your interests."

Tank felt sick to the core, politics and politicians were his worst nightmare, always lying to each other and never mind the consequences for the public that they served. The confidentiality of the whereabouts of every Western agent, officer and military employee and their families had been compromised, but it had been kept a secret. No one was given any warning, because rather than changing access codes nationwide at huge expense to the defence budget, a gamble of incredulous proportions had been played. They couldn't possibly change codes every time someone left the service, but they took a gamble when key personnel left acrimoniously. On this occasion, they had lost, at the cost of over a dozen lives so far.

"Perhaps if our confidential files hadn't been hacked we wouldn't need to follow your precautionary advice, Secretary Walsh," the American politician added sarcastically.

"Oh, come now Foreign Minister, I don't think that this is as much of shock to you as you're pretending it is. Your military advisor is here and he seemed to know that our missing agent was in possession of 'top secret' information, as he put it so eloquently earlier," Janet Walsh parried the American aggression away acidly.

Tank looked at the uniformed American. He was holding his head in his hands, covering both eyes with his elbows still on the table, shaking his head in quiet disbelief. Janet Walsh had laid the trap and the Americans had walked right into it with their eyes wide open. They were not as innocent as they were pretending to be. Tank was tiring of the political tennis.

"Can we get back to the point in question please, we can hold an inquest when we've dealt with the terrorists," Tank interrupted. Janet Walsh looked at him and raised an eyebrow; she wasn't used to being interrupted. Tank didn't care.

"I couldn't agree more," Doctor Graff said, "the fact of the matter is that we were given information from a key Palestinian insurgent, under interrogation."

"You mean you were torturing him," interrupted the American military advisor. He felt aggrieved and took the opportunity to strike.

The Israeli doctor paused and raised his eyebrows, surprised by both the interruption and the hypocrisy.

"I'm not going to get into a debate about extraordinary rendition right now, but our men were trained in interrogation techniques by your CIA," the doctor countered. The American flushed red again, and for the second time that day, he wished he'd kept his big mouth shut.

"Everyone in this room knows full well that some of the information gathered during interrogation is pure fantasy," the doctor continued, "the plot that was described by this man was so sophisticated in its content that we didn't believe him. The plot relied on large amounts of radioactive material being acquired, transported and then deployed half way round the world. It would take an organised professional mind to plan it logistically. Not to mention the financial cost was so high that it was completely disregarded as nonsense." No one in the room could disagree.

"Well, we know that radioactive material has been brought here, and that a well organised assassination campaign is in operation, but how sure are you that Jerusalem and New York could be attacked?" Tank asked.

The idea that Jerusalem could be turned into a contaminated wasteland could indeed provoke terrible retaliatory strikes against Muslim targets. If New York was attacked, again there would be no telling what America's response would be this time. What if the response from Israel and the West was to destroy Islam's holy cities? The possible connotations didn't bear thinking about.

"We really didn't take any of it seriously until you contacted us for information about the men you captured and killed," the Israeli Major answered.

"Now we can only share what we were told with you. The source told us that Axe had sourced the thermoelectric generators somewhere in the old Soviet Union, and we now know that strontium-90 has been traced here and on the Syrian ship. That is definitive proof that the source was telling the truth, about that part at least. We also know that there must be more strontium-90 somewhere, because the radioactive imprints that you've found are not large enough to contain all the material," the doctor explained.

By measuring the glowing rectangles from the photographic evidence that had been recovered from the tower, a projected real size could be calculated. The figures didn't add up.

"We were also told that Axe had acquired access to important files, but we didn't know what those files contained. Obviously, they have used this information to target your people. So that part of the information we received is also true," the Israeli Major continued.

"What we don't know is if the rest of the plot is factual, or fantasy. The source's condition was deteriorating rapidly, but he told us that, and I quote, 'the Christians and Jews would not be able to visit their temples for a thousand years', hence we think that he was alluding to an attack on Jerusalem."

"And what was said about New York?" asked the American military advisor.

The Israelis looked at one another, and then the doctor placed his hands together and formed a triangle with his fingers while he chose his words carefully.

"He was almost delirious at this point, and we weren't taking much notice of what the interrogators were recording. We were sure he was rambling, but now we know differently we must take it seriously," said the doctor.

"Trust me, I'm taking it seriously," drawled the American, nodding his jarhead.

"The source indicated that the rebuilding of the twin towers site would never reach completion, he said quote, 'they can't rebuild what they can't reach', which we can only assume means that an attack on the financial district could be planned," the doctor finished his explanation, shrugging his shoulders, his palms facing the ceiling.

"We need to follow the British response and evacuate the area immediately," the American military advisor spoke to the politician on the screen. A radioactive attack on that part of New York would render the entire area a no go area, including ground zero.

"Don't be ridiculous," the woman on the screen responded sharply, "you cannot seriously compare a city like Liverpool with the financial centre of the United States of America. Evacuating a shopping mall and some corporation housing in England is hardly the same as clearing downtown Manhattan, it would cause nationwide panic, not to mention cost billions of dollars."

The uniformed man remained silent and shook his head slowly in response. He looked Tank in the eye and Tank understood the hopelessness in his eyes. Liverpool is a huge international port and home to several million people. Tourism is part of the city's lifeblood.

"What do you plan to do in Jerusalem?" asked Tank, looking for some support for the American military advisor.

The Israelis looked to each other again, and both of them bowed their head slightly, shoulders sagging. Their body language displayed their inner feelings. They were not comfortable with what they were about to say. The Israeli response had obviously been decided by men much farther up the political ladder than them. Don't shoot the messengers.

"We cannot allow this threat to become public knowledge. The city of Jerusalem is the religious capital of the world, and we can't compare it to this city, whatever we do it must be a covert operation. We cannot evacuate the city without causing a religious conflict which could spiral out of control," the Israeli Major spoke grimly.

"Well I hope your right, because if you're not all three cities will have something in common, they'll glow in the dark." Tank said, heading for the door. The talking was over. It was time to take action.

"Where are you going Agent Tankersley?" Janet Walsh asked. Tank's broad back was already squeezing through the doorway. Chen stood up and spoke.

"I think we've learned everything that we need to know for now. We'll be in the shopping mall as soon as the evacuations are complete; our men are ready to move. It's absolutely vital that we find this device quickly, so that you'll know what to look for in your own cities."

Chapter Forty

Yasser Ahmed

Yasser tried to decipher what the helicopter pilot was saying to his mate but it was useless, he couldn't make head or tale of it. The helicopter engineer was in the back of the dark grey machine; his voice was muffled and interrupted by banging and clanking noises. The pilot was sitting up front switching banks of monitors on and off, some were above his head and some fixed to the dashboard in front of him. They laughed while they chattered. The pilot saw that Yasser was stood in his cage watching them, and he drew his index finger across his windpipe slowly as if he was cutting his throat. He was goading Yasser that this trip would probably be his last.

The pilot made an unheard comment to his mate and they both laughed aloud and pointed at Yasser through the windshield. The pilot's mate jumped from the sliding cargo door, out of the grey helicopter, onto the sand. He was wearing a green military vest, which emphasised his fat beer belly. It looked like it hadn't been washed for centuries. He tucked his arm inside the singlet mimicking a one armed man. He turned over his bottom lip and placed it over the top one, pretending to cry. Yasser stared into the man's very soul with his shark like eyes.

The helicopter mate was the man that had stamped on Yasser's festering shoulder during the journey here. The man saw the venom in Yasser's eyes. He coughed up phlegm and spat toward the cage, and then he turned away and carried on with the flight preparations.

Across the runway in the near distance, dust and sand spewed upward from the earth as a herd of goats and sheep stampeded toward the guardhouse. Yasser could see the Bedouin children chasing them with their sticks and crooks, shouting and laughing as the chased the animals. The pilot and his mate heard the racket and stopped what they were doing inside the helicopter. They both climbed down onto the sand and watched as the animals galloped closer and closer to the guardhouse. They were less than three hundred yards away from the helicopter now, and were running at full pelt, fear driving them on.

The pilot was bare-chested, wearing green coloured combat pants and high-necked army boots. He had his automatic pistol pushed into his waistband near his spine. The pilot took his gun out of his pants and aimed it at the centre of the approaching stampede. He leaned his right shoulder against the dark grey metal of the helicopter for support as he aimed, and closed his right eye to sight the shot. Suddenly the door to the guardhouse screeched open as the Eygptian guards came out to investigate the kafuffle outside.

The hooves of the approaching herd were thundering across the runway now. The animals had left the Bedouin children far behind. One of the guards spotted the pilot about to shoot into the approaching herd and he shouted over the noise. Killing a Bedouin animal carried severe consequences, as animals were the lifeblood of a nomadic tribe. The pilot heard the guard, but chose to ignore the warning. He looked at him without lowering the gun and sneered. He had visions of taking a carcass of lamb to sell wherever it was that they were heading to. He closed one eye again and fired into the stampeding herd.

The pilot's gun jerked as he fired and a loud retort echoed across the airfield, clearly audible over the bleating animals. As the shot rang out, completely unexpectedly, the back of the pilots head exploded, spraying the hull of the helicopter with blood and brain matter. A triangular piece of skull bone hung from the metal, adhered with sticky fluid. Yasser noted that there was skin and hair still attached to the bone.

The wounded pilot turned away from the stampede and looked toward Yasser, his mouth was hanging open and his eyes were wide and shocked. There was a ragged bullet hole in the centre of his forehcad where a bullet from the Bedouin chief's M16 had hit him. His legs buckled and he toppled forward onto his knees, still staring into Yasser's eyes accusingly. Yasser ran his index finger across his windpipe slowly, returning the pilot's throat cutting gesture, just seconds before he disappeared beneath a tidal wave of bleating animals.

The pilot's mate jumped up into the cargo hold of the helicopter out of the path of the stampede. He stared in amazement at the bloodied carcass of his pilot being trampled in the sand, and then he looked at the blood splatter up the side of the helicopter, which made absolutely no sense at all to him. The Eygptian guards were none the wiser either. The stampeding animals were causing havoc all around the helicopter, and their hut. The noise was deafening. The pilots mate turned to Yasser and watched him intently, trying to understand what was happening and why.

Suddenly, without warning the pilot's mate was simply knocked of his feet backwards into the helicopter. Yasser smiled as he watched the man's boots twitching, knowing that the mate was injured but not dead yet. The guards were too busy watching the animal madness in front of the guardhouse to realise what had happened to the helicopter's pilot and its mate. They were clutching their ancient Enfield rifles, more for comfort than anything else.

When the Bedouin tribesmen mounted their camels and headed toward them they didn't realise that they were hostile until it was too late, not that it would have made any difference.

The three Egyptians placed their weapons down against the guardhouse and raised their hands in surrender. One of them was babbling his apologies for whatever offense had been caused to the Bedouin chief, who was sat on his camel watching the scene and cleaning the sights of his sniper rifle, oblivious to the man's pleading. Melad pointed his Kalashnikov toward Yasser's cage, and the guard that had given him water everyday ran over to it and opened the door with his keys. Melad and Megdah approached the one armed terrorist leader and offered him fresh water, Yasser drank slowly from the flask, stared at the frightened guard, and then he drank again. The guard had always sensed the evil that pervaded from Yasser but now that there were no metal bars between them the feeling was tenfold. Yasser turned to Melad.

"Shukraan," Yasser thanked the men and bowed his head in respect.

"Ahlan wa Sahlan," the two Arabs said that he was welcome, and they kneeled before him.

"We are here to take you to a place where you will be safe and free caliph," Megdah said.

"We will never be truly free until we have driven the crusaders from our lands, and the Jews are wiped from the face of the earth. I'm not sure who is worst, them or our Muslim brothers that collude with them," Yasser cocked his head to the side as he looked at the terrified guard. The man stared at the floor trying to avoid eye contact with Yasser or the others. He was holding his hands together loosely in front of him, and his feet were crossed one in front of the other, visibly trembling.

"You brought me water every day didn't you?" Yasser asked the guard. He didn't answer he just nodded his head rapidly in the affirmative.

"I asked you a question," Yasser said quietly.

"Yes, yes I brought you water every day sir, please don't kill me," the guard whispered.

"Every day that you brought me water, what did I say to you?"

"You said thank you."

"And every time I said thank you, what did you say?"

The guard started to shake, his lips quivered and he screwed his eyes closed tightly together, trying to make the scary world disappear. He didn't answer, because he couldn't.

"Answer me!" Yasser screamed in his face. The sudden shouting made Melad and Megdah jump, startled.

"Every time that I thanked you for bringing me water, what did you say to me?"

"Nothing, I didn't say anything to you, I was ordered not to," the guard shrunk further into himself, his shoulders hunched up and his chest sank.

"Exactly, you said nothing to one of your Muslim brothers, because the Kufur 'ordered' you not to," Yasser hissed the words in the guard's ear.

"You will wish that you used your tongue when you had the opportunity to. Cut his tongue out and feed it to the goats," Yasser said to Melad.

"What?"

"I said cut his fucking tongue out!" Yasser shouted at Melad, and the look in his eyes defied contradiction.

Megdah moved first, not as squeamish as Melad. He kicked the guard at the back of the knee joint and the guard fell to his knees. Megdah positioned himself directly behind the guard, and pulled the man's arms up his back and secured them with his elbows. The arm lock was unbreakable. Melad took a wicked looking Bedouin dagger from his robes. The handle was ornately decorated, the blade was curved and razor sharp. He forced the man's head backward placing his forearm under the guard's chin. The terrified Egyptian clamped his teeth together, trying to avoid the terrible punishment that awaited him.

Melad couldn't force the guard's mouth open no matter how hard he tried. Yasser watched the men struggling with distain. He eventually lost his patience. Yasser took the narrow blade from Melad and pushed it slowly into the guards left eyeball. The orb burst spilling aqueous humour and blood down the Egyptian's cheek. The guard wailed in agony, screaming for his life in an incoherent gurgle. Yasser handed the dagger back to Melad and grabbed the screaming man's tongue between his finger and thumb. Melad took exactly forty six seconds to saw the guard's tongue off at the root.

Chapter Forty-One

Grace Farrington

Tank climbed into the Jeep that had transported him to the meeting. The uniformed driver loosely saluted again, and then handed him his pager.

"You dropped this on the passenger seat earlier," the soldier said.

"Thanks." Tank glanced at the screen and it indicated that there were several messages stored.

"It hasn't stopped beeping since you went in, sir, but I didn't want to disturb the meeting."

Tank read the first message. He reached the end of the digital text and then he read it again. He looked up through the windscreen down the long sandstone tunnel, which stretched off into the distance, and then he looked down at the screen again. The driver wasn't sure where he wanted to go, but he knew it would be down the tunnel toward the city centre somewhere, so he engaged first gear and drove on without asking. Tank reached for the coms unit, which was attached to the green metal dashboard, above the heater unit.

"Control, this is pilgrim one," he spoke into the microphone. He sat back in the seat; still a little shocked by the message, and put his size twelve feet up against the dash.

"Come in, pilgrim one."

"How long do uniformed division estimate they're going to need to evacuate the designated areas?" he asked.

"The last communication confirmed that the city centre is clear, and that the housing estates in close proximity will be cleared by five o'clock this afternoon."

"Have they met any resistance?"

"Negative that; they're broadcasting on local television and radio that there are a number of suspected gas leaks, caused by the earlier explosion at the St. John's Tower, so it's going smoothly at the moment."

"Are the Task Force ready?" Tank asked, trying to work out a time line for the operation.

"Roger that, they're all ready and waiting."

"I need one unit of six men, use Chen's team, in full NBC gear. Everyone else is to work on finding the missing insurgents," Tank ordered. It was pointless sending the entire squad into the subterranean delivery basement, looking for the suspect radioactive device. It was also against Task Force protocol to endanger the entire platoon simultaneously.

"Roger that, what about you, Tank, how long will you be?"

"I'll be there in one hour, over and out," Tank cut the dialogue before he needed to elaborate any further. He needed to get to the hospital quickly.

"Take me straight to the Royal," Tank ordered the driver. The driver glanced sideways at the big man, unsure whether he should question the order or not. The military vehicles that operated below the city never left the tunnels. They were taken into the tunnels in boxes and crates, and then assembled below ground away from the suspicious eyes of the general population. If military vehicles were seen regularly coming and going from beneath the Canning Place headquarters, speculation would soon abound about the existence of the subterranean bunker. The driver glanced at Tank again for confirmation of the order.

"What's the matter?" Tank asked the soldier aggressively. The message on his pager had rattled him.

"Nothing, sir, but this vehicle is restricted to this specific facility, sir."

"Did you understand the order that I gave you, corporal?"

"Yes sir, I'm just not sure that I can follow it, sir," the soldier worked for the British army not the Terrorist Task Force. He was concerned that he could be court marshalled. He had been posted at the bunker as a reward for completing two tours of Iraq. The corporal had unfortunately started showing signs of posttraumatic stress disorder, when it was rumoured that his unit was being sent to Afghanistan. His commanding officer didn't think that he would cope with another tour of duty so soon; hence, he ended up driving senior officers up down the giant sandstone tunnels.

"Do you need me to draw you a fucking diagram?" Tank asked in a deceptively calm voice. It was a voice many people had heard just before they died.

"No, sir, I don't require a diagram, sir. I do require permission to take the vehicle off the facility though, sir," the soldier stuck to his guns. He was a big solid man, not easily intimidated. He fancied his chances against anyone in a fair fistfight and he wasn't about to be intimidated by Tank.

"I'm giving you permission to take this vehicle out of the tunnel network, soldier."

"This is a British army vehicle, sir. Not a Task Force vehicle, with respect, sir. I'd need permission from one of my senior army officers, to take this vehicle of the base."

"Who does the British Army take orders from, corporal?"

"The British government, sir."

"Who do I work directly for, corporal?"

"I don't know, sir, it's a secret."

"Hazard a guess, corporal," Tank's voice was still calm, almost patronising and detached from the rising anger in his guts.

"The government, sir."

"Well done, soldier, you're correct."

"Thank you, sir."

"You're welcome, corporal, now are you going to take me to the Royal?" Tank asked, moving his hands like the conductor of a famous orchestra, his voice still balanced and calm.

"No, sir."

Tank pulled the hand brake up sending the Jeep into a screeching skid. The vehicle stopped sharply throwing the jobs worth corporal forward, hitting his head on the steering wheel. Tank grabbed the soldier by the scruff of his neck and slammed his head into the driver's door window. There was a dull thud as his skull connected with the toughened glass. The soldier moaned and struggled, but his protests became weaker when Tank threw a straight right jab, which landed cleanly on the side of his jaw. Tank's clenched fist was the size of a lump hammer, and the soldiers head rattled off the window again, rendering him unconscious. Tank grabbed him with one hand beneath the knees, and the other behind the head, and he heaved. He hoisted him into the back seat in one smooth motion, as if he was a sleeping toddler.

Chen and the fat controller pulled alongside the Jeep in a similar vehicle, and wound down the window.

"What happened to him?" Chen asked, gesturing to the unconscious corporal.

"Oh it's just a headache I think, he'll be fine. I need you to set up your team in full radiation kit," Tank said.

"Roger that, what about you?"

"I need to get to the hospital, I'll be an hour tops," Tank said looking at his watch, "cover for me till then."

Tank jumped into the driver's seat and slammed the Jeep in to gear. The wheels spun and sprayed grit into the air, as he sped off down the sandstone tunnel. The bunker facility was built during the construction of three massive traffic tunnels, which run beneath the River Mersey, joining the city to the peninsula of the Wirral. When you drive through the road tunnels there are numerous smaller service tunnels branching off in random directions, all with restricted access signs to stop normal traffic from entering. If you look close, enough you will realise that you can't actually see the end of any of them. They all disappear around sharp bends or into the darkness beyond eye view. In truth they were built as a part of the bunker system, some acted as supply routes for building equipment and the huge tunnelling machines, which actually dug out the underground facility; others were to become emergency exits and entrances for selected politicians and key military personnel to use in the event of an emergency. Tank weaved the jeep through the labyrinth of tunnels, using his detailed memory of their layout. Many of the tunnels looked like dead ends from a distance, only revealing sharp exits at obtuse angles when you had driven right up to them. The optical illusions had prevented inquisitive members of the public stumbling across the bunker system for decades.

Fifteen minutes later Tank was parking the vehicle outside the main doors of the hospital. The building looked like a modern office block, turned on its side, longer than it was high. The exterior was a dark brick facia, and smoked glass windows snaked round the entire circumference of the structure. To the left of the building was a public car park, beneath, which was the subbasement where Tank had shot Abu earlier. The incinerator chimneystack reached from the car park one hundred foot into the air above the hospital building. The main doors were guarded by armed police, and Tank approached them flashing his identification.

"Where are the Task Force people?" Tank asked brusquely.

"Fifth floor, sir," the uniformed policeman answered.

"Do me a favour, get someone to take a look at the squaddie in the back seat of that Jeep would you, he's not been very well." The policeman nodded and called over a hospital orderly.

Tank headed for the lift. There were people milling about all over the reception. The hospital shops and the reception desk were busy. An armed policeman was monitoring whoever entered the elevators; several other armed men policed the stairwells. Tank stepped into the elevator car and took a deep breath, trying not to let his emotions get the better of him. He couldn't afford to be carried away. The last few day's events rolled through his mind like an old movie, he paused some clips, rewound others, until he was remembering the call he'd received in the loft of the church at his grandmother's funeral. The doctor had said that Grace had demonstrated motor function in her hands. A twitch maybe, he hadn't dared to hope for anything more than that, until he read the message on his pager. It said that Grace had woken up.

Tank reached the floor where Grace was being guarded. He was greeted by one of his men. The Task Force man led Tank down the corridor to the small anteroom where she was being cared for.

"Is there any news on the Major?" Tank asked.

"They're not telling us anything, Tank; he's still in theatre though."

Tank nodded, looking through the glass into Grace's room. Grace was lying very still in her bed, just as she had been for more than a year. There was no sign of any change. Her mother was sat sniffling into a handkerchief at the left hand side of the hospital cot. Next to her mother was a tall, stainless steel, fluid delivery stand. Three drips were hanging from it feeding Grace with vital nutrients and essential medicines through clear tubes, which led to valves in her hands. To the right of the bed was her father, he'd seen Tank arriving and now glared at him through the glass. Tank couldn't be bothered what the man thought about him right now, or at any other time if the truth be known.

Grace was the first female soldier to cut it in the elite Terrorist Task Force. She had been critically injured in the line of duty doing a job that she loved. If he could swap places with her then he would, but he couldn't, and Grace wouldn't have had it any other way.

Tank wanted to hold Grace in his arms, but he couldn't even walk into the room while her parents were there without causing a scene. He stared awkwardly through the glass. He felt that he might as well be a million miles away. Her father was wearing faded denim jeans and a matching denim shirt, his hair was shaved at number one grade all over. The soldier in him had never really retired, despite hanging up his uniform decades ago. Grace's father stood up and walked around the bed to his wife. He helped her to stand up, holding her hand and talking to her reassuringly. Tank couldn't hear what he was saying but Grace's mother turned to look at him through the glass. Her eyes were red and puffy from crying, her eyes still full of tears. She nodded her head almost imperceptibly to Tank, and the slightest glimmer of a smile creased the corners of her mouth. She waved a weak hand to him and gestured him into the room. Tank smiled back at her and walked to the doorway. He stood face to face with Grace's father, just three feet separating them.

"She asked for you," Grace's mother said with a broken voice.

Tank looked past them to where she was lying. She didn't look any different. He wasn't sure what he had expected her to be doing. Sitting up and reading a newspaper, catching up on over a year's events; or tucking into her first solid food since she'd took two bullets. Ridiculous, but he hadn't expected her to look the same.

Grace's father placed his wrinkled black hand on Tank's huge forearm and squeezed gently, all the hate in eyes seemed to have disappeared, replaced by a compassionate understanding. Tank tensed his muscles reflexively, a little confused.

"We don't see eye to eye about Grace, but I want to thank you for sending your men here to look after her," her father said quietly, still holding Tank's forearm. Tank looked him in the eye. There was an inner strength behind his eyes. A strength that he had seen in Grace's eyes a million times. Her father had been the first black man to reach the rank of Regimental Sergeant Major in the British armed forces. He was Grace's hero, and the reason why she'd chosen to follow him into the service to be a career soldier.

"We don't see eye to eye because she's my little girl, she always will be. She woke up, Tank. She woke up and she asked why you hadn't been to see her today," tears filled his eyes as he spoke. The hand on Tank's forearm squeezed a little tighter. "She woke up and she knew that you hadn't been here today. Go and see her."

Tank felt a lump the size of an orange in his throat as he approached the bed. She looked so fragile, so small, so beautiful, but so painfully vulnerable. The memory of the black woman on the gurney returned. Jagged red holes drilled into her naked chest by an assassin's bullets. His stomach tightened at the thought of it. It made him feel protective and scared at the same time. Anger filled his mind as the sight of Grace's body being slammed against a land rover by a high-powered bullet in Chechnya returned to him. He reached out and touched her hand, scared that he might break her if he pressed too hard. He was scared that she might shatter into a thousand pieces beneath his touch. Her skin felt warm, alive. Her hand twitched, and her eyes flickered open.

"You're late. Where've you been?" she whispered. Tank held her and cried like a baby.

Chapter Forty-Two

Yasser

"You should have used this when you had the chance to," Yasser said waving the severed tongue to the screaming Eygptian that it had belonged to. He was covering his ruined eyeball with one hand, and the other was over his blood-filled mouth. There was a thick gurgling sound coming from his throat as he screamed in pain and tried to breathe at the same time.

"Put him into my cage. Make sure that he has fresh water to drink," Yasser ordered. Melad and Megdah dragged the man away looking a bit bemused. They couldn't understand the significance of giving the man water to drink when you'd just cut his tongue out. It made perfect sense to a psychopath like Yasser Ahmed, one good turn deserves another. Yasser walked toward the Bedouin tribesmen and exchanged formal greetings with them.

"Shukraan, Ahlan wa Sahlan," the chief greeted him as he would another chief. Yasser returned the respect that he'd been shown by bowing his head slightly.

"What are we to do with these bastards?" the chief asked spitting phlegm toward the Egyptian guards. The Bedouin despised the Egyptian government and their minions, especially those that aided the West.

"Put them in the cage for now," Yasser said, and the Bedouin tribesmen herded them toward the cage. The terrified guards were falling at Yasser's feet as they were dragged to the cage, begging for mercy. They had seen what had become of their colleague. One of the Bedouin approached the wounded helicopter engineer.

"Not him," Yasser shouted, "bring him to me first."

The Bedouin dragged the injured man to Yasser. His military boots dragged two lines in the sand. He was shot in the shoulder, injured badly but well aware of what was going on around him.

"This man mocked my disability," Yasser addressed the gathering as if he were presenting a sales pitch. He circled slowly round the man, and the two Bedouin that held him as he spoke.

"He mocked my disability and he showed me no mercy at all. A Muslim who was willing to berate and inflict pain upon his brother for no reason at all," Yasser explained to his audience.

"In the back of that flying machine he stamped on my wound," Yasser pointed to the festering stump, making some of the men grimace at the thought of how painful that must have been. The stump was scabbing over and drying out, a collage of blackened blood and purple flesh, mixed with creamy patches of infected puss. As he displayed the terrible wound, several bloated flies flew away, disturbed from their feeding.

"He saw a brother, injured and in pain, and he offered me no solace, no sympathy, no mercy, only more pain and humiliation. Can somebody explain to me why one man would treat his brother in such a terrible way?" Yasser raised his good arm questioning the crowd. The gathering stayed silent. Yasser continued to circle the man. The man was looking around the crowd of Bedouin in a panic; the grip on his arms was unbreakable, which scared him. The fact that Yasser was circling him was even more terrifying, especially because what he saying was one hundred percent correct. He had been the second man on rendition flights for over a year now, never once stopping to think about the pain and terror that was being inflicted on his unfortunate prisoners. He'd lost count of how many men and women he'd kicked, punched, stamped on and raped in the back of that grey helicopter, but he had a feeling that the reaper was coming to repay him for his kindness.

"Why?" Yasser stopped directly in front of the man.

He stared into him with his glassy eyes. The man looked into Yasser's eyes. It was like looking into a milky bottomless pit. There was a terrible logic in them, which made it more frightening. Yasser felt aggrieved, and he wanted an explanation for that, an explanation and recompense of course.

"Why did you mimic me for only having one arm?" Yasser leaned forward and whispered in the man's ear. "Having one arm isn't funny, but having no arms is even less funny than that. You can tell me what it's like soon."

The man's bottom lip started to quiver and he squeezed his eyes closed, tears spilled over and ran down his face.

"Why did you stamp on my wounded shoulder?"

"Muta' assif, I'm sorry," the man spoke in poor Arabic, terrified of what Yasser might do to him.

"Oh, I have no doubt in my mind that you are sorry now my brother, but are you sorry because you're no longer in control, and because you're scared, or have you seen the error of your ways?" Yasser started to circle him again.

"No, I am truly sorry, please don't hurt me," the man cried, spittle dribbled from his mouth and his knees sagged. The Bedouin had to support him.

"My brother, why do you cry so?" Yasser addressed the gathering again.

"When you stamped on my shoulder, did you think that it would make me cry?"

"Please, I didn't think at all. I'm sorry I followed orders," the man sobbed.

"What, why didn't you say so?" Yasser cried out loudly. He waved his hand dramatically.

"We must let this man go immediately. He was only following orders. Tell me who ordered you to stamp on my shoulder," Yasser sneered in the man's tear stained face.

The man jabbered but he couldn't answer. Yasser bit hard into the man's nose and crushed the cartilage between his teeth, feeling it crunch and crack under the pressure. The man screamed and jerked violently trying to escape Yasser's vice like grip, but he couldn't. The Bedouin held him too tightly. Yasser released his teeth and spat blood and saliva into the man's face.

"Tell me who ordered you to put your arm inside your vest and mimic me."

The man moaned a garbled reply that no one could understand.

"Tell me whose orders you were following and you are free to go," Yasser spoke calmly.

There was no reply except the shuddering sobs of the man.

"This is your last chance. Whose orders were you following when you stamped on my wounded shoulder?" Yasser whispered the question into the man's ear. There was no reply. Yasser sunk his teeth into the man's ear, twisting his head and ripping a chunk of flesh away from the lobe.

The man's knees buckled. The Bedouin repositioned themselves and restrained him by twisting his arms behind his back. They bent his hand in an awkward angle, applying wristlocks to him. He cried out as one of the locks was applied a little harder than was necessary to restrain him.

"Where do you feel the pain?" Yasser bent over and asked him, his mouth close to his ear.

"My hand, he's breaking my hand," the man cried through gritted teeth.

"Remember that sensation in your hand. Remember it well because you will yearn for that feeling one day. The chance to feel anything in your arms is a gift from god, even if it is pain. I'm going to teach you how to become humble. I will teach you how to become a man with no arms and no legs at all. You will thank me eventually, I promise you that, and I promise that I will show you the same mercy and compassion that you have showed to me," Yasser said.

The man started to sob uncontrollably. He had a vague idea of what was coming to him, but he was way, way short of what was actually going to happen to him. If he'd known, his heart would probably have exploded at the idea that one man could feel so much agony at the hands of another.

Melad and Megdah pushed their way to the front of the Bedouin crowd to listen to their leader.

"There will be a workshop on this airbase somewhere," Yasser spoke to them directly.

"There is one at the other side of the guardhouse," Melad said. They had been able to see it from where the Bedouin set up camp, but it had been hidden from view from Yasser's cage.

"Perfect, take him there, and bring me all the tools that you can find. Let the lessons begin."

Chapter Forty-Three

Nasik/ St. John's

Chen opened the access door, which led into the stairwell that serviced the subbasement delivery areas beneath the St. John's shopping precinct. Five members of the Terrorist Task Force peeled away one at a time, entered the stairwell and descended in perfectly practiced combat formation. They were all dressed in heavy leaded jump suits, which were designed to offer some protection from nuclear, biological or chemical attack. Progress was slow and laboured. Tank was the last man through the doorway. He entered the stairwell then headed down the stone steps to take up the lead position, by overtaking the other Task Force men. Once a member of the team is positioned in the lead position, the man at the rear of the formation then passed everyone else, to take up the lead, and so on. The man at the rear moved to the front in rotation, one man taking the place of the next as the unit moved forward by the numbers.

At the bottom of the stone steps was another fire door. Chen approached the door, held the handle in his left hand and signalled with his right, two men break left, and two break right. He pulled the door open and the Task Force men streamed through the doorway into the cavernous subbasement, and took up low covering positions. Tank and Chen followed them through into the delivery area. The delivery area stretched out half a mile left and right in both directions. They were positioned on a raised platform, which ran the full length of the service roads. Five foot beneath the raised platform was the tarmac surface of the road, which was an inch deep in rainwater from the streets above, and littered with discarded cardboard boxes and rotting vegetables. Liverpool's street cleaners hadn't been down here for a while. Still, what the tourists couldn't see wouldn't hurt them. The walls of the raised delivery platform were punctuated by metal floor to ceiling roller shutters, which were symmetrically spaced out as far as you could see in either direction. Across the service road was another raised area, which completely mirrored the one that the Task Force men were positioned on. Behind every huge roller shutter was a delivery and storage warehouse belonging to the retail units that traded in the three-storey shopping mall above.

"Take a reading off the Geiger counter," Tank instructed. The device could be hidden in any one of over one hundred and fifty storage units, each of which contained its own stairwells and goods lifts linking them to the stores above. It was going to be like looking for a needle in a field full of haystacks, even using handheld scanners. The shopping mall had been thoroughly scanned from the air already, but the thousands of tons of concrete and steel just couldn't be penetrated.

Chen's tech guy scanned the platform with his electronic unit, and it emitted loud clicking noises as he passed it over the concrete. There was nothing there to detect. The tech guy shook his head to communicate that the machine was coming up blank.

"This is pilgrim one," Tank spoke into the coms. "We need to start checking the empty units first, which is our closest target?"

"Roger that pilgrim one, from where you are, I would say that unit eleven is the closest to you. It should be on your side of the road, to your right," the fat controller was directing operations from the Task Force office, using detailed plans to guide them in.

Tank signalled to the team and they moved as one fluid unit along the platform to the shutters, which were marked with a giant number eleven. To the right of the shutter was unit number nine, and to the left was unit number thirteen, all odd numbers on one side of the road, and all evens on the other.

"Scan it," Tank ordered into the coms.

The tech guy moved forward protected by his Task Force colleagues. The Geiger counter clicked noisily, the pitch varied as he moved it around the concrete platform. He neared the metal roller shutter and the tone changed again sensing the difference in its surroundings, but there were no radioactive traces to detect. He shook his head again and moved away from the unit door.

"This is pilgrim one, nothing here, what's next?" Tank asked into the coms unit.

"Next door, number thirteen," the fat controller directed them. The shopping centre was incredibly busy all year round, especially so since Liverpool won the City of Culture status in 2008. When the shopping centre management refurbished units, they carried out the work in small blocks, so as not to spoil the cosmetic impact for the tourists.

"Number thirteen unlucky for some," Tank said, signalling the team to move to the unit next door.

The tech guy moved forward and started his sweep pattern in front of the huge shutters. The Geiger counter clicked as he scanned the concrete platform. The result was the same. There was nothing to detect. He went through the pattern sweeping left to right as he approached the metal shutters.

"How many more empty units are there after this one?" Tank asked into the coms, fearing that the results outside unit thirteen would be as fruitless as the previous ones.

"There are nine more after number thirteen."

"I've got something," the tech guy whispered into the coms. He was standing in front of the metal roller scanning the handle, and the pitch of the Geiger counter was oscillating wildly. He took the scanner away from the door and it settled again. The tech guy looked at Tank and nodded, sweeping the gadget over the handle again the tone registered a positive reading.

"What is it?" the fat controller asked, as the tech guy analysed the reading that the Geiger counter had recorded.

"I'm not sure, the reading is very weak, give me two minutes to analyse it."

"Don't worry about analysing the substances; just tell me what type of rays it is emitting?"

"It's very weak, but it's definitely beta rays, probably from the hand of someone who has been in contact with a beta emitting substance, or its container," the tech guy explained.

"What do you think?" Tank asked the fat controller.

"If it's definitely beta rays, then it`s strontium-90. I think that is what we are looking for; the odds of anything else giving that reading are a million to one."

"Roger that control, we're going in, pilgrim one out."

Tank called Chen over to him and they both approached the metal clasp, which fastened the door to the concrete platform. Chen wiggled it up and down, as there was no padlock. Tank had to assume that whoever had taken the lock off, had refastened it on the inside, both locking the roller, and making the padlock inaccessible from the outside.

"Get Flash over here," Tank whispered to Chen. Flash was the unit's explosive expert. Everyone in the Task Force was adept with explosive compounds and their different applications, but Flash loved the stuff, hence the nick name Flash Bang, or Flash for short. Flash looked at the clasp and then gave thumbs up signal. He pointed to four spots along the base of the roller, two to the left of the clasp, and two to the right, and then he pointed to the clasp itself.

Tank gestured the team to take up sheltered positions left and right of the roller, while Flash got to work. He removed a black webbed pouch from his belt and opened a stainless steel zip, which fastened it. Flash took a lump of plastic explosive, a Semtex based product used by demolition experts when liquid explosives like Tovex weren't suitable. Then he took four brass rings, the size of a large wedding band from the bag and stuffed the plastic explosive into them. The brass rings had the effect of directing the blast in a preordained direction, concentrating the explosive force of the blast tenfold. He positioned the packed brass rings beneath the edge of the roller shutter.

There was a narrow metal receiver well running beneath the shutter door, the full length of the opening. The brass rings combined with the metal well that they were inserted into, would concentrate the force of the blast upward. Flash removed a small electric drill from his utility belt and fitted it with a metal drilling bit, the diameter of a one pence piece. He drilled a hole through the clasp and out the other side, only stopping when he felt the bit had completely penetrated the warehouse and was drilling fresh air. Then he took a fibre optic flexible camera and inserted it through the hole. Twisting the fibre, he could see the interior of the warehouse. He signalled to Tank that there was one bandit visible in a seated position to the right hand side of the storage unit. The fibre optic was removed and then quickly replaced with a long thin latex sleeve, which resembled a kid's party balloon.

Flash poured half a litre of the liquid explosive Tovex into the balloon, from a storage flask, which was in the pouch. The balloon, full of demolition grade liquid explosive, now breached the metal roller shutter, and more importantly was positioned beneath the metal padlock, inside the warehouse unit. Combined with the four preset brass compressed charges that he had already set, the roller shutter would be blown upward into its housing at about ninety miles an hour, taking anyone inside completely by surprise. Flash stepped away from the door and jumped down from the raised delivery platform onto the service road with a splash. He summoned Tank and the others to follow suit, as it was a much safer position, and it offered a brilliant line of sight to open fire at any bandits that were revealed inside the unit.

Tank checked that the unit was ready to go, and then he signalled that he was going to remain on the delivery platform, to the left hand side of unit number thirteen. Standard Special Forces protocol when attacking a possible suicide bomber is to shoot the bandit in the head as many times as possible until they stop moving, in order to prevent them detonating an explosive device with a remote switch. The more angles they could shoot from the better.

"When you're ready Flash, we're moving on your mark," Tank whispered into the coms.

"Roger that, on my mark, three, two, one," Flash counted down and detonated the charges.

Chapter Forty-Four

New York

Sabah had been born in Mogadishu, Somalia in the mid sixties sometime. He was orphaned at a very young age like millions of other children from that country. Somalia has been torn apart by civil war for decades. Muslim extremists have fought a string of corrupt governments fuelled constantly by famine and poverty. The United Nations sent troops in to try to stop the genocide in the late eighties and early nineties, resulting in the ambush and massacre of twenty-four Pakistani peacekeepers. America became heavily involved resulting in the incidents immortalised in the movie 'Blackhawk Down', but to no avail. The war still rages today, and the tribal and religious divides run deeper than ever. Islamic extremism in Somalia is like a cancer, which has been spreading and taking a stronger grip every day for over thirty years. Sabah was one of its victims.

Sabah couldn't remember ever not holding a machine gun when he walked outside on the streets of Mogadishu. He'd been recruited into the local militia at a very early age, joining his four older brothers in the back of a converted Toyota pickup truck. The truck is what is known as a technical; a civilian vehicle converted to carry a fifty-millimetre belt fed, heavy machinegun, powerful enough to punch holes through brick walls. They patrolled their residential block, looking for enemy militia or government soldiers that had dared to wander into their territory. Life was cheap, and death was a daily occurrence.

His four older brothers were all dead, three of them were victims of sectarian killings, and the fourth brother became one of Africa's millions of aids victims that die every year. Sabah became a well-respected member of his militia, dedicated and focused, fearless and brutal. During the infamous conflict with American forces in the early nineties, he rose through the ranks quickly. The higher up the militia ranks that he climbed, the more religion became the driving force, as opposed the tribal issues, which fuelled him as boy. He was chosen to travel to a religious terrorist training camp in the mid nineties, to study explosives and the manufacture of improvised explosive devices. It was during this training that he met and studied under the nefarious Yasser Ahmed and his cohorts.

Yasser spotted that Sabah was a fast learner, and had a much higher IQ than the average student. He soon picked up explosive methodology, and started to display an interest in the helicopters and light aircraft that supplied the base with food and munitions. Yasser encouraged him to learn, and arranged for the pilots to teach Sabah. Six months later, he had his first solo flight, and using a forged pilot's licence he became the regular airborne camp deliveryman. That was fourteen years ago, since which he'd become a very accomplished pilot.

It was as an accomplished pilot and dedicated follower of Islamic Jihad that he had been given the honour of striking back at his Western tormentors. It was a plan that would rival the attack on the twin towers in its magnitude, and would echo across the Western world for decades.

Sabah was sat at the controls of an Antonov-124, which is a Russian built, record-breaking cargo plane, used by several Eastern European air forces. On May 1987, a world record flight was made by an Antonov-124, which flew for twenty-five hours and thirty minutes without refuelling, covering twenty one thousand, and one hundred and fifty one miles. This incredible aircraft can fly over four thousand miles fully laden, carrying a payload of one hundred and twenty two tons. The plan was incredibly simple. On board was a crate wrapped in a dozen layers of aluminium. The crate was the size of a small saloon car, weighing about three tons. The inside of the crate was lined with a ton of strontium-90, which had been salted with cobalt, all of which was packed around a core of military grade high explosives.

The explosives were set to explode when the pilot detonated them by a remote switch positioned in his cockpit. The blast would compress the radioactive mixture to a critical state. The aluminium jacket was then designed to disintegrate into a cloud of metal confetti, showering a huge area with radioactive particles. Strontium-90 has a half-life of about twenty-eight years, rendering anywhere it contaminates radioactive for decades. Sabah simply had to take-off from the west coast of Africa, and then fly the airplane as close to the financial district of New York as he could; then detonate the device in the air above the city, spreading the contaminated material as far as was physically possible. All he had to do was deceive the American radar operators, and air traffic control as he approached American airspace, but that was all part of the plan.

Chapter Forty-Five

The St. John's

Flash detonated the five charges simultaneously, shattering the padlock inside the warehouse and propelling the huge metal roller shutter upward. It slammed into its housing with a deafening rattle. Nasik was rudely woken from his troubled slumber, confused and disorientated. He lifted head to see what was happening. He was surrounded by armed men in black protective suits.

"Don't move a muscle or I'll blow your head off," Tank shouted at Nasik, shock tactics to frighten and confuse the enemy.

"Put your hands behind your head right now asshole," Chen closed in on the bandit, Nasik.

Nasik looked drunkenly from one man to the next. He tried to follow their instructions by lifting his hands, but they were heavy and difficult to control. He notice a deep throbbing pain in his right hand, which was now the size of a spade, purple and bloated so that it looked like a lobster's claw. He stared at it as he lifted it up in front of his face. Nasik didn't remember hurting it; in fact, he didn't remember much about anything. He lifted his left hand, which felt even heavier, and the men in black started to shout louder, very loud indeed, their voices echoed off the warehouse walls intensifying the noise.

"Drop the weapon!"

"Drop the gun now!"

All he could hear was shouting and balling. He looked at his left hand and in it was the Colt revolver. Nasik wasn't sure why he had a gun but he did, and he needed to drop it. He shook the gun trying to free it, but his fingers had swollen and they were stuck between the trigger guard and the handle. He was still confused when the Task Force opened fire. His head was physically torn to pieces in seconds, splattering blood and brain matter across the grey breezeblocks.

"This is pilgrim one, we have one bandit neutralised, I repeat one bandit down," Tank spoke into the coms. "Chen get your men to check him for booby traps."

"Roger that."

Chen signalled and two of his men approached the headless corpse." They scanned beneath his legs and behind his back for wires or pressure pads. The body was clean, and they searched his pockets. There was a wallet, which according to the photograph inside it had belonged to a middle aged white European, and a bunch of labelled keys.

"He's clean, there's nothing on him."

"What about the keys?" Tank asked. Chen tossed them to Tank. They were all different cuts, different applications, and they were all clearly labelled.

"Who do you know that labels their keys?" Tank asked.

"My father," Chen replied. Tank shook his head in despair.

"The warehouse area is clear," the Task Force men had scoured the storage area and found nothing.

"All the readings from the floor space are clear," the tech guy called in after checking the concrete floor with the Geiger counter for radiation.

"Ignition key, van door key," Tank was reading the labels. "Lift one key, basement key, shutter key, and lift two key."

"Okay, the van is how he arrived," Chen speculated. "The van door key was needed to remove the device from the back of the van."

"Which would put the lift one key possibly at the tower," Tank was turning the keys through his fingers as they spoke.

"The basement key gave him access to the delivery area, and the shutter got him in here."

"Which leaves the lift two, key," Tank said holding it in the air, looking around the warehouse.

"There's a goods lift set in the rear wall," Flash pointed out.

"Scan that door," Tank said into the coms. "Pilgrim one where does the goods lift from unit thirteen service?"

"According to the plans, it services just one unit on the second floor," the fat controller replied.

"Is the elevator car there?" Tank asked. The tech guy was scanning the metal doors for radiation traces. The Geiger counter clicked loudly as he waved it across the door handle. There was a six-inch sight glass fitted into the door just above the handle, which allowed the operator to see if the goods lift was there or not.

"Negative, but the handle is reading that someone has been in contact with beta emitting material," the tech guy answered.

"Pilgrim one here, get an extraction team down here to remove the bandit, you'll need to get it to Graham Libby immediately for analysis," Tank said. "We're going to use the stairwell to reach the second floor."

"Roger that, look I would advise that if the lift is in working order, and it hasn't been rigged, that you bring the device down to the subbasement," the fat controller said with his usual amount of tact. "Obviously if it was to explode it would be better that it's below ground, not that I think it will explode, but you know what I mean don't you?"

"Roger that control, and thanks for the advice," Tank said sarcastically.

Tank pointed to the stairwell and the Task Force men started up the first flight in combat formation. Chen took the lead to the first landing, and then took up a covering position as the man at the rear overtook him and started up the second flight. The second flight brought them level to the ground floor of the mall, but there were no entrances or exits connecting them. The stairs were covered in once white vinyl, now cracked and peeling up at the edges, countless black blobs of chewing gum spotted them. The formation turned the second landing and headed up to the first floor level. Again, there was nothing of note, just the tattered white staircase covered in discarded gum. It was obvious that the shopping centre management never used the stairwell to access the warehouse below.

As the Task Force approached the second floor, they were faced with two sets of double fire doors, one directly facing the stairs, and the other branched from the small square landing to the right. Tank reached the small landing and studied the doors. They were made from compressed chipboard, and covered in green fire retardant paint. There were eight-inch rectangular windows fixed in each door, positioned in the centre of each set, where they met in the middle. Tank looked through the doors to the right. There was a long corridor with several doorways leading off it, probably a backup area containing office space and staff facilities. The double doors in front of him had hand written notices pinned to them. One said 'If the customer isn't smiling, then give them one of yours', and another ordered, 'No chewing gum on the shop floor', which would explain the state of the staircase.

"This is the entrance to the retail unit," Tank nodded toward the double doors. He pushed them but they were locked in the middle with a mortise lock, but they moved enough to indicate that they wouldn't be much of an obstacle.

"It's locked," Chen said. Tank shook his head slowly.

"I can see that," Tank answered looking through the glass window for tripwires or booby traps that could have been rigged on the doors from the inside.

"Check the bunch of keys," Chen said.

"Negative that," Tank said taking two steps back, and then launching his massive shoulder into the centre of the doors, just below the glass windows. The mortise lock shattered beneath the weight and the wooden frame split down the centre. The Task Force poured into the empty shop unit like a well-oiled machine.

"Shop floor is clear," they started to sound off, a well-practiced military procedure.

"Men's changing rooms are clear."

"Ladies changing rooms are clear."

"Scan that lift," Chen ordered his tech guy. He approached the lift doors cautiously, checking the floor for tripwires, and began to run the Geiger counter over the metal. The clicking noise oscillated loudly and the pitch changed as he moved the monitor away. He seemed unsure and he looked through the sight glass in the lift door.

"What's the score?" Tank asked, waiting for his verdict.

"There is a large plastic tough box in the lift, and we have beta rays registering on the Geiger," the tech guy sounded like he wasn't sure about something.

"There sounds like there should be a, 'but', at the end of that sentence," Tank said. "What's the problem?"

"Well, if you look at that box," he said moving aside for Tank to look through the sight glass. Tank looked and then moved so that Chen could see it too. "If that box contained enough strontium-90 to make an effective dirty bomb, then this Geiger counter would be doing summersaults, but it isn't."

"What are you saying?"

"I'm saying that that tool box isn't full of strontium-90."

"Check it out Chen, and then send the lift back down to the basement," Tank said. "Pilgrim one here, did you hear that control?"

"Roger that," the fat controller said. "The bomb squad are on standby and ready to come down there. Doctor Graff, the Israeli, is there too. He wants to see the device."

"Now why would he want to do that?" Tank asked.

"My thoughts exactly," replied the fat controller.

Chapter Forty-Six

Yasser

Yasser was sat in the Bedouin chief's gazebo eating a watery lamb stew. It had been so long since he'd eaten a proper meal that it tasted like the most wonderful food on the planet. The Bedouin women and children were preparing the caravan ready to depart, and continue on their eternal journey across the deserts. They were herding the sheep and goats into manageable flocks, ready for departure. The elder tribesmen were seated in a wide circle enjoying their meals and chattering in a dialect that was difficult for Yasser to follow. Megdah and Melad were sitting on either side of him, eating in silence. Megdah was pushing pieces of lamb round his plate aimlessly, having completely lost his appetite. His pallor was pale, as if he was about to vomit. He couldn't get the visions of Yasser and the helicopter engineer out of his mind.

Melad on the other hand had been fascinated by it all, even helping a couple of times when Yasser's single arm grew tired of sawing. At one point, he'd changed the blade on the hacksaw, which had snapped on a particularly thick piece of thighbone, while Yasser had a rest and spoke kindly to the screaming man. Yasser had spoken none stop as he cut the man up, explaining that you couldn't be cruel to people for no reason at all. A man had to have a sense of justice, an eye for an eye, a tooth for a tooth; Yasser had a cause, a belief from which he would never deviate. He was fighting to revenge all the injustice that had been caused by the capitalist heathen invaders from the West; were as the helicopter engineer had stamped on Yasser for no reason at all, and so he had to be taught humility by having his limbs sawn off, one at time. In Yasser's mind, it was a just punishment.

Melad had gone up in Yasser's estimation, especially when he'd stumbled over a five-gallon drum of battery acid. They used it to cauterise the ragged wounds, causing unbelievable pain, and stopping their subject from bleeding to death before Yasser had finished teaching him his lesson. Megdah couldn't believe how long the man had screamed for, he'd prayed for him to have a heart attack or bleed to death, just so that the screaming would stop, but he hadn't. He was still screaming when all his limbs had been hacked off, and Yasser dragged him to the front of the guardhouse and nailed him to the door by his ears. Megdah eventually threw up at that point, as did two of the Egyptian guards in the cage, when they saw what terrible fate had befallen their colleague.

"What is wrong with your food?" Yasser asked Megdah.

"Nothing, there's nothing wrong with it. I am not hungry," Megdah explained nervously.

"Don't insult our hosts, eat your food," Yasser turned and looked at Megdah in the eyes. Megdah turned away quickly, breaking the eye contact and began to eat his food without any further protest.

"How long do you think it will be before they realise that you are gone?" asked Melad.

"They were preparing the helicopter to leave earlier," Yasser replied. "We don't have long, it must be expected somewhere."

"Our sponsor sent me because I have a pilot's licence. We can take the helicopter, and I'll take you to our sponsor," Melad said.

"No, it will be tracked as soon as it takes off," Yasser answered. "We will travel with the Bedouin until we can find transport."

"Our sponsor was most specific that we were to bring you to him as quickly as possible," Melad kept his voice as calm as possible, so as not to annoy Yasser. He really didn't want to be on the wrong side of him.

Yasser turned to him and stared angrily. "Then your sponsor will be disappointed, although I'm grateful, I'm not inclined to dance to somebody else's tune."

"There are plans afoot which he thinks will interest you," Melad spoke quietly.

"What kind of plans?" Yasser asked, shovelling a spoonful of the stew into his mouth.

"Plans that involve many of your followers, Caliph, members of Axe," Melad whispered the name of the organisation.

A muffled scream disturbed the conversation. It was coming from the front of the guardhouse. The Egyptian soldiers had been buried naked in the sand up to their necks, facing their colleague who had been nailed to the door.

"It sounds like the insects have found them," Yasser commented with nonchalance.

"We could take one of the small airplanes," Melad suggested.

"Okay," Yasser said without any hesitation. He ate another mouthful of stew and turned toward Megdah, who had finished his food, and was sat staring at the line of heads protruding from the sand near the guardhouse.

"We are going alone though," Yasser said. "I don't like your friend. He will remain here."

Melad nodded and stood up without offering any protest. He would arrange for Megdah to be picked up as soon as they arrived back in civilisation. He walked off toward the distant yellow airplanes, to check if they were serviceable. They were covered in a layer of the shifting desert sand, but they looked to be reasonably modern aircraft, probably Piper Cherokee, he couldn't be certain from here.

Yasser spoke to Megdah without looking at him.

"You go and make sure that the guard in the cage has water to drink, and set fire to the helicopter."

"What about the guardhouse?" Megdah asked, trying to redeem himself. "Should I burn that too?"

"No, you'll need that for shelter," Yasser answered as he stood up and walked away without another word.

Chapter Forty-Seven

The Mid Atlantic

Sabah had barely said a word to his co-pilot since take-off. He had no idea that the Antonov-124 he was co-piloting was carrying a three ton, cobalt salted, dirty bomb. The hotel mogul, Abdul, had advertised through his hotel staff recruitment service, for a pilot with experience of flying cargo airplanes. He'd been hired purely for satisfying airport regulations on take-off. Two pilots are essential. Abdul had selected the co-pilot for this mission, because of his appalling record. He was an unreliable fifty eight year old alcoholic, who hadn't flown an aircraft for two years. Getting him into the co-pilot seat without asking too many questions had not been too difficult.

Sabah could smell whisky on his breath when he arrived at the airport. He was a short, fat, man from Somalia, and he smelled like he had walked all the way from Mogadishu with a dead rat in his pocket. Sabah took an instant dislike to him as soon as he met him, which was good because he would have to kill him before they reached American airspace.

The flight had been uneventful so far. They had no problem getting the cargo plane airborne, and there were rarely any issues from Africa's air traffic controllers. The smell from the co-pilot had become incredibly more pungent as the flight went on, yellow sweat patches were spreading from beneath his arms across the back of his already soiled shirt. They were two and a half hours from American airspace, but they would already have appeared on their long-range radar.

American airspace is controlled by twenty-two different control centres, which make up the national airspace system. Each centre owns certain sectors of domestic airspace and international sectors too. The Atlantic sectors are divided by Aeronautical charts, and aircraft are identified by their individual transponders. When a transponder is identified entering a certain sector, then the relevant control centre picks it up.

"This is charter flight 14-8, requesting permission to alter course heading to Albany, Warren County, over," Sabah made his first communication with American air traffic control. He thought it was safer to pre-empt communication, rather than wait for the Americans to pick them up on long-range radar.

"Roger flight 14-8, good afternoon, could you state your destination and authorisation codes please," came a crackled reply.

"We are heading to Floyd Bennet airfield, Warren County, we're part of the Adirondack hot air balloon festival," Sabah answered confidently. The balloon festival was due to be held the following week, an annual event that was watched by millions across America.

"Congratulations sir, that's one hell of an event, could you confirm your authorisation codes for me please," the air traffic controller wasn't going to be fobbed off with chitchat. The co-pilot looked at Sabah, and then looked away again.

"Could you take the helm for a moment I don't feel too good," Sabah said to the co-pilot. He stood up and walked out of the cockpit quickly, avoiding any more questions from air traffic control.

"What about the authorisation codes?" shouted the fat co-pilot, but Sabah had already gone. The co-pilot shook his head at the pilot's incompetence. The radio crackled again.

"Charter flight 14-8 we require your authorisation codes before we can grant you a new heading," the air traffic controller was being very professional, unlike the pilot.

"Roger that, this is charter flight 14-8, I'm afraid the pilot has taken ill and had to use the toilet. As soon as he returns I'll communicate the required authorisation codes, over," the co-pilot explained, as best as he could.

"That's a negative charter flight 14-8, we need those codes within the next five minutes, American aviation regulations I'm afraid, but all pilots and co-pilots should have access to those codes at all times. I am taking it that you don't have them, and the pilot does."

"Roger control, I'll get back to you before five minutes are up, and thank you, I must apologise for the pilot's behaviour," the co-pilot went right over the top on the polite scales.

Air traffic control didn't reply, immediately. There was a brief silence.

"Roger that charter flight 14-8. Could you just confirm the destination that you're heading to please?"

The co-pilot grabbed a clipboard from the document shelf.

"Roger control, Floyd Bennet airfield, for the Adirondack balloon festival," the fat co-pilot answered.

"Roger flight 14-8, you can see that written on your manifest, but the authorisation codes aren't beneath the destination," the controller remained calm and professional, but there was an edge to his questions creeping in.

"Roger control, Floyd Bennet airfield is written on the manifest here, and the Adirondack balloon festival, but I'm afraid that the pilot must have the authorisation notes on his person. I do apologise for the inconvenience," the co-pilot did his best to keep relations on an even keel.

Air traffic control remained silent, and Sabah returned into the cockpit. He climbed into his seat in silence. The co-pilot shook his head and handed Sabah the clipboard, making a drama out of it.

"You need to communicate the authorisation codes immediately; you young pilots today have no consideration for anyone else but yourself. If I had done that in my day I would have been fired immediately," the co-pilot said in an acidic tone.

Sabah appeared to ignore the man, and then swung his right hand in a wild arcing movement, slamming an eight-inch combat knife into his chest. The blade ripped his heart in half and killed him instantly.

"Consider yourself fired," Sabah said as he strapped himself into his seat, ready to pilot the final leg of the journey alone.

Chapter Forty-Eight

The Terrorist Task Force

Chen used the lift key to open the concertina style door, and he searched the elevator car for booby traps. When he was satisfied, he closed the door and pressed the basement button, sending it down to the warehouse below. The lift slowly settled into its housing at the bottom of the shaft, where Tank and the bomb squad were waiting for it.

"It's all yours boys," Tank said opening the lift doors to reveal the large black tough box.

The bomb squad moved forward and surrounded the lift. The men were dressed in heavily armoured clothing, dark blue in colour, resembling human two legged Armadillos. They checked and double-checked the box and the surrounding elevator for wires or sensors before eventually wheeling it out of the lift.

"The suspect device is contained in a large toughened plastic utility container, mostly used in the construction industry for transporting tools," the bomb squad men had to broadcast a running commentary on everything they did for obvious reasons. If the explosive devices that they tried to disarm exploded, then there would be few people in a position to explain what went wrong, and why.

"Approximately one hundred litres in capacity, secured by two plastic quick release clasps, which are self folding," he continued.

"There is metal inside the box," he said scanning the device as he spoke.

Tank thought that was odd, but his thoughts were disturbed by the sound of footsteps approaching from the delivery platform outside. Graham Libby and his team had already recovered the corpse, and he wasn't expecting anyone else. A Task Force man turned into the unit accompanied by the Israeli scientist, Doctor Graff.

"Doctor," Tank said nodding an unfriendly greeting. He really didn't have the time or the patience to mollycoddle a foreign politician right now. The doctor nodded back in an equally belligerent manner. He seemed worried and eager to see the device.

"I can understand your unwillingness to be courteous, agent Tankersley however it is absolutely vital that I see this device before it is dismantled," the doctor said walking by Tank as if he wasn't there.

"Be my guest," Tank said under his breath.

"I am releasing the clasps now, left side first," the bomb squad communication continued.

"And now the right side," he said, as he inserted a narrow wooden blade that looked like a lolly ice stick, and ran it around all three sides of the lid, looking for filaments. There was nothing. They lifted the lid completely open and peered inside. The Israeli doctor walked around the gathered men and found himself a good vantage point. He removed a silver digital camera and began to video the process.

"Does he have to that right now?" the bomb squad man looked at Tank for an answer.

"He's from Israel," Tank shrugged as if that was reason enough, and no one argued.

Inside the plastic box was a shallow grey plastic inner tray, designed to hold screwdrivers and screws. It was moulded to fit snugly into the box, and was fitted with a carry handle in its centre, so that it could be lifted straight out. It was empty apart from a soft packet of cigarettes. The bomb squad lifted the carry tray gently and proceeded to insert the wooden blade around the edge again, repeating the earlier process.

"I am removing the inner tray," he said lifting the grey plastic tray.

"The Israeli doctor looked shocked as he leaned over and studied the contents of the plastic box. The bomb squad team looked at Tank and gestured him over to the device. Inside the box had been lined with a shiny metal foil of some kind, similar to what is used for cooking a turkey.

In the centre of the storage space was an eighteen inch, cylindrical section of drainpipe, stuffed with a substance that Tank didn't recognise. Surrounding the section of pipe was a grey sludge, resembling thick porridge in consistency, too thick to move like a liquid, but not thick enough to stand on.

"Where is the detonator?" Tank asked.

"There isn't one," the Israeli answered, unexpectedly.

"I think we need slightly more information than that doctor. Would you mind telling us what this is?" Tank said getting annoyed.

"There doesn't appear to be any explosive material in here either," the bomb squad man said taking of his protective helmet.

"I think that the strontium-90 is in the pipe. The grey substance surrounding it is sludge, radioactive sludge, a waste product."

"So why are there no detonator, and no explosives?" Tank asked the obvious question.

"Because it`s a hoax. This device is a decoy," the doctor said shaking his head slowly.

Chapter Forty-Nine

CIA Headquarters, Langley

The news that was coming into Director Ruth Jones was the worst that she had heard in her short tenure as head of the CIA. The Foreign Secretary had just called from the Whitehouse to inform her that, CIA personnel files had been stolen by the British, and then disclosed to the terrorist organisation Axe. Every current file and personnel detail would now need to be rewritten and encrypted, which was a mammoth task. On top of that, there was an imminent threat of an attack against New York's financial district.

Director Ruth Jones was under the microscope as the first female operative to achieve such elevated status within the intelligence agencies. Following the disinformation surrounding Saddam Hussein's weapons of mass destruction, Washington had decided that their intelligence agencies would benefit from talented female leadership, rather than the egotistical male dominance, which had plagued the agency since its conception. The government believed that women in senior leadership roles were less likely to make macho decisions, and more likely to make intelligent, fact based decisions.

They also had the propensity to be open and honest. Ruth Jones was indeed a talented leader, but she was also a tough one. The office staff called her, Ruthless Ruth, because of the increasing number of agents she had axed. She had no tolerance of incompetence at all, and even less if someone's integrity was brought into question. Trust was the crux of the way she ran her operation.

"What do you mean we don't know where he is?" Ruth Jones asked politely down the telephone.

"Just that director, we were expecting the helicopter to take off from the airfield eight hours ago, but it failed to. All communication with the base has been lost," agent Japey tried to explain.

"And you're sure that he was being transported when this happened?" Ruth pressed, unhappy with the vagueness of the situation.

"I wasn't informed that he was being moved, until I was informed that he wasn't accounted for director," the agent back peddled.

"Don't insult my intelligence or your own by bullshitting me Japey, why wouldn't you know that he was being moved?" she spoke very assertively down the line.

"I didn't officially know director. I mean we, never officially know where he is, or when he is being moved, for obvious reasons."

"Bullshit, if you think I'm swallowing that then I'm afraid you don't know me very well Agent Japey. Now you have five seconds to explain this fucked up situation before I fire your ass," assertive became aggressive.

"Okay, I'll tell you what I know."

"You'd better, I'm waiting."

Ahmed was held for interrogation in Chechnya for a couple of months. At first, we were getting some good information from him, but it soon became evident that he was feeding us with the names and locations of his rival militias. "We were doing his dirty work for him," Japey opened up, realising that Director Jones was not a woman to mess about with.

"What do you mean, doing his dirty work for him?"

"We sent special operations to a number of target addresses given to us by Yasser Ahmed."

"And what?"

"Well, we neutralised the insurgents at those sites," the agent was losing his grip. Lying was second nature to him, but telling the cold hard truth stuck in his throat.

"How many?" the director asked.

"How many what?"

"How many insurgents did you neutralise, on behalf of Yasser Ahmed?" she had him on the ropes now.

"Err; I don't have the details in front of me."

"Bullshit, how many."

"Sixty five, I think," he didn't sound convincing.

"Thank you. At last, we have a smidgen of truth Agent Japey. What happened?" she pushed further.

"The information was becoming increasingly more untrustworthy, and he was in a weakened state, so we felt that another approach was useless. We were about to hand him over to the British," he explained sheepishly.

"Do they know that he is missing?" she asked.

"We aren't really sure that he is missing ourselves director. All we know is that the helicopter didn't leave on schedule, and that communications are down," he tried to recover a modicum of control.

"Have you looked at the airfield on satellite pictures?" the director knew that all avenues would already have been explored before the news reached her level. He was stalling.

"Yes they are inconclusive."

"Bullshit, you're suspended with immediate effect, bring your gun and your badge into my office on your way out," Ruth Jones hung up, sat back and watched the telephone. It rang almost immediately.

Apologies director, but this is difficult. The satellites show the helicopter has been torched, along with some light aircraft and a hangar. The airfield appears to be deserted, we've lost him," the agent sighed, almost relieved that the truth was out.

"What have you done about it?" Ruth Jones needed a solid response to this situation.

"We are preparing a Delta Force unit to attend the airbase on a recon mission to find out what happened."

"I don't want American troops setting a foot anywhere in the Middle East, especially on a wild goose chase. He's gone and we can be sure of that. Where's our nearest carrier?" the director had to clean up the mess before it became public knowledge that the most wanted terrorist on the planet had escaped from the clutches of the American forces.

"There's a fleet in the gulf."

"Wait until nightfall and destroy that airfield, make sure there isn't a single brick left standing. I'll prepare a press release explaining that we have discovered a terror training camp, and have taken the relevant action to destroy it," as Ruth Jones put the phone down her secretary handed her a fax from civilian air traffic control. It appeared that there was an unauthorised aircraft heading toward American airspace from the African continent. It was going to be one of those days.

Chapter Fifty

The Task Force/ Holyhead

Ryan Griffin and his unit of Task Force men were positioned on a stake out. Information received from one of the Palestinians, who was still in hospital suffering from burns, had led them to their preordained rendezvous point. The Palestinian terrorists had agreed to meet up when their individual missions were completed. The agreed rendezvous was the rear car park of a bar called the Bay Leaf, in Treaddur Bay. The Task Force had coerced their doctors to withhold pain relief from the terrorist, until he surrendered information about his associates. Bearing in mind that he had fifty percent burns on his body, he soon starting talking.

They were sure that two insurgents hadn't been accounted for, and they were sure from the way events had panned out that they would be heading for the hills anytime now. The attacks on Britain's security chiefs had been swift and brutal, but the wave seemed to have subsided, which indicated that the terrorists were about to leave. If the Syrian vessel hadn't been impounded then it would be due to leave port, and it made sense that the Palestinians planned to leave the same way that they had arrived.

Ryan Griffin was sitting at a table, at the rear of the white building. The Bay Leaf was a tall rectangular building, painted brilliant white and topped by a black slate tiled roof. The windows were square frames, dissected into smaller symmetrical squares. Every third small square was fitted with a thick bubbled glass pain, giving the bar an ancient maritime look. At the rear of the pub was a raised wooden deck. Long wooden tables were laid out, with brightly coloured parasols drilled through the centres of them.

Ryan was sitting at one of the tables in a sleeveless tee shirt, which showed off his well-toned arms. He was blond and had chiselled features. He could pass as a beach bum, which made him blend into the surfing crowd that filled up the tables around him easily. He was drinking a bottle of cider, which had turned warm hours ago, studying every vehicle, which entered the car park. Four of his men were in similar positions in the beer garden, and two more were sitting in their car pretending to read a map. The Bay Leaf was so close to the shore that they could hear the waves breaking over the chattering and laughter of the tourists.

A Honda Blackbird turned off the main Treaddur Bay road into the lane, which led to the car park behind the pub. There were two men on board, one dressed in motorbike leathers, and the other in jeans and a waterproof jacket. The motorbike engine purred as the driver steered it toward the back of the lot. Both men were looking around the parked vehicles as they past them. Ryan couldn't be sure if they were the terrorists, helmets and gloves covered their skin, making it difficult to identify them. The bike weaved through parked cars and then pulled up to a stop right next to Ryan's men in their car.

The pillion rider climbed off the motorbike and removed the chinstrap. He grabbed the helmet by the chin guard and pulled it off. Ryan and his agents tensed in readiness. He was dark skinned.

"Check them out," Ryan whispered into the coms unit. The two agents in the car opened the doors and climbed out, startling the pillion rider. He stepped back in between the motorbike and the two advancing men. The Task Force men pointed Glock nine millimetres at the pillion rider, and one of them flashed his identification. Before the Task Force men could speak, the pillion rider spread his arms wide to protect the driver, and then rushed at the Task Force men shouting at the top of his voice.

Ryan Griffin and his agents sprang into action. The beach crowd had been stunned into silence by the unusual sight of men waving guns. Some of the women bolted for the back door of the Bay leaf, escaping as fast as they could. Most of the men were too intrigued to move. The pillion rider was dropped before he'd moved two yards by a thundering blow to the bridge of his nose. The heavy metal Glock smashed the fragile bones in his nose to pieces instantly. The scuffle gained the rider precious seconds, and before his passenger had hit the floor, he had spun the motorbike one hundred and eighty degrees. The Honda Blackbird has one hundred and ninety brake horsepower, and the terrorist was twisting the throttle open as far as it would go.

The motorbike's front wheel reared up in the air as the engine thrust the machine from zero to sixty in seconds. The Task Force men didn't even have time to release a shot, because the bike was too quick, and there were too many innocent bystanders looking on. Ryan and his men sprinted to their vehicles, as the Blackbird accelerated off into the distance. The Task Force men were driving three and a half litre BMW's sports saloons, with all the badges and trimmings removed, so that they looked like bog standard family cars. Beneath the bonnet was the best German engineering that the famous car manufacturers could muster. Gravel was flicked up in the air as the two vehicles roared off in pursuit, wheels spinning.

"Have you got a visual?" Ryan asked his driver.

"I think he just turned the bend at the top of the hill."

The motorbike had taken the main Treaddur Bay road, heading toward the town centre and the port beyond. The road climbed a long sloping hill, through a mishmash of expensive beach houses and large bungalows, before twisting left out of view. The BMW's burned rubber as the powerful torque propelled them up the hill after the motorbike. There was no sign of the fugitive until the vehicles broke clear of the coastal residential area.

The blur of houses on either side suddenly disappeared and was replaced by farm meadows on the right and a golf course on the left. The road between the two was long and straight, and the Task Force was granted a long-range view of their target. They could see the motorbike reaching the end of the straight. The road opened up for them allowing the drivers to floor the accelerator, pushing the speeding vehicles to their limits. The Task Force vehicles were gaining ground as the long straight stretch of road began to run out. It twisted to the left sharply and dipped simultaneously, allowing the motorbike to speed out of view again momentarily. The motorbike was entering the outskirts of the built up area, which was situated at the edge of Holyhead. He was now two miles from the port, and the Syrian vessel that he was desperate to reach.

"He's headed for the port, he's riding in a panic," Ryan said, more to himself than anyone else. There was no sense in the rider's actions. He couldn't outrun them, and he wasn't about to be allowed to board a vessel back to the Middle East, but he was in fear of his life, behaving irrationally. Ryan punched a button on the dashboard and the computer screen brought up a GPS view of their location, in the form of a map. They were depicted as a red arrow moving swiftly across the image.

"Control, this is pilgrim six," Griffin wanted to communicate with their air support.

"Go ahead pilgrim six."

"Does air support have the bandit on visual?"

"Roger that, the bandit is eight hundred yards north of you heading directly for the Irish Sea," the helicopter pilot answered.

The Palestinian on the motorbike opened up the throttle and bent his chest down to touch his petrol tank, trying to reduce the wind resistance and increase his speed further. The bike screamed down Kingsland hill at over a hundred miles an hour. As it reached the bottom of the hill, the pursuing BMW's were only just reaching the top. The cars rocketed over the crest of the hill, all four wheels leaving the tarmac for several heart pounding moments, before finally crashing back down onto the road, tyres squealing, and sparks flying as they roared down Kingsland in hot pursuit.

The motorbike approached a three-way junction as he belted past the town's fire station. On the left was a row of Victorian terraced buildings, three storeys high. The street levels were all shop fronts, a taxi office, a diving shop and a bakery. People stood outside chatting and pushing children in prams, saying hello to neighbours and the like. To the right hand side was a busy dual carriageway, which had been built to carry the thousands of juggernauts, which travelled, through the town, en route to the ferry terminals. Directly in front was granite built Humpback Bridge, which crossed the port's railway lines. The roads all converged at a multiple set of traffic lights on the crest of the bridge. The lights were set to red, stopping the traffic, and a long queue had already started to form.

The Honda Blackbird had reached one hundred and twenty miles an hour as it approached the back of the traffic jam. The rider stamped on the back brake trying to slow the speeding machine down, but to no avail. Thick black smoke billowed from the rear tyre as the rubber burned on the tarmac. He aimed the bike at a gap between the stationary cars, and it screamed through the jam, stopping just short of the bridge. The chasing BMW's roared past the fire station and slammed on the brakes as they hit the back of the queue. There was no obvious way through for them.

The Palestinian dropped the motorbike into first gear and edged the Honda slowly through the traffic, weaving it in and out of the cars. He reached the front of the line as the traffic lights turned to green again, and opened up the throttle, leaving the pursuing Task Force men for dust.

"This is pilgrim six, he's away from us and we can't get through this traffic. It`s up to air support now," Ryan Griffin said banging the dash board with his fist.

"Roger that pilgrim six we're on top of him," the helicopter answered.

"When he gets to the port there will be nowhere left for him to go. He might start shooting," Ryan said looking at the GPS map. The rider was cornered.

"Roger that, what do you want us to do?"

"Take him out," Griffin answered.

"Roger that."

Chapter Fifty-One

Terrorist Task Force

Tank entered the control room of the subterranean bunker. Everyman and his dog were packed into the glass walled room waiting for the latest information about the impending plot. The large screen had been dedicated to live footage of operations by the bomb squad, as they dismantled the radioactive materials, and disposed of it into protected containers. Every telephone in the room was being used as intelligence networks the world over communicated with the control centre.

"There are no explosives in the container," said the lead member of the bomb squad on the screen.

"What is the likelihood of the detonator and explosives being carried separately?" asked Janet Walsh, the Prime Minister's secretary.

"It's very unlikely," Tank answered.

"I'd have to agree. The carrier was operating alone. I can't envisage them separating the two, increasing the chances of failure or capture," Chen added.

"I am very concerned that this is a smoke screen. The attacks on your key personnel, and the discovery of radioactive materials have been arranged to detract from a bigger more sophisticated plan altogether." The Israeli doctor shook his head as he spoke.

"What are the chances of the plan being an extension of this, aimed at somewhere else in this country," Janet Walsh asked.

"I think that the real target is either New York or Jerusalem, possibly both. The strontium in this device was enough to register on your scanners, and to make those who came into close contact with it sick. I cannot believe that there is enough material to create a substantial long term effect," the doctor explained.

"Why are you so sure doctor?" asked Chen.

"The Russian thermoelectric generators were originally built to power spacecraft and satellites. Thousands were built to power remote beacons, as you already know, with the projected lifespan of twenty years. This requires at least one hundred times the amount of strontium that you have found, for each unit, and we think that they are in possession of two," he held up two fingers to emphasise the point.

The room remained silent while the information was digested. The container that had been found was big enough to contain a much more devastating amount of strontium, had it been packed full of it. The space had been filled with a much less lethal radioactive sludge. It appeared that the plastic tough box device had been designed with deception, rather than devastation in mind.

Graham Libby appeared on one of the smaller screens, patched directly through from the autopsy suite. He had just finished analysing the remains of the Palestinian Nasik.

"What can you tell us Graham?" Tank asked.

"Well I can tell you that our terrorist was already on the point of death when he was shot," the scientist began.

"How do you explain the irradiation burns that he suffered to his hands?" the Israeli doctor was intrigued. There didn't appear to be enough strontium to cause such severe burns.

"I think that he may have carried the isotopes before they even built the device. He may not have realised what he was carrying, but if he had been in close proximity to both gamma and beta radiation then we would expect to see such extensive burning. The irradiation has penetrated the skin and burned deep into the bone marrow, as well as any tissue in between."

"That would explain the extent of the burns," the Israeli agreed.

"Yes, the rest of the body is showing typical symptoms of radiation sickness. The white blood cells are depleted, and the liver and kidneys contain massive amounts of radioactive plasma. He was only a few hours away from complete organ failure in my opinion," Graham Libby finished.

"Have we accounted for all the insurgents?" the Prime Minister's secretary asked.

"There is a Task Force unit in pursuit of the last remaining bandit as we speak," Chen replied.

"Where?" asked the American.

"They have headed back to the port where they arrived, Holyhead. They were obviously expecting to board the Syrian vessel that brought them here."

Another small screen sprang to life and the American director of intelligence services, Ruth Jones appeared in the picture. She looked flustered.

"Director, we were expecting to talk to the Secretary of State," Janet Walsh greeted her cautiously, as agency involvement allows signalled big trouble.

"We have a problem," the American said.

"How can we help?"

"We need to know if the Israelis extracted any specific information about the nature of the potential attack on New York."

All the heads in the room turned toward the Israeli doctor. He flushed red a little under the scrutiny and appeared to be considering his response.

"No, I'm afraid there was no specific detail," the doctor answered.

"Is it possible that the attack could be delivered from an airborne position?" the American director asked somewhat cryptically.

Chen looked at Tank and shrugged his shoulders. The fat controller removed his glasses and cleaned them with his tie, while he thought about the question. The Israeli doctor coughed and cleared his throat.

"May I ask why you're considering that scenario?" Tank asked. He was asking the question that everybody else wanted to know the answer to.

"We obviously need to consider every possible connotation of how this threat may materialise," the American lied.

"As long as the attackers are willing to destroy the aircraft while it is still airborne, then it would be the perfect way to contaminate a large area. The radioactive dispersal would be assisted by the wind, especially at a reasonably high altitude," the Israeli answered.

"Is there any specific reason why you are considering that particular scenario?" Tank pushed the issue.

"Doctor Graff, do you have any idea how large these devices may be, taking into consideration the negligible amount of radioactive material that has been intercepted in the United Kingdom?" she asked completely ignoring Tank's question.

The fat controller chewed the edge of his glasses and smiled at Tank. It was becoming obvious that there was something driving the direction of the American's questions.

"We can only estimate, but there would be several tons of isotopes in two generators. That is always assuming that they only acquired the contents of two units," the Israeli answered slowly and in a concerned voice.

"Do you have some inkling that the supposed attack is airborne?" Tank asked a third time. Janet Walsh shot him a withering glance, trying to make him back off.

"What would you estimate the possible dispersion radius of a device that size could be?" again, she ignored the question.

"If the wind was blowing on shore, up the Hudson River, then you could contaminate Manhattan completely with a device of a reasonable size," the Israeli was uncomfortable speculating.

"Thank you doctor," she said. Everyone was waiting for her to elaborate.

"If we have any new information regarding this issue we'll bring you up to date immediately. I do have some unrelated information for you regarding Islamic extremist activity," she completely changed tack.

"This morning at zero four hundred hours we executed a missile attack on a known terror training camp, which was situated on the Sinai Desert. The aircraft carrier USS Eisenhower carried out the attack using conventional Tomahawk missiles. The strike was a success," Ruth Jones communicated the missile attack as if it was completely unimportant, just another day at the office.

"We don't have any suspected training camps in the Sinai," the fat controller said astonished. He stood up and pulled his pants up above his waist, and then began rooting through his files looking for information to back him up.

"Obviously our data is a little more current than yours Agent Bell, I'll keep you informed of any political repercussions," the screen went blank and the connection was broken.

"What on earth was all that about?" Janet Walsh asked flabbergasted.

"One thing is for certain. She was lying through her teeth, and they're expecting an airborne attack on New York," Tank said.

Chapter Fifty-Two

Yasser

Yasser didn't wake up through the entire airplane journey across the Sinai desert. He'd seen three bright yellow light aircraft, which looked almost abandoned next to the hangar at the far end of the runway. Megdah had inspected the dusty aircraft, which Yasser had spotted on his arrival, and found them all in flyable condition. They were serviced, and full of fuel, ready for takeoff. The Eygptian government had dozens of light airplanes dotted all over the country, ready for a quick getaway, in case of an unexpected Israeli invasion. In 1968, the Israelis had launched an attack, which destroyed the entire Egyptian air force in one afternoon. The government built small remote airfields all over the desert to act as emergency backup facilities, in the event of hostile action. The light aircraft were kept ready and serviced, to act as a means of escape for the government's key officials.

Yasser climbed into the small yellow Cessna, strapped himself in and fell asleep before the aircraft had even taken off. It was the first time for as long as he could remember that he didn't fall asleep afraid of waking up. The pain in his infected shoulder was subsiding more and more, as it was left alone, and allowed to heal. The horrors of his months of incarceration melted away and he slept like a baby.

Megdah flew the aircraft across the desert to an airfield north of the Red Sea resort of Taba. Officially a military airport, it is also the main tourist entry point for the northern part of the country. It consists of one single, purpose built, air conditioned building. The building was split into two sections, arrivals and departures. The runway had been reinforced to accommodate the huge commercial jets full of tourists that landed, bringing people from all over Europe.

Apart from the modern terminal building, the rest of the airfield resembled the one that they had just left. Small flat roofed buildings were dotted about. There was a larger hangar building, which had three yellow light aircraft parked inside it, a water tower, and a guardhouse for the soldiers who were stationed there. Abdul had considerable influence in the area, owning three of the larger hotels in the resort. He had wangled a landing permit for the yellow Cessna and had a car there to greet Megdah and his notorious passenger. A significant amount of money changed hands, and the guards turned a blind eye.

When they landed Megdah tried to wake Yasser, but he couldn't rouse him from his sleep. The driver of the car that had been sent to pick them up, helped Megdah to carry the weakened terrorist, and placed him flat out on the back seat of the car. Yasser slept all the way through the road journey until they reached the coast. The road from Taba airport, to the Red Sea, was cut through a winding, twisting valley, which snaked through towering granite mountains on its way to the shore. As the vehicle approached its destination the driver called Abdul on the car phone.

"We are nearly at the hotel Abdul," the driver said.

"How is our distinguished guest?"

"Asleep. Where do you want us to take him, the hotel?" the driver hadn't been given any specific instructions.

"No, take him to the staff quarters, the doctor is waiting there to see him. I will join you there the day after tomorrow," Abdul said.

"And how are Megdah and Melad, my loyal friends?" he asked.

"I am fine Abdul," Megdah answered, "but we had to leave Melad behind. We will need to send someone back to pick him up."

"Oh, why did you leave him behind?"

"Yasser didn't like him I'm afraid," Megdah explained.

"I see," Abdul said slowly, not really understanding but wary that Yasser could hear the hands free conversation.

"I will explain when you arrive," Megdah said.

"No, don't wait until then. Call me when you arrive at the hotel," Abdul answered concerned.

"I will, Maa As-salaam," Megdah said goodbye to his employer.

"They arrived at the gates of just one of Abdul's hotels. The gate was built to impress the tourists as they arrived. It was fifty feet high and eighty feet wide, rendered with smooth plaster, which had been painted a terracotta colour, almost salmon pink. There was a high archway cut through it, which was edged with marble coving, through which a nonstop convoy of coaches arrived and departed. In the centre of the archway was an ugly wooden hut, which had a steel barrier on either side of it. Three security guards checked vehicle authorisation in and out of the hotel complex. The driver and the security guards exchanged brief greetings and the barrier was raised allowing the vehicle to pass, containing the sleeping terrorist leader.

When Yasser finally awoke he felt completely disorientated. He was lying between crisp cotton sheets in a room that he didn't recognise. The room was bright and airy, its furniture was made from carved mahogany, and there was the gentle hum of an air-conditioning unit. He sat up and looked around the room, trying to familiarise himself with his surroundings. The wound on his shoulder had been cleaned and dressed, and it smelled of antiseptic. There was a clear tube attached to a drip, which was fixed into his hand. He didn't know what was in it, but it didn't concern him. He felt better than he had felt for as long as he could remember.

"Ahlan Wa Sahlan," Abdul welcomed Yasser back from his slumber. He stood up from the chair that he had been sat in and walked over to the bed.

"Shukraan," Yasser greeted Abdul and thanked him for his freedom. He raised his hand and Abdul squeezed it gently in greeting.

"How are you feeling?" Abdul asked.

"Better than I have felt for a long time," Yasser answered.

"The doctor has injected you with some antibiotics, your shoulder was infected," Abdul explained.

"Thank him for me. How long have I been asleep?"

"Two days. We were very lucky to get you out of the airfield Yasser," Abdul's tone became very morbid, as he emphasised the situation.

"I am grateful for your intervention Abdul, you are a true Mujahideen," Yasser stroked his ego.

"Yes Yasser, I appreciate your kind words, but we were truly lucky to get you from the airfield in time."

"You seem to be making a point that I'm not grasping Abdul," Yasser was becoming bored with the man's inane self-preening.

"Yesterday morning at sunrise the airfield was completely destroyed. There was an attack, which left nothing standing at all. We were truly lucky to get you out in time," Abdul laboured the point.

"So the Americans know that I'm no longer enjoying their hospitality. It is good that the airfield will never be used for rendition flights ever again. They have done us a favour Abdul," Yasser couldn't care less. If he had the hardware, he'd destroy the lot of them.

"That is true Yasser, and realise how you have suffered at their hands, but my friend Melad was still on the airbase when they destroyed," Abdul had gone all around the houses to get to the point. He thought that it was extremely ungrateful and disrespectful of Yasser to leave Melad behind, but he didn't want to offend him.

"Your friend Melad was a coward, and he is better off dead than living his life slithering around on his belly like a snake. We are fighting a war Abdul, I have no time for cowards, and no time for the friends of cowards," Yasser looked into Abdul's eyes and saw fear. He too was a coward, but a useful one for the time being.

"Of course, you're correct, he's a casualty of war, expendable, his death is of no consequence," Abdul waffled, trying to placate the psychopath.

Megdah had told him everything that had happened at the airfield. He had told Abdul that he had unleashed a beast.

"Good, then let's not waste any more time talking about him," Yasser took the drip from his hand and stood up, making Abdul even more nervous.

"You have woken up just in time Yasser Ahmed, we've put plans into action in your honour, Yasser Ahmed," Abdul rolled the name off his tongue as if he enjoyed saying it.

"I'm both rested and intrigued," Yasser said humouring him.

"Your students have been busy in your absence Yasser, a plan of extraordinary proportions has begun to gather pace as it unfolds," Abdul explained.

"What is the objective?" Yasser asked.

"The complete destruction of the Jewish state of Israel."

Chapter Fifty-Three

America

Director Ruth Jones was sitting in a padded leather chair, chewing the end of a pencil. She had been notified earlier that an aircraft was flying from the African continent, directly across the Atlantic, heading into American airspace, without the proper authorisation codes. America was in a state of heightened alert. Normally the threat would be dealt with by the military, but because terrorists were suspected, the intelligence agencies were in the driving seat.

"What type of aircraft is it again?" she asked confused.

"It is an Antonov-124, Russian made, and last registered with the Ukrainian air force. There is a sale registered from the Ukrainian air force to an Egyptian construction company two months ago," Japey answered.

"And it can fly across the Atlantic unnoticed?" she asked sarcastically.

"No director, we have noticed it. As soon as it was noticed, it was challenged for the proper requirements, which it has failed to disclose. It is definitely up to no good, and we need to deal with it as an unidentified enemy aircraft," Japey tried to keep his cool.

He really didn't like working for Ruth Jones. She was too abrupt, too analytical, and she had sussed him out far too quickly. It made him very uncomfortable, working for a woman, especially one as sharp as Ruth Jones. Japey was a raving homosexual, but he really didn't want everyone to know that he was. He was fully aware that the new director of operations had realised that he was a poof the first time she met him, and that worried him. Nothing had been said about his sexuality, but there was something in her eyes, something that mocked him. She was far too sharp for his liking.

"Where did they say that they were flying to?" she asked for clarification. Shooting down a civilian aircraft had certain protocols that needed to be followed.

"They reported that they were flying to Floyd Bennet field, to take part in the Adirondack hot air balloon festival," Japey clarified the airplanes supposed destination.

"Why is that not feasible?"

"Floyd Bennet Airfield is situated on Long Island. It was New York's first municipal airport, and it closed to aircraft in 1971 director. The balloon festival is held annually at the Floyd Bennet memorial airport, which is in Queensbury, Warren County. They are two completely different places, but easy to confuse, " he expanded.

"Someone hasn't done their homework then," the director said thoughtfully.

"Some bright spark at the Federal Aviation Authority only picked it up because the pilot reported his authorisation codes as lost. He is saying that they have been mislaid and that he doesn't have enough fuel to turn around and go back," Japey explained further.

"Have we tried to divert the aircraft?"

"Yes director, the pilot has refused to alter course," Japcy said.

"Bearing in mind that we are expecting an extremist attack against New York, we have to treat this aircraft as a suspected potential threat to American lives," Ruth said, thinking aloud.

"The Israelis suspect that an airborne device could weigh upwards of a ton. A cargo plane would be the ideal vehicle to deliver a dirty bomb across the Atlantic," Japey clasped his well-manicured hands together.

"Then we have no other option. I'm going to have to recommend to Washington, that we shoot it down, before it reaches New York airspace.

Aren't we keeping the air force busy this week?" Ruth Jones put the pencil on the desk calmly.

Chapter Fifty-Four

Holyhead

Ali Rasser twisted the throttle of the Honda Blackbird, propelling the bike over a hundred miles an hour. A row of three pubs known locally as the three sisters, the Dublin Packet, the Blossoms and the Holland Arms went passed in a blur of colour as the engine roared down the road. Ali Rasser blasted past the bus station, heading for the harbour. He didn't know what he was going to do when he got there, but it seemed like the only place to go. Ali had shot Boris McGuiness and his sons, and he didn't think that the British police would allow him to go home unpunished. They would try and shoot him, he was certain of that. If he could get to the Syrian ship then he may be able to hide somewhere beneath the decks. It wasn't much of a plan, but it was the only plan that he had.

The Task Force helicopter kept pace with the speeding Honda motorcycle as it headed toward the harbour. The motorcycle raced headlong through the town, past the cenotaph memorial and down Land's End. The Land's End road runs past the back of the high streets shops. The buildings are built on top of what was once a cliff face, and the road is built at what would have been sea level, a thousand years ago. The buildings are an ugly mishmash of old and new, rusting fire escapes snake down the scruffy facades, adding to the unsightly effect. On the right hand side of the road is a high sandstone wall, topped with razor wire, built to protect the railway lines on the other side of it. It was only a mile from the jetty.

The helicopter pilot flew over the speeding bike, and overtook it. The pilot manoeuvred the helicopter to a position five hundred yards in front of the Honda, placing it between the fugitive and the harbour. He slowed down the rotor blades, dropping altitude quickly and positioned the machine three feet from the road surface. The helicopter turned slowly as it hovered, completely blocking the road. There was a small crowd of men drinking outside the King's Head, shocked into silence by the alien aircraft hovering above the main harbour road outside their local pub. It was not a sight that you see every day. A Task Force sniper opened the sliding door of the silver helicopter. He twisted his body and lowered his legs out of the machine, standing on the skid, but still strapped in by a harness. He raised a powerful 7.62 millimetre M21 sniper rifle, which is favoured by American Special Forces, and pulled it snug into the shoulder. He placed his right eye against the telescopic lens and focused on the speeding Honda. He had less than a few seconds to take the shot. The sniper mentally drowned out the noise of the helicopter and squeezed the trigger.

Ali Rasser watched the sniper taking aim and slammed the rear brakes on. The back wheel of the motorbike snaked along the tarmac dangerously, almost unseating the rider. He leaned the bike to his left, as far over as the machine would go. The exhaust pipe scraped on the floor creating a shower of sparks as it banked to the left. The snipers bullet nicked a three-inch gash in the arm of his leather motorbike suit, but caused him no injuries. He pointed, more than steered the bike off the Land's End road, and roared up Boston Street away from the helicopter.

The helicopter pilot upped the revs and the machine gained height rapidly. They were too low to see where the motorcycle had gone. The machine flew up and over Boston Street, and the pilot sighted the racing bike speeding down Newry Street toward the harbour. Newry Street ran parallel to Land's End, but was lined on both sides by narrow terraced houses. The sniper remained outside the helicopter, perched on the skid. He had the rider in his sights but he couldn't take the shot in a built up residential area. The bike was travelling at such a high speed that if he killed the rider, it could catapult through someone's front door. From their elevated position, they could see where the road was leading to. Four hundred yards on, the road breaks free of the houses and opens onto a sloping grassy area, which runs the length of the marina. There was a main road running parallel to the seashore, which was perpendicular to the one that the motorbike was on. The sniper would have a ten-second window when the motorbike left the houses, before he hit the blind junction, and had to turn left or right. He waved toward the beach area and the pilot flew over the speeding motorbike, lowered the revs and brought the helicopter down to within a few yards of the grass, waiting for the bike to break the cover of the buildings. The sniper took aim.

Ali Rasser had seen the helicopter losing altitude, and realised that it would be waiting for him up ahead. He had seconds to choose which option he was going to pick. Stay on the motorbike and die, or ditch it and try to lose his pursuers. As he reached the end of the terraced housing, he noticed an alleyway to his left hand side. The bike was travelling too fast for him to steer. He made a split decision, and parted company with the Honda, at over sixty miles an hour. The brakes screamed, and rubber burned and squealed. Ali hit the grass at the side of the road and rolled across it, flipping like a rag doll. The bike slid down the road in a shower of sparks. Hard plastic faring shattered and splintered, as the Honda tumbled down the street. Ali shook himself when he finally came to a standstill. The protective armour plates in his leathers had worked well. He was still in one piece. He stood up and bolted for the alleyway.

The bike clattered to a halt against the kerb, and bounced into the snipers line of fire. He almost squeezed the trigger, such was his state of readiness, but quickly realised that the rider was nowhere to be seen. He signalled upward to the pilot, who increased the revolutions of the rotor blades, dust and debris blew across the marina, and the helicopter climbed steeply.

"Take us over those houses there," the sniper shouted over the noise of the rotor blades as the helicopter gained height.

The pilot nodded affirmative and the helicopter banked sharply to the left, leaving the sloped grassy areas behind them. Directly beneath them was a row of red-bricked Victorian terraced houses. The terrace was six houses long and each house was three storeys high. From the air, it was easy to see that the terrace was serviced at the rear by a narrow alleyway, designed for refuse collection and coal deliveries. The alleyway ran from the rear, along the side, and onto the main Newry Street, where the rider had been seen last.

"He must have taken that alleyway there," the pilot spoke into the coms unit, pointing to the back of the terraced houses.

"Roger that, take us over the alleyway and onto the road beyond," said the sniper, studying the area through his scope.

The helicopter circled the block several times, flying low over gardens, checking behind garages and wheelie bins. As they circled Ryan Griffin and his support team were arriving on the scene, having finally cleared the ferry terminal traffic and caught up with the action.

"What is the situation there?" control asked over the coms unit.

"This is airborne, we've lost him."

"Roger that, where was his last location?" Griffin asked. He was leaning out of the window of the BMW, craning his neck to see what the helicopter was looking at.

"He must have taken that alleyway to the side of the tall terraces, and that leads to the housing estate behind it," the pilot explained.

The pursuit vehicles screeched around the corner, and pulled to a stop. The helicopter was circling above covering a much wider search area than could be viewed from the ground. To the left was a four-storey brick house, detached from its neighbours, and surrounded by plush gardens. In the side garden was a single storey building which looked like a double garage that had been converted into a granny flat. The brickwork wasn't square, and it looked like it had been built on the cheap, probably by the 'Chuckle brothers'. It was enclosed in thick vegetation.

On the opposite side of the road was a long single storey building with a black slate tile roof. Once a jewel on the coastal road it was long since derelict. The building was painted beige over a rough stippled concrete render, now turning green as moss ravaged the crumbling facade. The tiles on the roof were hanging loose in some places and missing completely in others. It was built so that from the air it would have been a T-shape, one longer section perpendicular to a shorter one. There was an old wooden pub sign swinging from a rusted metal bracket, which identified the building as the Royal Naval Club. The holes in the roof and the boarded up windows gave it a neglected sad appearance.

"You take the house and gardens, and we'll take the old Navy Club," Ryan shouted to the Task Force men in the other car.

"Pilgrim six, cover us we're splitting up and searching on foot," he said into the coms to the airborne unit.

"Roger that pilgrim six, we're in a search pattern above you, heat sensors aren't showing anything from the garden area's we'll check the buildings as you enter, over," the pilot replied.

Ryan Griffin opened the boot of the BMW and took a Remington pump action shot gun from the weapons box. He cocked the slide-loading ratchet and pushed five heavy gauge shells into the breach. He clicked the shotgun again and pushed one into the pipe. He was now ready to knock an elephant over at a hundred yards. The Task Force team from the second car followed suit, one man armed with a pump action, and the others with Glock nine millimetres. Their cover blown, the Task Force men took battle vests from the weapons boxes and strapped them on. They checked their own equipment and then checked their colleague next to them.

The second team moved in formation toward the ramshackle granny flat at the rear of the big house. Ryan Griffin and the first team headed for the derelict public house. They moved down a short flight of stone steps, which dropped from the pavement onto the over grown car park. Tall thistles sprouted through the deteriorated tarmac. The front door was boarded over with a single sheet of chipboard, which was screwed to the doorframe and had been marked with the words keep out.

They hugged the mossy walls as they moved around the low building. They reached a window, which was also boarded up. Ryan tugged at the wood but it was screwed down tight to the frame. No one had gained access through there. He nodded his head and the unit moved on. They turned the corner of the building and the sea breeze hit them. The grassy areas which sloped gently down to the beach road, and the marina beyond, stretched out from the edge of the building's car park. Ryan looked at the dozens of white yachts that were moored symmetrically in the marina, swaying gently in the wind.

They reached a walled area at the end of the building. The wooden gate that once prevented unauthorised entry, was hanging from a single hinge. The planks were split and warped. The paint was badly cracked and peeling off in long strips. Ryan kneeled and pointed the Remington pump action into yard. There were old aluminium beer barrels upended amongst the weeds. The contents of half a dozen refuse bags were strewn across the concrete; milk cartons, fast food wrappers and broken bottles. He signalled silently for the unit to move into the yard, and the Task Force men overtook him silently.

Ryan entered the yard, his team were positioned either side of the rear doorway. The door had been boarded over with two pieces of chipboard, and the bottom section had been ripped away from the frame, allowing someone to gain access. He approached the chipboard and studied the screws that had fastened it to the doorframe. The heads were rusted and aged, but the threads were still shiny and new looking, having been protected from the elements by the wood.

"Pilgrim six, entering the building, we've evidence of a recent break in," Ryan whispered into the coms unit.

"Roger that pilgrim six, scanning the building now," the pilot moved the helicopter over the old building and looked at the thermal images on his screen. Three wobbly green blobs appeared, Griffin and his team in the rear yard, which was positioned at the end of the shorter section of the building. At the far end of the longer section of the building was another larger green image.

"Pilgrim six, the building is positive for occupancy, one reading at the far end of the elongated sector, to the right of your position."

"Roger that, moving in."

Ryan Griffin headed under the barricade followed closely by his unit. Inside the old social club smelled rank, although it had been years since people frequented it, the smell of cigarettes and stale ale still pervaded from the walls. There was also the unmistakable smell of stale urine. The walls and ceilings had been hacked to pieces, because scavengers had ripped out the electric copper wiring and water pipes to be sold as scrap. The floors were an obstacle course of bricks and debris. The unit tiptoed through the rubbish silently. The only sounds in the building were a dripping tap, which echoed through the dank walls, and the muffled helicopter engine.

As they progressed, their eyes became adjusted to the gloom, and they became accustomed to the choking stench. The elongated section of the building was in fact the old barroom. The remains of the bar were still standing, but the mirrors and fixtures had been ripped from the walls a long time ago. A ceiling fan hung precariously lopsided from a thin electric flex, one of the blades snapped in half. It was swinging almost imperceptibly, as if it had been nudged gently sometime ago. The unit fanned out and headed toward a doorway at the far end of the room. There was a shuffling noise from beyond the open doorway, which made the Task Force unit freeze, weapons raised. The darkness beyond was impossible to penetrate.

"Come out with your hands up," Ryan shouted into the gloom.

"Don't shoot, or I will kill this man," came the reply in broken English.

"No one needs to die here today, as long as you throw your weapon out, and then come out with your hands raised," the Task Force man replied.

"I want to talk to your senior officer, I have a hostage," Ali answered, his voice shaking with fear.

"I'm the senior officer," Ryan answered.

"I'm coming out," Ali spluttered. A bulky shadow appeared in the gloom beyond the doorframe. It was difficult to distinguish the form, but it appeared to be more than one person.

"Come out and show yourself, drop the weapon."

Ali shuffled toward the doorway. He had the ugly silver Bulldog revolver, which he'd used to shoot Boris McGuiness and his sons with in his right hand. In his left arm was a tramp, being held tight by the throat in the crook of his elbow. The huge fat revolver was pressed against the tramps head, deep into the matted tangled hair.

"I'll kill him," Ali snarled in a threatening voice.

"This is your last chance, drop the weapon," Ryan swiped his fingers across the side of his neck in a slashing motion. The team understood the silent signal, and move a few yards closer, trying to get a better shot.

Ali pulled the tramp closer to him, trying to hide behind the dishevelled bundle of rags and bone, but he'd hesitated a second too long. The Task Force men opened fire in unison blasting the terrorist and his smelly hostage into oblivion. The terrorist's body was disposed of secretly. There was nothing to be gained from parading his demise except more public unrest. As for the other fatality, no one even knew the vagrants name as he was incinerated in an undisclosed crematorium. If he had been given a headstone, it would have said, 'collateral damage'.

Chapter Fifty-Five

Sabah / Charter flight 14-8

Sabah took a long gulp of cold water from a stainless steel flask. He swallowed the cool refreshing liquid, and the aftertaste of plastic thermos container clung to the back of his throat. He wiped the sweat from his brow with a handkerchief, and drank some more. There was less than a mouthful of water left, so he poured it onto his handkerchief and cooled his brow with it. It was becoming increasingly more difficult to tolerate the stink coming from his dead co-pilot.

The co-pilot's body had rid itself of all the waste products that were stored in the bladder and lower intestine. The putrid smell of human excrement mixed with the sour smell of stale sweat, which was already pervading from the co-pilot before he died. Sabah couldn't stand it any longer. He switched the Antonov-124 onto autopilot, and shuffled over to the co-pilot's seat. Despite the overall size of the cargo plane, the cockpit area is relatively cramped. It wasn't designed for dragging dead bodies around.

He grabbed the fat man beneath the arms and tried to lift him from the chair, but he was a dead weight. Sabah heaved again and the body lifted slightly but wouldn't budge from its seat. He couldn't understand why he was so immovable. Sabah leaned over the body, holding his breath to avoid the smell of faeces and urine. He swore aloud when he realised that the fat co-pilot was still fastened in his seat by his safety belt. He unfastened the clasp at the front of the body, recoiling when his hands touched wet soiled patches of material. This time the body moved from the seat with one fluid movement. He dragged the corpse off the chair, through the cabin door, into the rear cargo. Sabah paused to catch his breath, tired from the excursion of moving the fat co-pilot. He reached for the damp handkerchief and wiped sweat from his forehead again. The hold was empty, bar the aluminium wrapped crate. Sabah heaved the body from the floor and dropped it by the three-ton radioactive device.

Sabah heard the radio cackling from the cockpit. Air traffic control hadn't communicated with him for over an hour. They'd tried to divert him from his flight path several times, offering a series of alternative landing sites outside of American airspace, where he could have landed and refuelled while the correct authorisation codes were acquired. Sabah had bluffed most of the suggestions away and he'd pretended that his understanding of English wasn't great. They had stalled and accepted all his excuses until he'd reached the position of no return. Sabah tried everything.

The co-pilot had taken ill. The authorisation codes had been mislaid, or forgotten at the airport. The balloon festival organisation hadn't forwarded the correct information in the first place. Both the pilot and co-pilot were agency staff, and were not aware that the codes had been forgotten by the other. Every time he offered another inane excuse, the airplane flew a hundred miles closer to the American continent.

Every single weak excuse that Sabah had invented had done nothing to appease air traffic control. The more he stalled, the more concerned the aviation authorities became. Their requests that the plane divert became demands. They were now convinced that the Atropov-124 was on a bogus flight.

There were hundreds of bogus flights every year, trafficking drugs, arms or illegal immigrants into American airspace. The federal air controllers couldn't possibly intercept them all. Sabah knew his excuses would not be accepted in the long term, but it had allowed the airplane to fly closer to its target. The Americans had extended every single alternative to the pilot, but to no avail. They now had no options left open to them. Since the attacks of 9/11, the responsibility for the defence of the continental United States lies with the newly formed Northern Command. They are responsible for the protection of America, Canada, Alaska, the Caribbean and northern Mexico. Any vessel, airborne or otherwise, entering a five hundred mile exclusion zone, without proper authorisation is treated as a lethal threat.

Sabah heard static crackle coming from the cockpit radio again, but it was not direct communication; it was more like interference. It sounded like there was some other communication taking place close to the aircraft, but on a different wavelength. His heart missed a beat when he noticed movement outside the cargo hold's windows. A huge dark shadow blocked the sunlight coming through the starboard windows. The airplane was flying at over thirty thousand feet, and he wasn't expecting any company so soon. He ran to the starboard window and peered through. There were two F-16 Fighting Falcon jet fighters, flying in close formation less than one hundred yards from his starboard wing. The dark grey coloured jets were a terrifying sight. The missile racks beneath the wings were loaded with, air-to-air, sidewinder missiles.

Sabah ran to the cockpit and climbed into the pilot seat. Although it was pointless, he fastened his seatbelt. Somehow, it gave him comfort. He looked through the side windows and stared at the two powerful, grey jet fighters. This was the end of the road as far as the attack on New York was concerned. He was still over five hundred miles from the target.

Sabah wondered if he could get the cargo plane diverted onto somewhere else, under escort, and blow the plane up anyway. He had never really expected to reach American airspace without a serious challenge, but he had expected to be allowed to land at Floyd Bennet airfield under escort. That would have allowed him to enter New York's airspace and complete his mission, but it now seemed that the Americans were not going to be so accommodating. If he accepted a set of new coordinates, he could still explode the device over a built up area. Wherever it was that was contaminated, it would make headline news and highlight the Islamic struggle. He decided to try.

"This is charter flight 14-8, requesting that the escort take me to an alternative landing strip, I have American jets escorting the aircraft," Sabah looked at the jets, but they had gone. They were nowhere to be seen.

"American control this is charter flight 14-8, I must remind you that we are a civilian aircraft, and request an alternative set of coordinates," Sabah craned his neck trying to see where the jets had gone.

"American control, can you read me? This is charter flight 14-8, can you read me?" Sabah climbed over the seat to look out the other side, but again there was no sign of the F-16s. They had either gone, or were directly behind him. The radio crackled but air traffic control ignored his requests. He ran into the cargo hold, peering through the port side windows, but there was no sign of the warplanes. They were gone. Sabah ran back into the cockpit, and grabbed the microphone. He was starting to panic, but he couldn't understand why. The mission was always going to end in a violent death, but it would be at his own bequest, not someone else's. This scenario was far more frightening. He didn't even know where the jet fighters had gone.

"American control, this is charter flight 14-8 requesting emergency coordinates, are you receiving me?"

"Mayday, mayday, this charter flight 14-8 requesting immediate communication, is anybody receiving me?" Sabah twisted in his seat to look behind the aircraft. There was nothing there. The radio crackled again, distant voices ghosting across another channel close by.

"Control, there is a misunderstanding, flight 14-8 is requesting an alternative landing destination," Sabah found the silence deafening. He couldn't understand why they were ignoring him.

He was still thinking about what to do next, when six sidewinder missiles blew the Antonov-124 into pieces of metal confetti. Larger pieces of burning aircraft tumbled through the clouds. The F-16s fired heat seeking air-to-air missiles, blasting the bigger sections into smaller pieces of debris. The Russian Antonov-124 and its radioactive cargo drifted down to the Atlantic Ocean. To all intents and purposes, it might never have existed at all.

Chapter Fifty-Six

The Terrorist Task Force

Tank and the Task Force senior officers, Chen and David Bell, left the bunker headquarters and climbed into an unoccupied military vehicle, which was parked in the huge sandstone tunnel. Chen jumped into the driver's seat, started the engine and waited for the fat controller to climb into the back, before engaging first gear and heading the armoured Jeep down the rock channel. They were leaving the politicians to talk politics, and headed back to the office on the top floor of the Canning Place police headquarters. They needed to plan the Task Force's response to the day's events, and summarise the cleanup operations, which had been searching for the remaining insurgents.

"There have never been any terrorist training camps in the Sinai Desert," the fat controller said, thumping the back of the passenger seat with his podgy hand. He was frustrated by the American's arrogance. They had unilaterally bombed an uninspected facility. The international protocol was clear, suspect facilities had to be inspected by the core members of the Security Council, before any military action could be taken. He shook his head and made a noise with his lips at the same time, sounding like a horse snorting.

"I would state my reputation on it. Mubarak is far too deep into Bush's pocket to annoy the Americans, that aside, when have the Egyptians allowed extremist camps on their lands?"

"Not to our knowledge," Chen agreed.

"Mubarak has been fighting the extremists himself since they bombed his predecessor President Sadat, and then there's the suicide bomb attacks on Western tourists in Sharm el Sheikh and Hurgada, he wouldn't allow them to operate in Egypt, not anywhere," Tank added.

"So why would the Director of the CIA, stick her neck out if there was no camp?" the fat controller asked. He was leaning his head in between the two front seats like a fat child annoying its parents on a long journey.

"Well, we have to accept that they attacked and destroyed something in the Sinai Peninsula. What we need to do is work out what they blew up, and why," Tank said.

"Do you think it was sabre rattling maybe, a live military exercise to scare the Iranians?" Bell asked aloud.

"There is no way it was a terrorist training camp. Our satellites would have picked up that kind of activity immediately," Chen insisted.

"What else could it be, an airstrip?" the fat controller speculated.

"It is the most likely answer. The Sinai is dotted with small remote airfields. The Egyptians have been paranoid about an Israeli air attack since the airstrike in 1968," Tank explained.

"Exactly and why would anyone attack an airfield in the northern deserts? There is absolutely nothing there of any military value. Those airstrips are only big enough for light aircraft and helicopters," Chen mulled over the conundrum.

The Americans had to own up to the attack, but the details they had released were little short of useless. They hadn't gone to the extreme of excusing it as a mistake or military exercise. It would have triggered an international outrage to deny that it was anything but a premeditated military attack. The war on terror could be used as a trump card for a myriad of evils.

"Unless the airfield was being used for something that the Americans uncovered, and decided that they didn't like what was going on," Tank thought aloud.

"Arms smuggling, drugs, I mean we could speculate forever," Chen answered.

"Rendition," the fat controller said, raising his voice unnecessarily.

"What in the Sinai?"

"Yes in the Sinai. We received information from our men in Cairo a while back, that there were rumours about rendition flights being allowed into Egypt," the fat controller was remembering a memo from months ago.

"There were suggestions that President Mubarak was allowing the Americans to use remote airfields, via third part allies, for extraordinary rendition flights."

"Okay, if we assume that the information was correct, then why would the Americans bomb a site that they were utilising?" Chen asked.

"Maybe something went wrong," the fat controller speculated.

"What if someone of political value was being held there, maybe a double cross or an argument over jurisdiction?" Chen mused.

"Or maybe they're trying to cover something up, using the cover of a supposed terror training camp as a smoke screen," Tank caught on with the theory.

It made perfect sense. Something had gone wrong in the deserts of northern Sinai. Something had happened that was so bad, that the Americans would risk international outrage to cover it up. Tank was going to make a point of finding out exactly what it was.

Chapter Fifty-Seven

Jerusalem

The old city of Jerusalem is situated inside ancient walls, which have been built and then destroyed, by both Christian and Muslim armies on numerous occasions. Outside the walls, the city has become a mishmash of modern and traditional townships, some of which are sectioned from the others by huge ugly security walls that snake along the valleys and hillsides. The old city inside the walls is dissected by a spider's web of narrow higgledy-piggeldy lanes. It's possible to touch the buildings on both sides of the street, at the same time in some parts of the old town. At the centre of the city is the Temple Mount. Its importance to the Jewish and Muslim faiths makes it the most contested religious site in the world.

The Temple Mount itself is a huge stone platform built over a hill. It looks like an Egyptian pyramid with the top half cut off. Built on top of the remains of Solomon's Temple, is the much-revered mosque, known as the Dome of the Rock, its immense golden dome is visible from miles around. Islamic scriptures tell that this rock is the point from which the great prophet Muhammad ascended to heaven, to receive instruction from Allah. The walls of The Mount are the remains of the original temple, and are the epicentre of the Jewish faith, the Wailing Wall.

Beneath the rock is a natural cave known as the Well of Souls. It was originally only accessible from a small hole in the rock itself. The Knights of the Templar hacked open an entrance from the south of the mount, looking for the Holy Grail, which can still be entered today. It was into this manmade fissure that Rahid Bindhi climbed under the cover of darkness. The ancient city's alleyways were starting to quieten down, as tourists and pilgrims drifted back to their hotels, most of which were situated outside the walls in the new city. Getting to the cave unchallenged had been relatively easy.

Beneath the lower platform of the Temple Mount is a series of enormous underground chambers. Some are built in the space between the bedrock and the temple floor, while others are cavernous manmade structures, ranging in historical age. The huge underground chambers were once built by craftsmen as temple sectors, dedicated to various tranches of worship, and are now used as cisterns holding the city's water supply. The biggest chamber known a cistern eleven holds seven hundred thousand gallons of water. It is built from the rock and is carved into the shape of a huge letter E, with beautiful pillars and ornately carved columns running all through it. Many believe it was built as part of the second temple, others believe it was once a mosque. For now, it was used as a big reservoir for the city's water and the hiding place for a two-ton dirty bomb, which had been built over a period of months by Rahid Bindhi and his affiliates.

The entrances to the old city were all protected by metal detecting scanners, trying to prevent suicide bombers from reaching the most sacred parts of Jerusalem. Inside the ancient walls is crammed full of Israeli soldiers and part time reservists. Every other person carries an M14 machinegun over their shoulder. Checkpoints are manned round the clock looking for Islamic insurgents. Despite Israel's best efforts, access to the city could be gained, using local geographic knowledge and a little help from a few determined friends. Rahid and his cohorts had painstakingly carried bundles of plastic explosives everyday to the base of the Temple Mount, and entered the series of cisterns, which led from the Well of Souls.

Two of his colleagues had become sick carrying the radioactive materials, which had been hidden inside plumber's toolboxes. The city employed an army of plumbers to combat the ancient leaking water supply system, which was constantly springing new seepages. Jerusalem is built in a desert, and the water supply is the city's life blood, therefore it's maintenance and the upkeep are given top priority. Rahid and his affiliates never looked out of place, as there were local workmen coming and going all the time. Once all the components of the device were assembled, they worked night and day to make it functional, and the device had been completed a week ago.

Rahid had been born in the old city, the eldest son of a Muslim butcher. The city was then in Muslim hands, controlled by the state of Jordan. The Palestinian people were still the indigenous race. Jewish immigrants had started to arrive in Israel since the early nineteen thirties, and integration between Muslims and Jews was slow and difficult. Immigration became a tidal wave following the horrors of the Holocaust, during the Second World War. Rahid senior found his Muslim customers were being ousted from their homes, by the considerably richer Jewish families that were arriving in the city. Trade became a daily struggle as the demand for his meat dwindled, and the kosher butchers prospered. Eventually after many years of struggling financially, his family sold their house at a rock bottom price to a Jewish family from Poland, and the last Muslim family in the street moved outside the walls into the West Bank.

In 1967, during the Arab Israeli conflict, the Jews recaptured Jerusalem, and declared it the capital city of the new state of Israel. The only country in the world that recognises Jerusalem as the Jewish capital is Israel itself, everyone else classes their capital city as Tel Aviv. International opinion is that Jerusalem is of such religious significance, that to recognise it as the Jewish capital would provoke its Arab neighbours to reclaim her. That could only be achieved by all out war.

The terrorist group Ishmael's Axe were the willing vehicle for Abdul's plan to wreak havoc across the West with radioactive dispersal devices. The piece de la resistance however was to detonate one of them next to the Wailing Wall, contaminating the site and poisoning the city's water supply for decades. Jerusalem would become a radioactive wasteland, but it would no longer be under the control of the Jews. It would remain almost intact until the time when the armies of Islam were mighty enough to defeat the Christian Zionist invaders. Jerusalem was the jewel of the Middle East, but It had been stolen from the peoples of Islam, and Rahid was about to redress the balance.

Chapter Fifty-Eight

New York

Agent Japey had been with the CIA since graduating from university as a law major. He wanted a job where he could apply his considerable legal skills, and be exciting to his peers at the same time. He considered the military but ruled it out because of the discrimination shown to homosexuals that were out of the closet. He applied for the agency and that gifted him an aura of mystery, a secret agent, with a secret. It was the ideal career for a closet homosexual, who was ashamed of his sexuality.

Japey thought he could fit in with the heterosexual boys in the bar any day of the week. He could tell raunchy jokes, swear about the football game; even berate other openly gay men by calling them queers. He could act brash and macho as well as the next guy, or that`s what he thought. The reality was much different, as most of his colleagues had guessed that he was gay a long time ago. They often took bets on how many times they could get an offensive gay label into a conversation, without Japey realising. One of the agents got the word, 'fruit', in a story eight times once, while another made his first part time job in a laundry, as a 'shirt lifter', the topic of conversation every time the opportunity arose.

There was a spurious rumour about his sexuality once, started by a younger agent who had spurned his advances. Japey had misread the signals and ended up embarrassed and humiliated. Once the rumours found their way back to Japey, he fired the agent for a trumped up misdemeanour the following week, killing the rumour in its tracks. The only person who had seen right through his facade immediately was the new director of operations, Ruth Jones. She was sharp, but he thought that he was sharper.

The shooting down of the ex-Ukrainian cargo plane containing a potential dirty bomb attack, should have been used as a massive propaganda weapon. Billions of pounds of taxpayer's money could have directed into the intelligence agencies coffers to aid the continuing war on terror. It was a blinding opportunity for media manipulation. The Whitehouse could have claimed it was another reason why the war on terror was so vital to the nations well being, indeed its survival.

If he'd been the agency's director, he would have plastered it over every front page in the nation. A foiled Muslim extremist plot of that magnitude was an opportunity gone begging. He couldn't believe that the stupid woman running the department had pulled a complete media blackout over the whole thing.

Apart from senior members of the Northern Command, and the President's office, nobody was even aware of any incident or potential threat to the country's biggest city. Ruth Jones had insisted that going public with the incident would strike fear into the hearts of an already nervous American population. Islamaphobia would reach unprecedented levels, damaging the fragile relationships between America's indigenous people, and their peaceful Muslim neighbours. Japey thought that the Whitehouse would overrule the director, and that the media machine behind the President would shift into overdrive.

Unfortunately, the complete opposite happened and every agent involved in the potential attack had been sworn to secrecy. Every message between charter flight 14-8 and air traffic control had been erased. Even the records of the airplane's transponder being tracked by satellites had been wiped. The navy had swept the crash site to ensure that there was no tell tale debris floating on the Atlantic Ocean, but there was really no need. The F-16s had done a comprehensive job. There was simply no proof that anything had happened. The opportunity to get his face in front of the cameras had been ripped from him by that self-righteous bitch of a boss. To top it all she had transferred him out of the main office, which was the final straw.

There had been plenty of news coverage about the terrorist incidents in the United Kingdom. Images of the burnt out restaurant at the top of the giant St. John's Tower had been broadcast around the globe. It was headline news the world over, the smoking tower a poignant symbol of the religious war that was raging across the planet. The details of the attacks on high-level personnel from the intelligence agencies had been squashed, just like the rogue aircraft incident.

Scenes of hundreds of Iranians celebrating the attacks by burning the Union Jack, and the Stars and Stripes in the streets were being screened every time there was a commercial break on the news networks across America. The line in the sand between conservative Muslims, and their extremist relatives was being blurred by media frenzy, which was exactly what Ruth Jones wanted to avoid. They had to ride the wave of the British story, and then professionally manage the media aftermath, in order to placate the nervous American public.

Agent Japey had been sent to New York's field office on the premise that Ruth Jones needed him to quell any rumours of an imminent Islamic attack on the city. The truth was she wanted him out of the main office, because he was a liability, and because he had lied to her once too often. Japey knew that was why he'd been transferred, and Ruth Jones knew that he knew, and frankly, she didn't give a toss.

Japey wasn't going to just lie down and allow his precious career to be brushed under the carpet along with the shooting down of the airplane. The news from Britain was the perfect precursor to a terrorist incident in America, if only his superiors had grasped the opportunity. Everyone involved in the incident could have benefited from the publicity exposure that it would have attracted, but they had chosen to listen to that woman instead. He had an idea that would put the agency and its relentless battle against extremism firmly in the spotlight where it truly belonged. He was sat on a tall stool at the bar when his cell phone rang.

The bar was a seedy pick up joint for gays. The colour scheme had been chosen by someone of the more artistically camp fraternity. There was a certain stereotype running through the whole venue, pink, pink and pinker. It was the type of bar that Japey could never be found in by any of his heterosexual colleagues. If his tough butch colleagues at the agency could see him drinking beer in this joint, he could never look them in the eye again.

He twisted on his stool so that he could answer his cell, and turn away from the guy he'd been chatting up simultaneously, hopefully without offending him. He put one foot down on the sticky carpet, which was so discoloured by chewing gum and stale beer that it was difficult to spot a pink piece any more.

"Have you found anyone that fits the bill?" Japey asked, taking a deep slug on his bottle of Sol, it had a girly slice of lime wedged into the neck.

"I've done better than that, I've got two possible targets, and they share an apartment in Queens," the agent on the phone answered.

"What is their background?"

"You're going to love this. They are both currently under observation by the feds, because they worship at a mosque that's on our radar. One of the guys is related to an inmate being held at camp X-ray, Guantanamo Bay. He was arrested for travelling through Kabul, allegedly trying to fight with the Taliban," the agent was excited.

"Have these guys been fingered for anything yet?" Japey asked. He needed someone under suspicion, but not so hot that they were being watched night and day.

"Hey big guy, do you want another beer?" the man that Japey had been chatting up nudged him. He placed his hand on Japey's buttock and allowed it to linger just a little too long.

"I'm talking on the phone," Japey snarled at the man, pushing his hand away. The man shook his head like an offended drag queen and walked away to talk to some other guy.

"Who was that?" said the agent on the other end of the phone.

"No one, answer the question. Have they been fingered for anything, are they under surveillance?" Japey snapped back, batting the question away, annoyed that the chat up line had been heard by one of his agents.

"I just heard someone call you, big guy, but not in big guy kind of way," the agent joked.

"What the fuck are you inferring?" Japey snarled again aggressively, his stomach turned at the thought of his secret being discovered.

"Nothing, don't throw your dummy out of the pram, they're clean for now, no tails, no surveillance just like you asked me for," the agent said offended. All joviality had gone from his voice.

"Good, well done, I didn't mean to snap, it's been a long day," Japey apologised. He had protested a little too much, he thought.

"No problem, I was just joking that's all," the agent still sounded offended. He pouted and blew an imaginary kiss to his partner who was sat next to him in his unmarked agency car. The other agent giggled silently, his hand over his mouth so that Japey couldn't hear him in the background.

"Good, there is no offence taken on my part. I want them snatched tonight," Japey ordered, gaining control of his faculties again.

"Tonight, what's the rush? I'm not sure that we can set this up for tonight," the agent back peddled.

"I thought you said that your team was up for this gig," Japey tried to sound hip, but just sounded even more camp.

"Err; we are up for this, gig, as you put it. We need to stake these guys out first and make sure that we can pull it off without any hiccups," the agent tried to reign Japey in.

"Stake them out them, but I want them snatched tonight, absolutely no excuses," Japey said abruptly.

"Okay, you're the boss," the agent said resignedly.

"Yes I am, call me when it's done," Japey hung up and looked around the bar for someone who looked quick and easy. He had some pent up tension to get rid of.

Chapter Fifty-Nine

Yasser

Yasser looked down at the walled holy city of Jerusalem, from the top of the Mount of Olives. According to the scriptures, The Mount is the last place that Jesus was ever seen. At the foot of The Mount is the Garden of Gethsemane, where Jesus was betrayed by Judas Iscariot to the Roman centurions. The view across the valley into the city is breathtaking, one of the most historic views anywhere in the world. The beautiful domes and spires of dozens of mosques and churches dominate the skyline.

The slopes of The Mount are also the site of one of the biggest cemeteries in the Middle East. The scriptures say that when the dead rise and come back to life, that they shall rise from the Mount of Olives. Millions of Jewish people are buried on the slopes because of this prophecy. The graves are all topped with white stone slabs, carved with Hebrew prayers, and then piled high with smaller stones and pebbles. The smaller stones are placed by family members when they visit the grave, a gesture of their sorrow. Thousands upon thousands of white stone slabs are dotted across the sloping mount as far as the eye can see, from the top of the hill, all the way down to the valley below. During Jordanian rule, thousands of the graves were desecrated by the Muslims. Many of the graves have been smashed and desecrated, scattering the white stone over the hillside. Yasser took great comfort in looking at so many Jewish gravestones.

Across the steep valley were the thick walls of Jerusalem. The elevation from the Mount of Olives allowed Yasser to look over the ancient walls, at eye level with the huge golden dome, which topped the mosque called, the Dome of the Rock. In the background was the steeple of the Church of the Sepulchre, which encompassed the site where Jesus was crucified. Yasser stared at the giant flat stone platform, which topped the Temple Mount, and envisaged the network of caves and manmade chambers beneath it. He breathed deeply, and the hot dry dusty air filled his lungs.

It felt good to be alive, good to be free again, and good to kill Christians and Jews.

Abdul was standing one hundred yards away on a viewing platform further up the hill, surrounded by tourists. He was admiring his handiwork through binoculars from a distance that he felt comfortable with. He was also enjoying the distance between him and Yasser. Yasser was making him very nervous; in fact, he was scaring the life out of him. The man was a complete lunatic, ice cold inside, and completely focused on causing death and destruction. Although it was Abdul that had sponsored the plan, he had never anticipated being so close to the actual mechanics of the operation.

The gratitude that Yasser had shown for being freed by Abdul and his men was brief and abrupt, almost as if he felt it was their duty to do so. Abdul was getting the impression that Yasser didn't like him, and that frightened him. He sometimes felt that Yasser thrived on his fear, as if he could see it in his eyes. Abdul turned the binoculars toward Yasser to see what he was doing. He scanned the gravestones back and forth, left and right, but couldn't see him anywhere.

Abdul was almost relieved when he realised that Yasser had gone, he had disappeared. It seemed too good to be true. Abdul had regretted freeing the terrorist leader within hours of meeting him. He wasn't the benevolent father of the Islamic struggle that the myths and legends made him out to be. Abdul had pictured him as a chivalrous warrior fighting for the cause of the down trodden, poverty stricken Muslims everywhere. Instead, he had unleashed the beast.

Abdul stepped between two sections of a low wall, which allowed entry into the humongous graveyard that covered the entire hillside. He scanned the slopes again looking for Yasser, but to no avail. His hopes began to rise, could it really be this easy to get rid of the psychopath that he had unwittingly aligned himself with. He picked his way carefully through the shattered gravestones, which were strewn across the grassy slopes, causing trip hazards every way he turned. Abdul stumbled and bashed his toes against a chunk of stone. His open sandals offered him no protection. He leaned against a head stone and held his injured foot in the other hand, while cursing in Arabic. The toenail on his second toe had been torn away at the edge, and it throbbed painfully, blood seeped slowly from the small tear.

Abdul sat on the rectangular stone slab to catch his breath. The sun was blazing down and he was beginning to feel its effects. Sweat ran from his forehead into his eyes, blurring his vision. He wiped his eyes and looked back up the slope toward the tourists on the viewing platform. He had stumbled a few hundred yards down the hill from where he had been watching Yasser. Abdul lifted the binoculars and scanned three hundred and sixty five degrees. There was nothing but graves to be seen for miles. He dropped the glasses into his lap and swore again at his swollen toe. He crossed his legs to make it easier to inspect the offending injury. The nail was blackening already, and blood was congealing between his toes.

"It is good that you are bleeding on Jewish graves Abdul," Yasser appeared close to his right hand side, making him jump.

"Yasser," he gasped holding his heart in a gesture of fright. "I thought that you had gone."

"No Abdul, you only wished that I had gone," Yasser stepped in front of Abdul and stared into his eyes. Abdul felt as if Yasser was looking for the truth deep in his soul, his eyes drilling into his deepest thoughts.

"Not at all, I was worried that you had gone," Abdul wiped sweat from his eyes again and tried to look offended by Yasser's remarks.

"You are a liar Abdul, and a hypocrite," Yasser broke his stare and looked across the valley into Jerusalem. The massive golden dome was shimmering in the heat haze. The minaret seemed to be melting in the scorching sun. He watched a section of bedrock below the Temple Mount and saw a tiny figure in the distance appear from a rent in the shadow of the huge structure. He knew where the entrance to the ancient chambers was.

"I do not understand why you berate me so much. I was your benefactor, and I gave you your freedom," Abdul blustered, trying to gain a modicum of respect from Yasser.

"How dare you, assume to hold power over me Abdul?" Yasser span toward him in a whirl. He leaned his face close to Abdul. His lips were curled into a snarl.

"I don't try to wield power over you my Caliph, but I demand your respect. I gave you your freedom," Abdul leaned back away from Yasser, and broke his gaze. He wiped sweat from his brow again, fear was adding to the heat perspiration.

"You dare to give me my own freedom! My freedom was not yours to give to me or anyone else, because my freedom is my own. It can only be stolen."

"You are twisting my words, I deserve your respect."

"You can only dream of earning my respect Abdul. You are a rich selfish pig, sitting in your hotels, playing golf, whilst your brothers beg for money for food and water from Christian tourists," Yasser spoke very calmly.

"I create jobs and provide money for hundreds of Muslim families, and I donate thousands to your cause," Abdul stood up, and placed his hands on his hips belligerently. He was fiercely proud of his self-made status.

"Listen to yourself Abdul. You give me my freedom, and you have created, and you donate thousands, you're almost divine Abdul. We should all pay homage to all mighty one, Abdul," Yasser bowed deeply and swept his arm across in body in a dramatic fashion, but all the while, he never took his stare from Abdul.

"I will not be insulted by you any longer. I have given you your freedom, and now I will leave you to your own devices. I bid you farewell Yasser Ahmed," Abdul turned and walked away.

He picked his way carefully through the rock-strewn grass. Abdul had only taken a few tentative steps when the first crushing blow fractured the back of his skull. Yasser held a triangular chunk of gravestone in his fist, and he didn't stop smashing it into Abdul's head until it had been turned into an unrecognisable bloody mush.

Chapter Sixty

Queen's district, New York

Agent Japey approached an unmarked dark Crown Vic, which was the United States law enforcement agencies vehicle of choice. There were two men sat in the front of the vehicle smoking cigarettes. One of the men was going bald, but he was masking it by sweeping his hair from above his ears, over the top in wispy strands. Japey detested him. He had greasy skin, which was covered in deep blackheads, and his cheeks were pockmarked by years of acne. Japey hadn't had many dealing with him, but he remembered his name was Dewi. His unkempt appearance and bad personal hygiene disgusted Japey. He always smelled of sweat and stale cigarettes.

The second agent was the man that he had spoken to earlier on the telephone. His name was Anthony. Anthony was in his early forties, but looked younger. He kept his receding hair cropped close to his scalp, and he sported a Freddie Mercury moustache, which blended into designer stubble on his face and neck. Both agents were wearing loose black suits over open necked white shirts. Anthony's collar was clean, whereas Dewi's had a dark sweaty rim that was four days old.

Japey hesitated before he opened the rear passenger door to look up and down the street cautiously. The street was flanked on each side by five storey tenement buildings. Brick steps with low balustrades led to every rundown apartment's scruffy front doorway. Bags of refuse were piled at the foot of every set of steps, many of them had been rifled by local stray dogs and cats, scattering litter along the sidewalks. The area was bedsit land, and home to the poorest of the poor. Drug addicts and alcoholics, prostitutes and illegal immigrants made up the bulk of the street's inhabitants. Japey was interested in two illegal immigrants in particular. He climbed into the smoke filled vehicle, and waved his hand in front of his face fanning the stale air for dramatic effect.

"Can't you guys open a window or something?" he said as he closed the door.

"No way, the smoke would attract too much attention," Dewi replied sarcastically without even turning round to look at him.

"Very funny, I can tell that you're a very funny guy. Maybe you could tell your jokes down at the employment exchange. They could get you a job on stage somewhere," Japey slapped the headrest jerking the agent's head forward. Dewi turned in his seat and glared at Japey. He hated faggots, and this guy was a first class faggot, and everyone knew it.

"Can we get a grip please ladies?" Anthony said. "The two targets are safely tucked up in bed, no telephone lines and no mobile phones registered to their apartment."

"Do we have a snatch squad arranged?" Japey asked ignoring the glares from Dewi.

"Two good agents in the panel van parked one hundred yards down the street, on our left hand side," Anthony pointed through the windscreen.

"And you have explained the need for complete secrecy to them I assume?"

"They only know the location, and that we are snatching two terrorist suspects. Once we have them they don't need to know anymore than that," Anthony answered without looking back.

"Good, and what time are set to go?" Japey looked at his watch. There was a black curly pubic hair stuck in between two of the stainless steel links in his watchstrap, evidence of a sordid encounter earlier in the toilets of the pink pickup joint. He flushed red, plucked it from the watch quickly, and flicked it on the carpet. As he looked up the two agents in the front were staring at him. They looked at the watch, and then him, and then each other. Dewi smirked and turned away.

"We are set to go in fifteen minutes," Anthony answered, chuckling to himself.

"Right, good, and have we got access to the building down town?" Japey had flushed crimson, but he straightened his tie and composed himself. He was just being paranoid. No one could know that he was gay, could they?

"Director Ruth Jones is behind this operation, right?" Dewi asked.

"She can't be seen to be involved, and when it hits the fan she will deny all knowledge of it of course," Japey nodded and looked directly at Dewi, and he could see contempt behind his eyes. He was being paranoid again.

"Of course, but she will know who has been involved, right?"

"Oh don't worry, you'll all get yours, I'll see to that personally," Japey looked out of the side window avoiding eye contact this time.

"Where are we taking them?" Dewi asked.

"You don't need to know that for now," Japey gloated, as being in control gave him a buzz.

"What do you mean, we don't need to know? We are sticking our necks out here, at least let us know what we're getting ourselves involved in," Dewi twisted in his seat and glared at Japey again.

"All you need to know is that we're set to go in thirteen minutes," Japey said looking at his watch. It was nearly time to put his plan into action.

Chapter Sixty-One

Tank

Tank hung up the telephone and turned to Chen. He had just been updated by his counterpart in the American intelligence agencies. They had a cordial relationship and a modicum of mutual respect between them, enough to inform each other of anything that could potentially put their people in danger.

"It seems that the missile attack in Egypt is off limits even to us," Tank said. He picked up the telephone again and punched in a number with a thick finger. The Americans were keeping their cards close to their chest, and there appeared to be little or no information forthcoming about the missile attack. In Tank's experience that meant only a hard core of senior people really knew exactly what had actually happened. The line connected at the other end.

"Have we got any information yet on rendition flights into the Sinai?" Tank asked.

"I was just about to call you, wait until you hear this," the fat controller was on the other end of the line.

"That sounds like you've got good news," Tank said.

"No, I certainly wouldn't call it that."

"Don't keep us in suspense."

"The Americans were due to hand over a tier one personality to MI6 agents last week, only the handover was suspended indefinitely," the fat controller explained.

"Who have they got that we're waiting to process?"

"Well, let me tell you what we do know first, and then I can tell you what we don't know."

"I don't like the sound of this," Tank picked up a pencil and bit down on the wood, crunching it between his back teeth.

"Neither did I, anyway, we do know that a rendition flight left Chechnya en route to the Middle East. It had two tier one personalities aboard. One of the bodies was transferred at a small airfield in Turkey, and handed over to the Spanish, something to do with the Madrid bombings a few years back," the fat controller paused waiting for Tank to comment, but he didn't. The silence at the end of the line spurred him to continue.

"The flight stopped several times to refuel and then rested at a small airfield awaiting instructions from MI6, guess where?"

"At a push I would have to say the northern Sinai area?" Tank answered sarcastically. He bit on the pencil again, splintering the wood. He could see what was coming a mile away, but he hoped he was wrong. His stomach turned.

"Correct, nothing too drastic so far, except the flight never took off from that airfield again," the fat controller fell silent.

"And then the Americans wiped it from the face of the earth with Cruise missiles," Tank added.

"Correct again, now here's the punch line. The only rendition subject that we are expecting from the Americans is, guess who?"

"Lord Lucan."

"Don't be silly, he's dead."

"I was joking."

"This isn't funny Tank," the fat controller knew that the news couldn't be any worse for Tank, especially with Grace the way she was.

"I know it isn't funny, but I don't want you to tell me that the Americans have fucked up a rendition transfer of a tier one terrorist personality, who just happens to be our old friend Yasser Ahmed," Tank snapped the pencil in half and bit his tongue at the same time.

"Correct again, I'm very sorry Tank. It has taken immense political pressure to get the CIA to admit that they've lost Yasser Ahmed, but they are saying that as far as they're concerned he was killed in the missile attack, trying to escape," the fat controller explained.

"That's bullshit, and they know it."

"I couldn't agree more, but that is the line that they're taking. He could be anywhere by now. The other news is that Northern Command have stood down their ground forces to amber alert, so they're not expecting anything else to happen on American soil," the fat controller added. "I call you when anything else comes through."

"They've stood their Northern Command ground attack forces down," Tank said thoughtfully, still holding the receiver in his hand.

"Did he say why?" Chen asked.

"When I spoke to my contact in Delta Force, he couldn't say anymore than that, except that they were very concerned that the Jerusalem issue could cause an international incident of unprecedented proportions, and that they weren't about to sit around and let the Israelis deal with the situation unassisted," Tank said.

"And are we going to sit back and let the Israelis deal with the situation, assisted by the Americans?" Chen asked very slowly, spreading the words out to emphasise that he understood what Tank was thinking.

"Absolutely no chance, get two squads kitted up and ready to go in an hour. We'll need an airlift to Jerusalem," Tank stood up a flexed his thick neck muscles and the sinews in his jaw line twitched visibly.

Chapter Sixty-Two

Queen's district, New York

Agent Japey stood at the bottom of some litter-strewn steps. Anthony and Dewi had already entered the brownstone tenement building, along with two members of an agency snatch squad. The two Middle Eastern targets were in a scruffy bedsit situated on the second floor. Japey waited until his men had climbed the second staircase, and then headed in the opposite direction, down the stairs toward the basement. The stairs were worn smooth with decades of use, and the further he descended the more cluttered with refuse they became. He stepped off the last stair into a pile of trash, it felt too thick and spongy. Suddenly the pile of trash moved and groaned beneath his feet. A tramp struggled to pick himself up from his makeshift bed, tiredness and cheap booze dragged at his senses, making him sluggish.

Japey took a telescopic baton from his belt. He held the handle in his palm and extended it out quickly with a flick of the wrist. He lifted the baton high above his head, and then brought it down diagonally in a vicious arc. The baton split the tramps skull open, dropping him to his knees. Japey raised the baton again and landed a second heavy blow, shattering the vagrant's spinal column, just below the first vertebrae. The tramp collapsed in a heap at the bottom step.

"Perfect," Japey said under his breath. He took a cigarette from a brand new packet, lit it and nearly choked on the vile smoke. He coughed into his hand as he placed the burning cigarette into the dead vagrant's hand. The tip of the cigarette glowed red in the dark stairwell. Japey placed discarded fast food wrappers around the tip of the cigarette and they started to smoulder. Japey ran to the basement door and slammed his shoulder into it, cracking the rotten frame and knocking the Yale lock from its housing. He pushed the door open and a smell of damp rushed out to meet him. Japey remained in the doorway as he removed a set of infrared imaging night sights from his jacket. He clicked them into place and looked around the basement to check that they were functioning. The body of the dead tramp appeared as a human shaped green blob, and the smouldering pile of litter that was starting to burn glowed brighter still.

Using the image enhancers, he moved quickly through the dank basement, until he reached the buildings fuse box. He pushed the main circuit breaker into the off position, plunging the entire tenement building into darkness. It was six short strides to the interior staircase, which would take him to the ground floor, and then nine creaking wooden steps brought him into the hallway. He could hear multiple footsteps moving above him on the second floor. There were muffled scuffling noises, and confused whispering. The agents had obviously been taken by surprise when the lights went off. Japey could hear shouting coming from several of the building's drunken inhabitants, annoyed by the sudden power shortage. Apartment doors opened and slammed closed, adding to the rising cacophony of noise.

Japey took two Saudi made nine-millimetre APS automatic pistols from his inside pockets. He attached black metal noise suppressors to each barrel and waited in the darkness at the bottom of the staircase. The shuffling snatch squad were making good progress and had already reached the first floor landing. He had heard several altercations as tenants challenged the agents, and hollered about the loss of power. There was a loud shout of alarm, and then a thudding noise as Dewi punched an enquiring drunk back into his stinking flat. The drunk crashed onto the floor and the door slammed closed, as the snatch squad turned at the top of the stairs, and started to descend.

Anthony was at the head of the group halfway down the stairs, feeling his way in the dark, and guiding the others verbally. Japey covered their descent from the bottom of the stairwell with his pistol. The snatch squad were half way down the stairs, and everything was going like clockwork. This was a textbook extraction. Japey moved the pistol from the darkness behind the descending team, aimed at the lead man and fired. The nine-millimetre kicked in his hand as he fired three shots into Anthony's chest. Three black patches appeared on his white shirt as he tumbled down the steps headfirst. Dewi reached for his gun instinctively, but a nine-millimetre slug slammed through his brow bone, liquefying his brains before it ripped the back of his skull off.

Japey swapped guns. He crouched down onto one knee and emptied a sixteen-bullet magazine into the remaining two agents, and the two Middle Eastern men. Within a few seconds, the snatch squad and their targets were slain, sprawled across the staircase. Japey sprinted up the stairs, taking them two at time, until he reached Anthony's bloody corpse. He reached inside his jacket and removed his Glock. Japey clicked the magazine into his hand, checking that it was full, and then he reloaded it. He emptied the magazine into the two Arabs, and fountains of blood splattered the walls and ceilings of the rundown tenement. The noise from the unsuppressed weapon thundered through the tenement building. Shouting and panicked screaming could be heard coming from the upper floors.

"What the fucks happening man?" the unshaven face of a white man appeared over the banister, peering into the darkness.

"Yes, who gone and killed the lights man?" a black face joined the first at the banister rail.

Agent Japey fired twice from close range, directly into the two enquiring faces. Anthony's un-silenced gun had woken everyone that wasn't already awake. Doors were opening all over the building. The two heads at the banister blasted backwards in a shower of blood and bone fragments. A woman on the third floor started screaming, and she was quickly joined by several others. The pitch-blackness and gunfire was spreading panic through the buildings' sober tenants, and confusion through the stoned ones.

A bright orange glow was spreading from the front door area, as the basement fire started to climb the floors. Japey ran toward the back of the building. He passed the basement stairwell, which was already a blazing inferno, and exited the building into an alleyway at the rear. He looked up and saw several of the buildings' tenants clambering out of apartment windows onto a metal fire escape. The fire escape was fixed to the brickwork, and snaked down the building in a series of ladders and landings as far as the first floor. There was an extending section connecting the first floor landing to the street, which was locked up to prevent burglars from using the fire escape as an easy entry point. Japey scoured the alleyway, and found a discarded mop handle. He pushed a wheelie bin beneath the fire escape and climbed on top of it. The mop handle made a perfect wedge, preventing anyone extending the final section of the fire escape down to the alleyway. There was gridlock and chaos on the metal ladings, screaming and fighting as people tried to scramble away from the advancing inferno. Japey jumped off the bin and disappeared into the night.

Chapter Sixty-Three

Jerusalem

Chen was stood one hundred yards away from the Wailing Wall. He was wearing khaki cargo shorts, with big square pockets on each leg, and a simple white tee shirt. There was a baseball cap on his head emblazoned with the New York Yankees. To finish the outfit he had a camera hanging from his neck on a cord. The hat was protecting him from the blazing sunshine, but not from the intense heat. He was sweating profusely, only the bottle of mineral water that he had, was keeping him from keeling over. He looked like one of a thousand Chinese tourists in the ancient walled city.

A group of Hasidic Jews walked past him on the way to prayer. They wore black leather shoes and black socks, which were revealed by the short pedal pusher trousers that their religion prefers. They had long black suit jackets, and wide brimmed hats, with thick black ringlets of hair hanging over each ear. Chen didn't think that they were in disguise, although if they were it would be a good one. They were just three of millions of similarly dressed Jewish pilgrims that entered the city every year.

Chen looked through his camera and scanned the square and the Temple Mount above it. The huge golden dome on top of the revered Islamic building, called the Dome of the Rock mosque glistened in the sunshine. He checked that six of his men were all in their various positions. He also identified four American agents, probably Delta Force, who were doing the same thing that the Task Force was, watching and waiting for something to happen. A voice came through on the coms unit in his ear, which looked like a normal MP3 player.

"Is everyone in place?" Tank asked. The link was direct to Chen and the Task Force men. There was no central control unit here, as they were in an operational no go zone. If the Arab states knew that British and American Special Forces were operating in Israel there would be hell to pay.

"Roger that, there are some friendlies in position too," Chen replied.

"I've seen a couple myself, Delta Force I think, and the Israelis have swamped the place with beggars," Tank added. He was referring to the numerous crippled beggars that worked inside the city walls, living off the generosity of the pilgrim tourists. Israelis intelligence agencies used the fact that there were beggars on every corner to disguise their troops. Jerusalem had never seen so many beggars, but the problem was that the locals knew most of the genuine cripples by name, and a sudden influx of strangers aroused suspicion that something was afoot.

"Every gate into the city is guarded by Israelis troops, they're searching everything that is coming into the city," Chen said.

"Roger that, keep everyone on their toes, we haven't a clue what we're looking for, but I am sure that whatever it is, is already here," Tank said.

He looked through a pair of binoculars over the walls into the city. He was stood on the viewing platform on the Mount of Olives, watching the comings and goings. It was as good a vantage point as you could get. Tank didn't realise that he was standing just two hundred yards away from the decaying body of the man that had financed the release of his nemesis, Yasser Ahmed. He was mouldering in the scorching heat, covered in a pile of broken gravestones further down the grassy slopes.

Tank looked through the binoculars again and scanned the length of the thick walls, left to right. The giant golden dome dominated the skyline. He didn't think that a radiological dispersion device could be hidden atop of the Temple Mount. Heat sensors would have picked it up by now. Wherever it was, it needed to be inside a building, out of site. Tank took the baseball cap that he wearing off his baldhead and wiped the sweat from his brow with the back of his hand. He was wearing thick denim combat shorts that went just past his knee, and a baggy white short-sleeved short shirt. Despite the tourist gape, he still stood out because of his muscular build.

Tank scanned the city again looking for a potential building, suitable for hiding a dirty bomb inside. It would need to be close to the Wailing Wall, or the Church of the Sepulchre, but nothing really stood out. He panned right past the golden dome and Temple Mount. It had to be inside somewhere. The city was a shambolic mixture of architectural designs, and every inch on the residential space had been contested for thousands of years, at the cost of millions of lives. There were residential buildings built into part of the old Temple Mount wall, just to the west of the mosque. They would be an ideal hiding place but the Israelis had already searched them with a fine toothed comb. Most of the inhabitants of that quarter were Muslims, and it was the first place the Israelis looked.

Tank elevated the glasses and located the spire of the Church of the Sepulchre. The Christians believed that it contained both the site of Jesus crucifixion and the rock slab where he was interned. The buildings around it were predominantly ancient retail units and narrow market lanes. It would be an ideal target, but there was far too much activity up there for a large device to be hidden for any length of time. It would take a conspiracy of biblical magnitude for a secret that big to remain a secret. Tank ruled out that section of the city and scanned down to The Mount again.

He scanned the bedrocks to the west of The Mount, and then remembered the tourist trip that he made here some years before. The guide had informed them about the ancient caverns and ornately carved chambers beneath the Temple Mount, which had been flooded to create huge underground reservoirs. It was probably a mile away across the valley. The device had to be inside of a building somewhere, or underneath somewhere better still.

He stood up and headed down a steep winding narrow path, which led from the Mount of Olives, through the graveyards to the Garden of Gethsemane, situated at the foot of the ancient city walls. It was slow going, and the gradient of the road, combined with the sweltering heat took its toll on the big man. His Glock was holstered in the small of his back beneath his baggy shirt. He kept the baseball cap in his hand as he made his way down the steep hill. There was a blind beggar on the left hand side of the road, but the way his head turned and followed passing tourists indicated that there was nothing wrong with his eyes. Tank tagged him as an Israeli agent.

A catholic monk was walking up the hill toward him wearing a long white hessian robe, tied around his fat belly with a pleated rope, leading a donkey. Tank wondered at the holy man as he approached, leading the animal that would carry Christ upon his return, according to the scriptures. He stepped aside to allow the man to pass with his beast.

Tank wiped the sweat from his baldhead again, keeping the baseball cap in his hand. It was too hot to wear it, despite its disguising properties. He plodded down the steep narrow lane avoiding the beggars sat on either side. There were low walls on either side of the lane, protecting the massive Jewish graveyards beyond them. A sudden bend in the road offered a view of the rock face beneath the Temple Mount, to the west of the city. Tank stopped and inspected it through his binoculars.

He studied the rocks and the walls above them, but he couldn't see where an entry point would be. The guide had told him that access was granted only to the city's employees, and that the entrance was a loosely guarded secret known to everyone except tourists. He looked oddly out of place standing in the narrow lane, looking through binoculars. He was a huge muscular bulk, with a shaved head. Several of the wrinkled old cripples studied him as he looked over the city, but one in particular was more interested than most. Tank looked back down the road that he had to negotiate, winding steeply down the mount. A hooded one-armed beggar past him and Tank glanced briefly at the man's face. An uneasy sensation crept into Tank's bones as his powers of recognition worked unconsciously. He suddenly stopped and turned around; facing back up the hill, but the one armed man had disappeared.

Chapter Sixty-Two

Director Ruth Jones

Everything that Ruth Jones had tried to avoid had blown up in her face. She was woken up in the early hours of the morning to the shocking news that a terrorist plot had been foiled in the Queen's district of New York, resulting in the deaths of four CIA agents, two terrorists and twenty-three members of the public. The tenement building where the incident had taken place had been burned to the ground along with most of the adjoining block. The shocking part of the breaking news was that the terrorist cell, which were killed in the swoop were planning a dirty bomb attack, targeted at the financial area of New York. Once the news reached the press, the area had been completely evacuated as a response.

Director Ruth Jones had been hauled over the coals by the Whitehouse, and she was struggling to explain why the Northern Command's ground troops had been stood down to amber alert, when an attack was imminent. They also wanted to know who had organised the swoop, and on what intelligence. Of course, she didn't know the answers, but she had a good idea who did.

Forensic teams were ploughing through mountains of charred remains, but there was little useful evidence untouched by the fire. There were secondary teams working outside the building, and they seemed to be having a more productive search. Recovering any good ballistic evidence was impossible, as the fire had melted the nine millimetre slugs. The victim's bodies were burnt beyond recognition, and it was only an anonymous tipoff that alerted the New York Police Department to the fact that it was a terrorist incident. The remains had been removed hurriedly before the rest of the building collapsed, destroying the crime scene.

"Tell me that you've found something useful," Ruth Jones said. She was sat in the back of an agency vehicle being driven through the suburbs of New York.

"It's a real puzzle Ruth," her science officer replied. "But we do have some solid leads."

"Okay, give me what we have so far," she urged.

"We have an anonymous call reporting agency involvement in a terrorist incident at one o'clock this morning. The police department informed the local agency office, and they confirmed that a four man snatch squad had been deployed to capture two suspected terrorists linked to the incidents in the United Kingdom."

"What, who deployed the snatch squad?" Ruth asked incredulously.

"According to the paperwork you did," he explained slowly.

"This stinks," she said.

"The fire started in a basement stairwell beneath the tenement building, and spread rapidly, destroying everything we have to work with," he continued.

"Can we prove it was set deliberately?" she asked

"There are human remains near the seat of the fire, probably a vagrant, meaning it could be accidental," the scientist explained.

"That's bullshit, and just too much of a coincidence," Ruth was getting frustrated.

"Try explaining that to a judge, reasonable doubt and all," he responded, playing devil's advocate.

"How much of the financial district have they evacuated?" Ruth Jones was mentally trying to assess the damage.

"All of it."

"Is there any sign of any radioactive devices anywhere," she asked.

"Nothing, absolutely nothing. We have scanned the whole area above ground, and our teams are searching everything below ground as we speak," he replied.

"How long will it take?"

"A minimum of two weeks."

"Fucking hell," she whispered under her breath. "Is there any good news?"

"Well there is some news. Whether it is good or not is for you to decide," he replied.

"Okay, let's hear it," Ruth needed a break.

"The agents' cars have been processed, and we have found some evidence that we can't explain," he began.

"What evidence?"

"We found a pubic hair in the back of the car, belonging to one of your agents, but not one that has worked in New York long enough to have left it there," he explained.

"Don't tell me, Agent Japey?" she was flabbergasted.

"You've got it in one, shall we bring him in?" he asked.

"Oh yes, bring him in. It looks like he's going to be taking it rough for the next thirty years," she smiled looking out of the windows at the massive skyscrapers. It was all the information that she would need to nail him to the wall. The knot in her stomach relaxed a little and she decided to get some coffee for the rest of her journey. It was going to be a good day after all.

Chapter Sixty-Three

Jerusalem

Tank leaned over the low wall that bordered the narrow lane he was on. There was nothing to see but acres of shattered headstones and grass. He turned and ran to the other side of the road and repeated the process, with the same result. Wherever the hooded beggar had gone would remain a mystery. Tank was almost certain that he recognised the shark like eyes that he'd glimpsed as they passed one another, but by the time the information registered, he was gone.

Tank saw movement at a bend in the hill; several beggars huddled together were walking up the hill away from him. He sprinted fifty yards up the hill toward them, holding the handle of his Glock behind his back. The group of men heard him approaching and stopped at the sound of the big man stomping up the hill. They turned around and stared at Tank. He looked into their eyes one at a time, left to right. Their eyes were old and watery, and not the eyes of a stone cold killer like Yasser. He leaned against the wall to catch his breath.

Tank pulled out his cell phone and dialled the fat controller at headquarters in Liverpool.

"Agent David Bell speaking," he answered on the first ring.

"Bell it's Tank, I need you to check something out for me."

"Okay, give me a second to grab my pencil and I'm all ears," he replied reaching across the desk to retrieve his writing implement.

"I need to know if Yasser Ahmed received any permanent injury from the shoulder wound I inflicted in Chechnya," Tank was almost certain that he had made a mistake. He was just being jumpy because of the seriousness of the situation.

"Oh, well I can help you there my big friend," the fat controller sounded as chirpy as only he could in a crisis. "He had the wounded arm amputated at the shoulder; it's all here in the file we've received."

Tank hung up immediately without another word and ran back up the hill to the viewing platform. He had run about two hundred yards, scouring every nook and cranny, looking for the one armed beggar, but to no avail. The narrow lane up the hill was a steep incline and he was sweating like a racehorse when he reached the top. He leaned on the wall to catch his breath, and then looked through his binoculars again. Tank panned the entire hillside cemetery from the summit to the valley below, but he couldn't locate the beggar. He focused in on the rock face beneath the mount, and felt torn between looking for the location of the dirty bomb, and finding the one armed man, that could have been Yasser Ahmed. He switched on the coms unit.

"Chen, I need you to locate the Israelis commander," he panted, still out of breath. The sun was blazing down on his baldhead, and sweat ran in rivulets down his neck, soaking his shirt.

"Roger that, what's the problem?" Chen moved away from the wall he was leaning on and headed across the square toward the Wailing Wall. There was a temporary checkpoint set up by uniformed Israeli soldiers, and their squad commander was positioned there, coordinating operations. The American Delta Force unit and the Terrorist Task Force were supposed to be acting in advisory roles, communicating via the Israeli officer. At least that's what the Israelis thought.

"Ask him if the chambers beneath the Well of Souls have been searched, I think they would be ideal to stash a device out of sight, plus the city's water supply is stored there," Tank said, getting his breath back.

"Roger that, the Well of Souls, sounds like an Indiana Jones film," Chen said nervously as he approached the Israelis soldiers. He approached the commander casually so as not to disturb the thousands of Jewish pilgrims who were waiting to pass through the check point to pray at the wall. The commander listened to Chen and then spoke to his men. There was a brief conversation, a shaking of heads, and then a realisation that they had missed something important. Orders were barked out and the Israeli officers broke away from the checkpoint flanked by a dozen of his elite men.

"The chambers were not part of the sweep," Chen said into the coms unit. "He is taking a unit down there now, shall we follow?"

"Roger that, you and three men assist the Israelis, leave the others in place, and tell them to be on the lookout for a one armed beggar. If they see anyone missing an arm they're to contact me with a location immediately and tail them," Tank ordered.

"Roger that, we're on our way," Chen replied without questioning the order.

Tank studied the rocks beneath the Temple Mount again, and a flurry of movement further to the east attracted his attention. Three canvas covered army trucks were pulling to a halt on the road, about three hundred yards east from the base of the rock face. Troops swarmed out of the vehicles and began to fan out, securing the area. Tank figured that Chen and his three-man squad were about fifteen minutes away from the area. The Israelis had obviously alerted a unit to secure the area until the commander arrived and took control. That gave Tank the opportunity to search for the one armed man.

Chapter Sixty-Four

New York

Agent Japey was sat on his favourite tall bar stool in the pink pickup joint, which was becoming his local haunt. The regulars knew that he was in law enforcement, and an agent of some kind. Japey enjoyed the mystery that surrounded him. He was munching on a bowl of peanuts and swigging his third bottle of Bud, while he watched the newsreels repeating themselves repeatedly. Pictures of the burnt out tower in Liverpool were followed by the burnt out brownstone tenement block in the Queen's district of New York. The international news agencies were linking the incidents, and calling them a coordinated terrorist attack on the Atlantic allies by Islamic extremists. The press was having a field day, Islamaphobia had reached fever pitch. Vigilante groups were burning and destroying Muslim businesses on both sides of the Atlantic. It couldn't have worked out any better if he had planned it.

The picture on the screen changed again, and Japey smiled as he watched himself walking out of the New York agency building, mobbed by excited reporters. He stopped in front of the cameras and gave a brief statement, flanked by his solicitor, claiming that he was the victim of a conspiracy and had been set up. The news footage was from earlier that morning upon his release from the agency's New York interrogation suite. Ruth Jones had him arrested and questioned about the Queen's incident, but apart from a single hair sample, there was little solid evidence to hold him on. Japey knew that he had covered his tracks. There was nothing to link him to the killings. He would be suspended, and investigated, cleared and reinstated in a higher position, to avoid any messy compensation lawsuits. So far, everything was going to plan.

Japey had especially enjoyed the frustrated look on the director's face, as he had walked free. It was great to get one over on the smug bitch. A real shot in the arm to prove to everyone that he was the superior being. The agents in the office were silent as he walked through; cold silent stares followed his every move. They had lost four of their colleagues, and the finger of guilt was pointing directly at Agent Japey. He had attracted the attention that he craved in many ways, but it would all pay dividends in the end. He smiled to himself again and finished his beer. The barman was leaning against the till watching the newsreel, along with a handful of gay regulars.

"You look good on camera," the barman said as he replaced Japey's empty beer with a full one. He put on an effeminate swagger, trying to earn a bigger tip, or something.

"Thank you," Japey flirted, and made a mock salute to the barman. They both laughed and Japey noticed a guy opposite laughing with them. Their eyes lingered a little too long and Japey knew there was an attraction immediately. How could the poor guy not be attracted to a handsome successful man such as Japey, and he was only human after all. His newfound fame was already proving fruitful. Japey was incredibly vain, and arrogant, and it would be his downfall.

The man who was sat across from Japey looked into his eyes, and smiled. He knew that he had him on the hook. He moved his beer and walked around the end of the bar to sit next to Japey, and Japey leered his slimiest smile.

What Japey didn't know was that the man was employed by the agency's black operations department, and was what is called a 'cleaner'. Ruth Jones sent him to tidy up the mess Japey had caused, and to renew the balance of justice. In his pocket was a small brown bottle of rohipnol, and a syringe full of heroin, strong enough to kill an elephant.

Chapter Sixty-Five

Jerusalem

Rahid Bindhi was struggling to stay awake. The light from his paraffin lamp was fading and the intensifying, as he watched the flame dance. There were rainbows forming around the light as watched it flickering. It cast shadows on the wall of the huge stone chamber. The chamber had been built long before Jesus was born, and had served as both a mosque and a Christian place of worship. The walls were carved by the best stonemasons of the day, huge arched alters were carved into the walls. Giant marble columns supported the rock ceilings, but the bases of them were covered by thousands of gallons of water. Only the top third of the chamber was visible above the surface of what was now the city`s underground reservoir.

Rahid was tasked with guarding the dirty bomb. It had been assembled on site over a period of weeks, and it was nearly time to detonate it. The radiation from the salted bomb was taking effect on Rahid. The white blood cells in his body were dying rapidly and not being replaced by healthy ones. His organs were poisoned with radioactive cells, which were lodged in his liver and kidneys. There wasn`t long left in this world for Rahid. He wiped his chin with the back of his hand, and thick chunks of his beard fell away from his face. He spat, trying to get rid of the metallic taste in his mouth, but it just became stronger. There were globules of blood in the phlegm.

The sound of gushing water echoed through the chambers, almost hypnotising in its quality. He had become accustomed to the sounds in the caverns beneath the Temple Mount, and he closed his eyes to rest them momentarily. The timer on the device ticked away. There was not long now, and then all would be well.

Chapter Sixty-Six

New York

Japey didn't feel well. He thought that the Bud had gone to his head all of a sudden. He was enjoying himself, flirting with everyone, enjoying his fifteen minutes of fame. He had been given three cell phone numbers already, but he wanted the guy he'd met at the bar. There was an attraction there, and the feeling was mutual, he could tell. How could the guy resist?

He stood up and squeezed the man's knee, and tried to smile sexily, but it transpired on his face as more of a snarl. His knees buckled slightly as he wobbled toward the gents, and he thought he was going to fall, but he was grabbed firmly by the elbow and supported. Japey turned and recognised the guy he'd been chatting up at the bar. He relaxed a little and allowed himself to be guided by the cleaner that Ruth Jones had sent. The cleaner had slipped the tranquilizer into Japey's beer twenty minutes ago. It was starting to take effect on his target. In another five minutes Japey wouldn't remember what his name was, never mind what was happening to him.

The cleaner pushed open the washroom doors with his foot and guided Japey into the washroom by the arm. The pink theme was continued throughout. A sticky pink carpet covered the floor for the first six foot, and then there was a second door. The door led into a tiled area, white porcelain urinals lined the left hand side, and cubicles lined the right. He pushed Japey toward one of the cubicles. Two of the other doors were closed. The cleaner pushed them, and they both opened revealing that they were unoccupied. He pushed the weakening agent through a cubicle door and held him against the wall by his collars, and then kicked the door closed behind them. It banged shut, echoing off the tiles with a clatter. Japey felt like he was watching the scene from above. This was what he wanted but the guy was getting a bit rough. Japey liked to control the pace, but he couldn't even control his tongue. He wanted to speak but he couldn't.

All the strength in his limbs had gone, and he felt compliant and helpless, but also excited about the encounter that was to come. He tried to smile but his facial muscles had ceased to work and his lips sneered into a twisted grin.

"What's up you fucking faggot?" The cleaner snarled into his ear, holding him up with one hand, and taking the booster syringe from his pocket with the other.

"Do you want me to make you feel good?" The cleaner showed Japey the syringe, waving it slowly in front of his face.

Japey tried to smile again, the drug was coursing through his veins. The sight of the syringe didn't register in his brain, but the promise to make him feel good did, selective hearing from his befuddled brain. The cleaner pushed the needle into a thick blue vein in Japey's neck, and then pressed the plunger. The heroin was in his brain in seconds, and his legs buckled completely. The cleaner undid Japey's belt and pulled his pants and underwear down. He turned the body and positioned it face toward the wall, bent over the porcelain pot, bare ass in the air. The cleaner put the syringe in his pocket, and removed another one. The new one was loaded with a much weaker dose of heroin. He shoved the needle into Japey's arm, just below the elbow, and left it there. It was half-full of blood and half full of the opiate.

The cleaner left the dead agent where he was. He bolted the cubicle door and then climbed over the top, leaving the agent locked in. It was much later when he was eventually discovered. A disgraced agent found in a compromising position in the toilets of a gay bar, killed by a drug overdose. It was perfect. The natural order of things had been restored, and a harsh justice dealt.

Chapter Sixty-Seven

Jerusalem

Tank watched Chen and his three-man team kitting up into black protective combat gear. The entrance to the Well of Souls, originally dug by Christian nights, had been scanned and traces of radioactivity had been detected on the rocks, which matched the profiles of cobalt and strontium. It seemed Tank was correct in his assumption that the bomb was hidden underground. Israeli Special Forces and units from Delta Force, and the British Terrorist Task Force entered the underground caverns equipped with night vision enhancing equipment and enough firepower to stop an army of terrorists.

The activity beneath the Temple Mount had drawn attention from locals, tourists and the media. The Israelis` troops were desperately trying to evacuate the area without creating widespread panic, but the number of curious onlookers was overwhelming. Tank scanned the growing crowds that were gathering, looking for Yasser Ahmed. Information gleaned from the first Soft Target campaign pointed to the fact that Yasser enjoyed staying close to the operations that he organised, watching from nearby and sometimes taking an active role.

There was no sign of his enemy amongst the gathering throng. Tank looked left and right, slowly searching the hillside graveyards for any sign of life. If Yasser was around watching events unfurl then he had to be on the Mount of Olives somewhere. He was convinced that he had seen him earlier, but realised too late. Tank tried to calculate the reasons why Ahmed would be here on the Mount of Olives. The more he thought about it, the more convinced he was that he was sightseeing, watching his affiliates carry out the plot first hand. Tank believed that Yasser was on The Mount to watch the action unfold as it happened.

The Mount was a safe enough distance away. Not close enough to be injured by the explosion, but close enough to see it, and hear it. Yasser could watch the ensuing panic as the Jews realised that the centre of their religion had been transformed into a smoking radioactive pile of rubble. The beautiful golden dome on top of the Temple Mount mosque would be contaminated too, but it wasn't as important a site as Medina or Mecca. It could be sacrificed for a few decades, as long as Jerusalem was returned to Palestine.

The viewing platform that Tank was on was situated near the top of the Mount of Olives. Between him and the valley below were a million white stone graves, some shattered some in better condition. He could only see what was on his side of the headstones. The opposite sides overlooking the city were hidden from him. Yasser could be hidden from view in any one of a million places. He scanned the slopes again and noticed a larger marble structure, which was similar to a Christian crypt. It was two hundred yards down the slope but offered a perfect view of the city. Yasser could be the other side of it watching the growing crowds below, and the disorganised military running about like camouflaged ants in the valley.

Tank spoke into the coms unit, while he watched the Israeli soldiers trying to erect barriers and roadblocks around the base of the Temple Mount.

"This is pilgrim one, who`s on The Mount?" Tank asked.

"Pilgrim one, this is pilgrim four, and I`m two hundred yards east of the golden dome, adjoining the west wall."

"Roger that pilgrim four. I need you to position yourself facing south toward the Mount of Olives, and signal me when you`re in position." Tank scanned the section of the wall that pilgrim four was situated on, and located him next to a huge stone buttress fortification.

"Roger that, I`m facing in that direction now."

"Roger, locate the viewing platform at the crest of the mount," Tank was watching his agent on the wall as he navigated him onto his position. The platform was becoming increasingly busy with curious tourists eager to get a look at what was going on in the valley below. Tank looked around the crowd, wondering if Ahmed could be among them.

"Roger that pilgrim one, I have you on visual," pilgrim four had sighted Tank in his binoculars.

"Roger, scan down the slope two hundred yards directly below me, and there is a marble structure there," Tank directed the agent.

"Roger that, I have it in visual."

"Roger, is there any sign of life there on your side of the building, it's out of my field of vision," Tank asked.

"Affirmative, there are three x-rays sat in the shade with a bird's eye view of the action, and they all look like locals to me," pilgrim four reported back.

"Roger that, how much detail have you got?" Tank moved away from the safety barrier and began pushing his way through the crowds, adrenalin started to pump.

"They're in the shade somewhat, I can't see everything."

"Roger that, are any of them missing an arm?"

"Negative Tank, I can't tell from here they're wearing robes and sitting down," pilgrim four answered.

"Roger that, get our sniper up there with you and have him cover that section of the slope. I'm on my way to check them out now," Tank pushed his way through the gathering crowds toward the small wall, which bordered the graveyard.

The noise of a helicopter engine began to oscillate down the valley, echoing off the slopes. Tank stopped and looked at it through his binoculars. It was a civilian aircraft fitted with cameras beneath it. He stumbled through the wall into the humongous graveyard and paused to inspect the helicopter. It was definitely civilian, probably the media. There was absolutely no way anything flew over Jerusalem without the Israeli air force knowing about it. Someone must have tipped them off. Tank pulled his cell phone out and dialled headquarters again.

"Agent Bell speaking," the fat controller answered on the second ring.

"What kept you?" Tank asked sarcastically.

"I was just about to ring you actually. The satellite news channels have a very disturbing story about an extremist bomb attack against the Wailing Wall. They have aerial pictures of Jerusalem as we speak," he explained gleefully.

"I was afraid you were going to say that. There`s a press helicopter above the Temple Mount, someone has given the thumbs up for the story to be leaked," Tank said.

"The American channels are crammed with the Liverpool attack, and they`ve linked it to a serious fire in Queens, New York. They evacuated the financial district this morning," the fat controller was linking everything up.

"It would seem that if the Americans have gone public then the Israelis have followed suit," Tank mused, looking up at the helicopter.

"There`s no doubt about it. The world and his wife are watching this on the television. The Americans and the Israelis will milk this for all it`s worth. They`ll turn Jerusalem and the rest of Israel into a fortress, an American aircraft carrier and missile silo all rolled into one." The possible connotations were endless.

"That`s if they stop short of a military strike in retaliation. All they have to do is bum up enough evidence that Iran is behind this and America has the perfect justification to blow it to bits," Tank answered, and the hairs on the back of his neck stood up as he watched the helicopter.

There was a slight rustle behind him and then the feeling of cold steel against his neck. The muzzle of a fat Bulldog revolver was jammed painfully into his carotid. He was held tightly from behind by at least two sets of hands. There was another rustle of footsteps and a slightly built Arab dressed in a scruffy robe stepped in front of him. The Arab had dead eyes and only one arm.

Chapter Sixty-Eight

Eternity

Small brown hands took the cell phone from Tank, and another pair removed his Glock nine-millimetre from its holster. Yasser reached out his scrawny hand and tugged the coms unit from Tank's ear, rendering him unarmed and very much alone. Yasser stared into his eyes in silence. Nothing was said. He nodded his head and the ragbag group of Arabs walked slowly down the hill toward the marble crypt, surrounding Tank and keeping him covered. One of them circled the group pointing here and there. From above it looked like Tank was strolling through the graveyard, being guided by local beggars. The crowds on the viewing platform were ensconced with the military activity to the east, below the Temple Mount. Yasser and his three cronies were leading Tank east out of sight of the growing crowds.

The group stopped momentarily and a hessian rope was tied tightly around the big man's wrists, digging into his flesh. Tank tensed the muscles in his forearms and hands, making them swell to their maximum potential. When the rope was secured, he continued to tense and relax the massive muscles in his arms. The fibres were stretching and weakening before they had finished securing their ligature. Tank took the respite to assess how bad the situation was.

There were four armed men, plus Yasser in the group, heading toward a crypt where he knew there was another three x-rays. He didn't know if they were bandits or just locals, but he had to prepare for the worst. Tank was eighteen stones of well-trained fighting machine. He could break these men in half with a flick of his huge wrist if all things were equal. Tank wasn't sure where he was being taken, but it appeared that they were heading toward the marble crypt. Tank was confident that his sniper could control several of the bandits, but the gun at his throat wasn't helping the situation. All four Arabs had robes on, hiding whatever weaponry they were carrying. He didn't know who had taken the Glock either. It was out of sight somewhere. The situation was fragile at best, and precarious to say the least.

Yasser led the way and never spoke or looked back at Tank once. Tank wasn't really surprised by that fact, because the man rarely showed any concern about anything. The good thing was that the group was still heading for the broken crypt, and the crypt should be covered by a sniper already. Tank liked the odds.

The four Arabs manhandled Tank down the slope toward the marble crypt. When they reached the marble mausoleum, Yasser turned the corner first and went out of sight. There were raised voices and a flurry of guttural Arabic as Tank was pushed round the corner of the crypt, out of sight from anyone watching from further up the hill.

Tank turned the corner and a heavy chunk of concrete flashed into his vision. It was a blur of rapid movement, which made him close his eyes instinctively. The concrete smashed into the bridge of his nose, splintering the small bones there to pieces. The pain in his head was excruciating, and his eyes watered blurring his vision. He felt blood run from both nostrils and the coppery taste stuck to the back of his throat.

Tank rocked his head backward trying to avoid any follow up but he was held too tightly. The second vicious blow caught him full on the mouth. His top lip burst like a squashed slug, and his two front teeth pierced the gums before being splintered into fragments of denture. White light exploded through his brain, the exposed nerves in his broken teeth burned like tiny supernovas of pain. Blood filled his mouth and he gagged, as the thick viscous liquid threatened to choke him. Consciousness was leaving him; his body was falling into shock. His survival instinct took control.

Tank opened his eyes to see the third blow heading for his face. Although he was badly stunned by the savage attack he only had two choices now, fight or die. The chances are he would die anyway. If he took another blow of such brutal intensity then death was a fore gone conclusion. He ducked at the last moment, bending his legs and twisting his body at the same time. The grip on his arms weakened as he twisted, allowing him to avoid the blow. The concrete block whizzed by his ear and into the face of the man holding the Bulldog revolver. The gun clattered onto the marble beneath them.

Tank launched his huge bald head as hard as he could into Yasser's jaw. The crushing blow cracked the lower part of his jaw, almost wrenching the muscles from the side of his face. The one armed man was flung backward by the force of the vicious head butt, dropping his concrete weapon as he fell.

Tank turned on his heels and drove his head backward and upward simultaneously. He caught one of his captors beneath the lower jaw. The man's teeth were smashed together by the blow, cracking and splintering into fragments. He screamed and pulled out a long thin blade from beneath his robe, waving it in front of Tank. There was a whooshing sound as the man's head exploded, destroyed by a 7.68 millimetre sniper's bullet. Before the man had hit the ground Tank had the blade between his wrists, in the space that he had stretched, and a second later he was free.

Two Arabs fell close by Tank, victims of the Task Force sharpshooter, but a third was closing in and pulling the Glock nine-millimetre from his robe. Tank bent down and scooped up a piece of marble headstone. He launched it at the oncoming man, striking him in the forehead. The heavy stone chunk knocked the man from his feet, spilling Tank's gun as he fell. Tank dropped onto the gun in a flash. He jumped across the stone and landed on the man's throat knees first, shattering his larynx and crushing the windpipe. The man gurgled as a fountain of blood erupted from his mouth.

Yasser was still on his back, stunned by the head butt, and that left two remaining bandits to deal with. One of them was kneeling inside the crypt, hiding from the invisible sniper that had killed his colleagues. The sight of his friends head exploding was enough to dampen his enthusiasm for a fight. The other was taking cover from the sniper behind a headstone about twenty yards away from Tank. He was kneeling down and peering around the stone in the direction of the city, facing away from Tank.

Tank switched the safety off the Glock and fired three bullets into the bandit behind the headstone. The three nine-millimetre bullets ripped into his back, punching ragged holes the size of walnuts in the flesh. His chest burst open like a scene from `Alien` as the bullets punched massive exit wounds. The rib cage was forced open by the devastating power of the hollow rounds.

Tank turned quickly and fired three more shots into the man in the crypt. He took them in the neck and shoulder area. Arterial spray splattered the walls of the mausoleum, as a ragged gash was ripped across the jugular vein. The man twitched violently as he lay bleeding on the marble. The contrast of white marble and a dark red blood was startling. Tank stood over him and fired two more rounds into his head. The twitching stopped immediately. Yasser Ahmed groaned on the floor. His mouth was hanging open awkwardly and an egg-sized lump had swelled from the shattered jawbone.

Tank wiped blood from his nose and mouth. His lips were three times the size of normal, and blood was running freely from both nostrils. He made an okay signal toward the city walls, knowing that his men would be watching him from their position. Tank spat blood on the grass. The gunfire would have attracted attention from the crowds above. He stepped inside the marble mausoleum and looked around. He saw what he was looking for. Tank had to make a decision quickly because there wouldn't be much time. There was one more thing to do. Tank reached outside the crypt with a big hand and grabbed Yasser's unconscious body by the foot. He dragged him out of the sunshine into the marble shrine.

At the back of the crypt was a gaping black hole in the floor. Obviously, it was once the resting place of very rich Jew, but it was now desecrated. Yasser weighed less than nine stones, and it was like carrying a ragdoll to Tank. The terrorist leader opened his eyes. His piercing shark like eyes suddenly became aware that he was in a deadly predicament. He lurched forward to escape Tank's grip. Tank straightened his right hand, and drove it in a stabbing motion into Yasser's throat. The terrorist grasped at his injured windpipe gasping for his breath. Tank bundled him into the empty grave. Yasser turned onto his back and glared into Tank's eyes. Tank smiled at him. He coughed blood and phlegm from his broken lips and spat it at Yasser, hitting him below the eye. Tank saw a flicker of fear flash across the terrorist's face and it felt good. He leaned over the grave and gripped the edge of the huge marble slab, which had once covered its dead Jewish occupant. Tank heaved and the slab squealed as it moved toward the hole.

Yasser realised what Tank intended and he tried to sit up. Tank punched him hard in the face, breaking his nose. Yasser closed his eyes as the crushing blow stunned him. He shook his head trying to clear his senses. As he opened his eyes, he could only watch as Tank dragged the giant slab the last few inches into place over the tomb. He cried out, a scream from the bottom of his Muslim soul. This was his reward for all his lifetime's work. He was to spend eternity in a Jewish grave, surrounded by the remains of a million Jewish souls.

His evil soul would be in torment for eternity.

Chapter Sixty-Nine

Liverpool-twelve months later

Tank walked into the meeting room in the underground bunker. Civil unrest had reached a new peak across the Middle East and the Western world, following the Jerusalem plot. Chen and his team had successfully helped the Israelis to disable the dirty bomb beneath the Temple Mount. There was a huge media circus watching and transmitting pictures across the globe as the device was carried out by men in ugly radioactive protection suits.

The incident left America with a diplomatic trump card. They turned their war on terror directly on the Palestinian, Israeli conflict. American forces were legitimately stationed on Israeli soil, airplanes, troops and missiles. Iran, Syria and the other Arab regimes could only watch in dismay as their Jewish neighbour became invincible.

In the West, right wing extremist groups across the Christian world were taking things into their own hands; religious vigilantes were striking at rival ethnic minorities.

Major Stanley Timms walked into the room. He was walking a little more stiffly than he used to, but he had made a remarkable recovery. Compared to the fate that befell some of his counterparts, he had been lucky.

Grace Farrington walked in to the bunker with Chen and the fat controller. They were laughing about something they were discussing before they entered the room. Tank caught her eye and that magnetism that they had always had sparked through his mind. She had been to death's door and back but her life force had brought her through. It glowed all around her like an aura. There was a mischievous gleam in her eyes that he loved.

There was serious stuff to discuss. Members of white extremist groups had been caught by uniformed police divisions, trying to blow up a mosque, using military grade explosives. It was going to need the Terrorist Task Force to investigate how widespread their plans were and how much military hardware they had acquired. Tank had a feeling he would meet them very soon.

Printed in Great Britain
by Amazon

79555089R00164